THE ROYAL ORDER OF
FIGHTING DRAGONS

OTHER BOOKS BY DAN ELISH

Children's Fiction

The Great Squirrel Uprising
Jason and the Baseball Bear
Born Too Short: The Confessions of an Eighth-Grade Basket Case
The Attack of the Frozen Woodchucks
The School for the Insanely Gifted
The Worldwide Dessert Contest

By Jason Robert Brown and Dan Elish
13

For Adults

Nine Wives
The Misadventures of Justin Hearnfeld

THE ROYAL ORDER OF
FIGHTING DRAGONS

DAN ELISH

The Royal Order of Fighting Dragons

Cover Credit: Original Illustration by Sam Shearon
Interior Illustrations: Original artwork by Sam Shearon
www.mister-sam.com

ISBN: 978-1-944109-54-7

VESUVIAN BOOKS

Published by Vesuvian Books
www.vesuvianbooks.com

Printed in the United States of America

10 9 8 7 6 5 4 3 2 1

For Andrea, Cassie and John

Chapter One

W ith ten minutes left in sixth-grade social studies, Ike Hollingsberry heard the faint *bring* of the incoming text. Though students at the Branford School in New York City weren't allowed to have their cell phones out in class, Ike wasn't able to resist glancing into his open knapsack to take a peek.

Click the link below to watch what happened to
your father on the set of *The Fighting Dragons.*

Ike sighed. *Really?* At this point, the only thing to do was to try not to laugh. When would these psycho bloggers leave him alone? The TV studio had made it clear from day one the accident hadn't been filmed.

As his teacher, Mr. Donadio, paced the front of the classroom, holding forth on the meaning of the American Revolution, Ike slipped the phone into his lap.

763-372-4667

As expected, he didn't recognize the sender's number. But Ike knew the type—another lunatic with too much time on his hands and nothing better to do than speculate about how exactly his poor dad had died.

"Ike?"

He looked up with a start. A black belt in karate, Mr. Donadio had once tossed a dictionary across the room, narrowly missing the heads of two talking students. Ike shuddered. What if the dictionary was only a warm-up act? What if the class terrarium was next?

"What do you think you're doing?" the teacher went on. "You know the rules on phones."

"I'm sorry," Ike stammered. "It won't happen again."

He dropped the phone back in his knapsack.

"Make sure that it doesn't," Mr. Donadio said. He smiled, perhaps a little too broadly. "Let's see whether you know as much about the Revolutionary War as you do about social networking. What year was the Constitution signed?"

Ike had done his reading—and carefully, too. But every time he received one of those strange texts, IMs, or emails, it was hard to focus on anything else.

"Well …"

His voice trailed off.

The answer was so close. He might have gotten it, too. But then he saw her, one aisle over. With stringy black hair and fingernails chewed down to their nubs, Elmira Hand held the dubious distinction of being the Branford sixth grade's biggest fan of *The Fighting Dragons*. She loved to surprise Ike at inopportune moments with comments or observations about the show. A glimpse of her was enough to wipe all traces of the American Revolution clean out of his head. All he could think about was his dad.

After letting him squirm for a few moments, Mr. Donadio scanned the class. "Who can help Ike out?"

Hands shot up.

"1787," a voice called.

"Very good," the teacher said. Then he tapped Ike's desk. "Perhaps you can tell us who our country's first president was?"

Laughter flittered across the class. Even in his addled state, Ike knew that one.

"George Washington," he muttered.

"Impressive," Mr. Donadio said. Then to the class. "Let's continue our discussion."

Ike tried desperately to follow the lesson. But how could he focus? It was maddening, actually. The mysterious text wouldn't shed any new light on his dad's accident. Even so, his heart was racing.

Because there was always that small chance.

What if, after all these years, there really was a video? Wouldn't that be amazing? Only four at the time, Ike still remembered walking down Broadway with his mother the day after the tragedy and seeing the papers at the local newsstand. With a crowd of people pointing and talking, it hadn't taken long to figure out what the headlines read.

Children's dragon-riding TV star Cameron Hollingsberry killed on set by fake insect.

Gigantic fake locust mauls TV actor in accidental death.

Star Hollingsberry slain by malfunctioning flying invertebrate.

Even seven years later, it was almost impossible to believe

3

something so ridiculous had taken place. Had his father, a mild-mannered British actor on a kids' TV show, really shown up for work one day only to be killed by a giant fake insect? Apparently so. What made it even crazier were reports that his dad had been engaged in a staged battle at the time, riding a fake dragon.

"Hey, Ike."

Somehow while thinking about his father, class had ended. To his dismay, Elmira was leaning over from her desk.

"Wanna grab lunch?"

"Lunch?" he said haltingly.

"Yeah. You and me."

He didn't want to be rude, but the last thing he needed now was to try and eat a Sloppy Joe while taking questions about his  dad from the class weirdo. "Gee, sorry, Elmira. I usually eat with Diego and Kashvi. In fact, I'm meeting them outside right now. But hey, another time, okay?"

Elmira objected, but Ike didn't wait. Grabbing his knapsack, he cut into the busy hallway.

As expected, Diego was already waiting, hair a mess, shirt untucked, and his belt missing a good half of the loops—his usual look.

"Yo," he said.

"Yo," Ike replied.

"Ready to eat?"

"Absolutely," Ike said. "But mind if I meet you there today?"

"Sure," Diego said. "Where you going?"

"My locker for a second. Save that seat, okay?"

Turning fast, Ike bumped smack into Kashvi.

"Where're you going?" she asked.

"That's what I asked," Diego said, coming up from behind.

"What's up, Ike?"

Out of the corner of his eye, Ike saw Elmira slip by, looking him over. No doubt he needed to move this along.

"Just my locker, guys," he said quickly. "See you in two minutes. Promise."

With that, he was off. Cutting around the corner to the back hallway, Ike glanced over his shoulder at his two buds. Since kindergarten, they had made an odd trio. Diego Miranda, the sloppy nerd who had immigrated with his family from Puerto Rico at age three, Ike Hollingsberry, the short nerd with a British dad and American mom, and Kashvi Changar, the nice-looking Indian girl who was so smart the word *nerd* didn't come close to covering it. The previous fall, she had taken apart her father's car engine on a dare and put it back together in less than an hour.

Ike hated to lie to them. Yes, he truly did want to drop his history book in his locker so he wouldn't have to schlep it to math. He also wanted to dodge Elmira. But mostly, he was too plain embarrassed to tell Diego and Kashvi the real reason he needed a minute to himself.

"I know it's hard," his mom had told him once. "But try not to think about what happened to Dad so much."

She had a point. Even after all these years, thoughts of his father came with a mountain of pain. Then again, how could an eleven-year-old boy *not* think about his dad?

After shoving his history textbook into his locker, Ike reached for his phone—legal during lunch hour—and called up Facebook. What else could he do? He had never known his dad all that well. But sometimes he just missed the guy.

Ike typed "Hollingsberry." A glowing picture of his father taken a week before his death popped up on the screen. His dad was dressed in full fighting regalia, atop a giant dragon.

Ike scanned down the page. A heading read:

5

Fan page of actor Cameron Rupert Hollingsberry who died tragically on the set of *The Fighting Dragons*.

Misty eyed, Ike glanced at the photo. Aside from the bright green eyes, he and his father had little in common. Although his father had been tall and broad with a strong jaw, Ike was skinny and one of the shortest kids in his class. Yes, his dad's golden armor, mighty shield, and brilliant sword were only props—Ike knew that—but even so, his father's powerful image, coupled with his fame as an actor, never failed to make him feel small by comparison. After all, Ike was no hero. Sure, he was a nice boy, and a decent student with a couple of good friends. But powerful? Brave? Not a chance. He could barely find the courage to kill a cockroach in his bedroom, let alone a monster locust from the back of a fire-breathing dragon.

Ike scrolled further down the Facebook page. He wasn't the only one who looked up to his dad. Not only did his fans think him a hero, but they still posted about it. Three from just that morning.

At 8:21 AM, DragonLove wrote:
"We love you, Cameron. The only good locust is a dead locust."

At 8:34, LucyLucy penned:
"OMG, I LOVED this brave man Cameron Hollingsberry. Remember Episode Four when he ripped out that locust's guts with his sword then used a piece of the antennae as dental floss? That was *drama*."

Then at 9:01 El-Peg 2 wrote:
"Hey, Dragon Fire-Breathing fans. Who out

there besides me thinks the whole show was real? I say Cameron Hollingsberry really *did* fly a dragon. I say he really *did* kill those giant bugs. I say the whole show was a set-up. Am I crazy?"

Ike grimaced. *Yes*, he thought. *You ARE crazy.*

It was weird enough that people were still so obsessed with the show. But the ones Ike couldn't take were the fans who thought the whole thing was real. Nutcases who wrote weekly blogs like, "How Cameron Rupert Hollingsberry Saved the Planet" or "The True Inside History of The Fighting Dragons." Other posts were online, too, being updated every day.

"Hey … There you are."

Ike sighed. Busted. Elmira, the one like a gnat he couldn't shake.

"Hey," Ike said.

He tried to move away from his locker, but the girl blocked him.

"Just a second," she said. "What was that text?"

Ike blinked. "What text?"

"I saw you looking at it in class. The one that had a link to your dad."

Ike focused on Elmira more directly. She had nice pale blue eyes and a friendly smile, he had to give her that. Of mixed race, she also had beautiful light-brown skin. But these more attractive features were coupled with off-beat ones—largish ears, a smattering of freckles, impossibly dry lips—that made her look more odd than pretty.

"What're you doing looking at my texts, anyway?"

Elmira smiled. "If you hadn't had your phone out illegally in class, I wouldn't have been able to look. So your fault."

Ike frowned. It was pure Elmira logic—annoying, even if

largely correct.

The girl leaned closer.

"Do you think your dad fought and killed those locusts for real?"

If only he could teleport straight to lunch. As it was, Elmira had him cornered—never a good thing. Along with her obsession with *The Fighting Dragons*, she had memorized the guest-star cast list of every *Star Trek* episode from the original series through *Voyager* and claimed to own thirty editions of *The Lord of the Rings*, some in foreign languages. This was a girl who had stood up in front of his English class and quoted the opening passage of *The Outsiders* in *Elvish*. A true oddball.

Even so, despite everything, Ike had always considered Elmira essentially harmless. Now he reconsidered. Was she one of those conspiracy freaks, too? Did she think his dad had been some sort of world savior?

"Listen," he said, "I don't want to be mean, but here's the deal. My dad was a Shakespearean actor who was offered a weird role in a kids' TV program where he flew a fake dragon to save the Earth from a horde of fake locusts. Get it?"

"Sure, I do, but..."

"Everything was fake, okay? *Fake*. Then on the sixteenth show, he died in a weird, tragic accident and it went off the air. That's it. He wasn't anything special. So please, just shut up about him. And shut up about the locusts, too."

Elmira's pale-blue eyes went wide. "So you want me to shut up, is that it?"

Annoying and also dense. "I have to go eat. See you later."

Ike cut around Elmira and hustled down the hall.

"But wait," Elmira said. "I have something to tell you. How about lunch? Have lunch with me?"

"Sorry," Ike called over his shoulder. "Like I said, I'm sitting with Diego and Kashvi today."

"But you sit with them every day," Elmira called. "And this is important. Tell you what—you get your tray and I'll find you later. I'll find you."

Ike kept walking.

Find him? He seriously hoped she wouldn't.

Chapter Two

T his was shaping up to be a terrible day. As promised, Elmira Hand had found Ike at lunch. To her credit, she had waited for him to finish his second helping of Sloppy Joes. She had even waited for Diego and Kashvi to clear their trays. Elmira had waited so patiently, by the time she appeared, Ike had forgotten about her altogether. But the minute Diego and Kashvi got up, she'd swooped in like a hair chewing, fingernail-biting bird and perched herself firmly across the lunch table.

"So here's the thing," Elmira was saying. "I think your father was a genuine real-live hero, not just an actor. In fact, I'm sure of it. See, I've done the research. I can back this up. Maybe you've seen my blog?"

"Your *blog?*"

"*Elmira Speaks. Google* it. No, forget it—don't *Google* it—I'll sum it all up for you right now."

Ike was determined not to let himself be drawn into a conversation.

"Sorry," he said. "I have to go."

"Go where?" Elmira said.

"Math. We have a quiz."

"But class doesn't start for ten minutes."

Ike once again looked Elmira over. For a girl who was generally ignored, she clearly wasn't someone to be underestimated.

"Or tell you what," she went on. "If you're in a hurry, I'll walk you there."

"No, no, don't walk me." Ike sighed. He had a chocolate chip cookie to eat anyway—might as well get this over with. "So really? You have a blog, is that what you were saying?"

Elmira smiled, proudly—a nice, open smile. Ike didn't think he had ever met someone with such a striking combination of strange and beautiful features.

"Do I have a blog?" she exclaimed. "Sure, I do. But first, hey, are you going to eat that cookie or what?"

Ike blinked. "My cookie? Yeah, why? Do you want some?"

"Only if you aren't having it," Elmira said. "I know. We'll share."

Without waiting for a reply, she broke off half and popped it in her mouth. Ike was almost surprised when she didn't down the rest of his milk in a single gulp.

"So," she said, wiping her mouth on a napkin. "I know I shouldn't have been looking at your text in social studies but I was so now we should finally talk. I mean, we've known each other since kindergarten, right? But we've never *really* talked, have we?"

Ike remembered a few conversations, but they hadn't been long or memorable—mostly Elmira talked *at* people. Though unclear on the exact details, Ike knew she had lost her parents at a young age and had been raised by a grandmother who spent much of her time travelling. Then there was her aunt's job, Sanitation Commissioner of New York, a position Elmira had used to talk the driver of a city street sweeper—a truck that brushed trash from the gutters—into giving her rides to and from school. No question about it, Elmira was weird all around.

"Listen," Ike said. "I appreciate that you care about *The*

Fighting Dragons. It was a cool show. But you know, nothing personal, I'm just not that into talking about it. Bad memories, you know?"

When Elmira nodded gravely, Ike thought she was going to get the hint and leave. Instead, she took his hand.

"It's been hard for you, hasn't it?"

Ike yanked his hand away.

"Are you missing what I said? I don't want to talk about it."

Elmira leaned forward, eyes wide. "Not even if I could prove to you that your dad was an actual hero? It is my belief your father really did fly a dragon. A real one. He really did save the world from those giant locusts. And better yet, when the locusts come back you're going to be called to duty, too—to fly on your own dragon and save the world all over again. And I might get to help."

Ike would have thought anyone else was joking, but Elmira wasn't known around school for her sense of humor. And she certainly wasn't smiling. In fact, eyes wide, fists clenched, her entire being radiated complete belief in what she had just said. Which meant only one thing. She was crazy.

Ike looked around, desperate for an escape. Unfortunately, Diego and Kashvi were long gone. Worse, seated at the only occupied table in the cafeteria were Harrison Opal, a red-haired boy, and his two main goons, Dirk Sher and Molly Willowinski. Large for their ages and with equally big attitudes, Harrison and his two sidekicks caused ninety percent of the grief in the Branford sixth grade.

Ike briefly closed his eyes. No, this was most definitely *not* his day—trapped by the class loser, fully on display to the class bullies.

13

Given Ike's own relatively low social standing, it was the last thing he needed. To make matters worse, when he opened his eyes, Ike saw Harrison, Dirk, and Molly looking his way with an enormous collective smirk.

It was time to shut this down.

"Bye, Elmira," Ike said, reaching for his tray. "I've got to get going."

To Ike's surprise, Elmira grabbed his arm and pulled him forcefully back to his seat.

"Give me a minute, okay? You won't regret it. I know it sounds nutty, but my conclusions aren't only based on my own personal research. *The Fighting Dragon* online community has shared information—lots of it."

Ike couldn't help himself.

"*Fighting Dragon* online community? It's officially called that?"

Elmira's eyes went wide. "Of course it is. And it's not the usual chat-room freaks. We've got some real powerhouses. Our main blogger is Hugh Seymour Livingston, Professor of Ancient Studies at Oxford in England. He's the one who got it all started." Sensing she might have piqued Ike's interest, Elmira kicked it up a notch. "See, a year ago Professor Livingston began his research on King Arthur—you know, the guy with the knights and the round table and Merlin the wizard? Well, check this out. Professor Livingston discovered the history that's recounted in the opening credits of *The Fighting Dragons* is true."

Ike wanted to scream.

"True?" he stammered. "The opening credits? The stuff about Merlin's spell and the portal?"

"Exactly," Elmira said. "And how the giant locusts rushed through that portal and destroyed old London. Then how King Arthur set up the Royal Order of Fighting Dragons to fight them."

"You are crazy," Ike shouted.

"No," Elmira said. "About a year ago, Professor Livingston was in the Dark, Dank Woods."

"Impossible," Ike said. "The Dark, Dank Woods is a made-up place from my dad's show."

Elmira shook her head. "Sorry. The woods were a *real* spot from King Arthur's times. They're a National Park now. Anyway, Professor Livingston found evidence—a dragon toe print and a locust fossil, too—that proves that the Royal Dragons were real. Do you hear me, Ike? *Real.*"

Elmira finished the thought, breathless, just as laughter exploded from across the room. Mortified, he glanced over his shoulder to where Harrison and his goons were cracking up.

"Hey," Harrison called over. "Has this professor dude done research on any other TV shows? Can he take me on a tour of Tyrion Lannister's bathroom?"

Ike felt like crawling under the table and staying there, forever if necessary. But he wasn't off the hook yet.

"Yo, Ike," Dirk yelled. "Take your new girlfriend to the Dark, Dank Woods. I hear it's way romantic."

"Yeah," Molly said with a laugh. "Maybe you'll get your own flying dragon."

Ike was too humiliated to respond. But Elmira was unfazed.

"That's a grammatical error, I'll have you know," she yelled back. "A dragon flies by its very nature. Which makes the term *flying* dragon redundant."

Ike shook himself. If he wasn't careful, Harrison and his goons would link him to Elmira forever. Who knew what kind of insults they would come up with then? And for once, he didn't know if he would be able to blame them.

This time he was up before Elmira could pull him back down. "I've really got to go."

"Great," Elmira said. "I'll walk you to math like we agreed."

"We *didn't* agree." Ike grabbed his tray. "Look, Elmira, I appreciate that my dad and his show meant a lot to you. But I'm going to go study. Don't follow me."

Ike half expected Elmira to still chase him. Apparently, she was smart enough to know when to cut her losses.

"Okay, but we'll chat soon about Sir Matthew Hollingsberry. He was a real guy, Ike, who helped King Arthur start the Dragon Order. And since he's your ancestor, that makes you an automatic member, too."

As Harrison, Dirk, and Molly's laughter filled the cafeteria, Ike felt his face turn bright red.

Sir Matthew Hollingsberry?

His ancestor?

This had to stop. At the cafeteria door, Ike wheeled around.

"Look," he called. "Leave me alone, all right? Find a hobby or something to do that isn't about my dad. Collect rubber bands. Learn how to ride a skateboard. Train a cat how to read French. Anything. But whatever you do, stop talking to me about that stupid show."

Elmira looked stunned. "But I have so much more to tell you. I'm a direct descendant of the royal order, too. At least, that's what my latest research suggests. So don't you see? You and I have to be ready to save the world—together."

Ike held up his hand. "Actually, know what? We don't."

He pushed through the cafeteria door, leaving Elmira chewing unhappily on a strand of hair while Harrison and his sidekicks snickered in the background.

Chapter Three

I ke stumbled through the rest of the day like a zombie, there in body but gone in mind and spirit. As much as he tried to block Elmira's rantings out of his head, he simply couldn't—so much he tanked the math quiz and then air balled two free throws in Phys Ed to lose a basketball game, creating another golden opening for Harrison Opal to tease him, first about his size—tiny—and his general athletic skill—minimal.

A total wreck by the time school was over, Ike had never been so happy to hear the final bell. After gym, he hurried through the Branford entrance gate to join Diego and Kashvi to walk home. Thankfully, to mark the first warm day after a bitterly cold winter, Ike's mom had slipped him twenty bucks to treat for ice cream.

"Hey, hey," he said, holding up the bill. "Look what I have."

"Well, well, well," Diego said with a smile. "Is that fine legal tender for us?"

Ike nodded. "Three cones. On my mom. Just have to bring her the change."

"I always liked that lady," Kashvi said.

Ike smiled. "She has her moments."

The thought of a coffee chip cone did wonders for Ike's mood.

But the day's strange events weren't quite over. With his first step out of the school entranceway, he caught an unfortunate flash of white out of the corner of his eye. A moment later, a street sweeper came rumbling down 89th Street and pulled to a halt in front of the playground.

"Oh, man," Ike said.

"What?" Kashvi asked.

Before he could stop himself, Ike ducked behind the school door. It was a little bit nutty, but the last thing he needed was another face-to-face with the class weirdo.

Diego scratched the back of his neck. "Um, are we playing hide and seek or getting ice cream?"

"First one then the other, okay?" Ike said. "Come on. I'll explain."

Diego and Kashvi exchanged a bemused glance but joined Ike behind the door—and just in time. Moments later, through a crack in the door jamb, the three friends watched Elmira run off the playground toward the sweeper.

"She cornered me at the end of lunch," Ike explained. "It got ugly fast."

Unfortunately, Elmira didn't appear to be in any hurry to leave. While the truck driver, a middle-aged guy with a droopy mustache, leaned impatiently out the window, she peered up and down the block.

"What did she say to you anyway?" Kashvi asked.

"Oh, nothing much," Ike said. "Stuff about how my dad rode a *real* dragon and how the locusts were also real and how she and I were going to ride dragons together one day, too."

Kashvi whistled. "No wonder you tanked that math quiz."

"I know, right?" Ike said. "I couldn't think." He shook his head. "My dad's fans are completely obsessed."

Diego smiled. "Remember what SpaceGirl8819 wrote on his

19

fan page?"

Ike knew what was coming. It was one of Diego's favorites.

"'It is my firm and undying belief," Diego intoned, "that *The Fighting Dragons* has been transmitted by radio waves to the Andromeda Galaxy where it is required viewing on Planet X-52.'"

Ike laughed. "Actually, that was Planet X-53."

"How about the guy who said your dad was a Greek god and his dragon had once belonged to Zeus?" Kashvi said. "Remember him?"

Of course Ike did. He remembered them all.

Diego draped an arm around Ike's shoulder. "Forget about Elmira and all those nutjobs."

"You're right," Ike said. "Thanks."

"It looks like you're safe for today anyway," Kashvi said.

Indeed, it appeared that either Elmira had given up or the driver had threatened to leave without her. After a final anxious look up the block, she jogged to the passenger side of the truck and climbed in. Seconds later, the sweeper rumbled down 89th Street.

"Coast clear," Diego said.

"Great," Ike said. He was a little bit embarrassed by how relieved he felt. "Let's hit it."

Ike didn't know whether to chalk it up to the first nice day of spring or the astonishing power of ice cream, but strolling up Broadway with his two friends, he cleared his mind. Better yet, once the trio had left the school grounds, Diego steered the conversation away from Ike's father to the latest addition to his family. Diego's new pet was a squirrel to accompany his three dogs, four cats, garden snake, and aquarium of rare Boeseman's rainbowfish. An animal lover, Diego was lucky enough to have a mother who was a vet and a father who worked at the Natural History Museum. Together, the family had started Snarl.com, a website devoted to experiments in animal-human communication.

"Cool," Ike said. "A pet squirrel."

"I hope he's nicer than that porcupine you snuck into school last year," Kashvi said. "I'm still pulling the quills out of my kneecaps."

"So is everybody," Diego muttered. "Anyway, this squirrel is totally safe. My mom gave him all his shots. He wants us to call him Scruff."

"He *wants* you to call him that," Ike asked, smiling. "What are you saying? He told you?"

"Well, not directly," Diego replied. "But let's just say I used some de-coding techniques on his chatters that I picked up from Dr. Bernie J. Wong."

"Dr. Bernie J. Wong?" Kashvi asked.

Diego nodded. "He's a new contributor to Snarl.com. Huge in the field of lost and undiscovered languages, both human and animal."

Ike and Kashvi exchanged a glance, but said nothing more. They knew better than to question Diego Miranda's dream of becoming a modern-day Dr. Doolittle.

"Anyway, it's way cool that your building lets you keep all those animals," Kashvi said. "We had to beg our landlord just to let us have dogs."

"Your building makes up for it in other ways, though," Ike said. "I mean, they let you run your shop in the courtyard, right?"

Like Diego, Kashvi had her own unique area of expertise. Over the years, she had worked up a mean side-business, fixing anything from fritzed out computers to jammed jet-skis, to broken down taxis. If it had a motor, Kashvi could make it work. Recently, she had taken in Mr. Donadio's 1986 Volkswagen for an overhaul.

"Did I tell you guys my dad and I are working on a two-man flying contraption thingee?" Kashvi said. "It's sort of like a

21

helicopter."

"Nice," Ike said. "I like two man flying contraption thingies."

"Me, too," Diego said.

"I found an 8.4 liter V-10 engine from an old Dodge Viper on eBay," Kashvi went on. "That thing has some serious kick. My calculations say we'll be able to circle the entire city front to back in ten minutes."

"Promise you'll take Scruff and me for a ride when you're finished," Diego said. "He'd like that."

"Deal."

Ike smiled. Nothing like having interesting friends. By the time the trio had meandered to his corner at West 97th Street, Elmira was a distant memory.

"See you guys tomorrow," Ike said.

"Yep," Diego said. "And remember, your dad's fans are insane. Every single one of them."

"I second that," Kashvi said.

"Yeah," Ike said. "Thanks."

With a final nod, he jogged down the block to his building, said a quick hello to the doorman and took the elevator to the eighth floor. Moments later, he was pushing through his family's front door.

"Hey, I'm home."

As usual, Ike's mother and sister were sitting at the small kitchen table. Snack time.

"Hey, honey," his mom called. "How was school?"

Ike wasn't big on delivering detailed descriptions of his day, regardless of what had happened—good, bad, or strange.

"Fine," he said. "Pretty good."

"Pretty good?" his mom said as Ike walked into the kitchen. "Well, I guess that's better than terrible."

Josie held an Oreo up to her mouth.

"See this cookie?" she asked.

"Yep, I sure do," Ike said. "Are you going to give me some?"

"Nope." She smiled, exposing a row of missing teeth. "I'm going to eat it and watch you suffer."

Ike knew the ritual. As soon as Josie popped the cookie into her mouth, he tickled. As always, his mother looked on with a smile for a moment, then broke them up.

"Careful, Ike," she said. "She'll choke."

With another squeeze, Ike let Josie wash down the rest of the cookie with a swallow of milk. When the tickling ceremony was over, Ike grabbed his own Oreo and moved on to his room.

"Hey," his mom said, "what's the homework situation tonight?"

"A math sheet and some humanities reading. I'm going to chill for a while."

"All right. I'll call you for dinner."

Moments later, Ike pushed into his room. It wasn't particularly big but he knew he was lucky to have a space, even a small one, all to himself—not all New York City kids were so fortunate. After tossing his knapsack on the floor, he grabbed his Nerf basketball and took a hook shot at his homemade hoop. *Score.* After sinking a few more shots, Ike flopped on his bed with his laptop. First things first.

Lying back on his pillows, Ike clicked on his email. It was incredible how much junk accrued in the course of one school day—messages from political parties, clothing stores, and assorted other sites with something to sell. Didn't they realize he was only eleven? He didn't even have a bank account.

With a sigh, Ike scrolled down his list, deleting emails as he went. Along with the ads and the requests for money were the usual messages from Locust and Dragon bloggers.

Now You Can Join The Locust And Dragon Fan

Club.

Delete.

This Starter-Kit Provides You With Everything You Need To Turn Your Family Dog Into An Actual Dragon.

Delete.

Win A Trip To The Spot Where Cameron Hollingsberry Saved The World.

Delete.

Once he had cleared his inbox, he moved on to his main mode of after-school relaxation, SIMS, a virtual world where he could be whoever he wanted. His most recent creation was an alter ego he named James B. Whitney, a six-foot-four boxer-chess champion.

"All right," Ike said to himself. "Let's see what I can do with James today."

But then Ike heard it again. The *ring* of another text. He had changed his phone number three times in the past year. Still, the wackos managed to find him.

Of course, he didn't have to look at it—not right away. But Ike had long ago resigned himself to the fact he was a prisoner of technology. With a frustrated sigh, he reached for his phone and took a peek ... then sat up so fast his knees slammed shut his computer.

It was the same message he had received in social studies.

And from the same sender. But wait. The message wasn't *exactly* the same.

> Ikey, click the link below to watch what really happened to your father on the set of The Fighting Dragons.

Ike gasped. Only one person in his entire life had ever called him Ikey. His father. But his dad was dead, right? Which had to mean one thing ... this text had been written by someone who had known his father.

Heart pumping, Ike grabbed the Nerf ball and took a wild shot at the basket. Then he paced his room, one question tumbling into the next.

Who was 763-372-4667 anyway? How did this person know his dad and why had they contacted him now? Was Elmira involved? Did the mysterious text have any relation to her decision to corner him that same afternoon at lunch? And most important of all ...

Should he press the link?

Yes, the TV studio had said there was no tape of his father's accident. But what if they were wrong—or lying? What if this link showed what the sender said it did?

His father.

His death.

Could he bear to watch?

Ike scooped up the Nerf ball then chucked it hard across the room. Then, before he could change his mind, he grabbed his phone. With his thumb over the link, he hesitated a final time, heart pounding so loudly he half worried that his mom and sister could hear it all the way in the kitchen.

"Just do it," he whispered.

So he did.

The screen of his phone went blank.

Ike leaned forward, waiting.

Chapter Four

L ike many online videos, an ad came first, this one beginning with a pickup truck climbing a snow-covered mountain road. But Ike didn't stick around long enough to find out exactly what was being sold. The minute an icon saying "Skip This Ad" came onscreen, he clicked on it.

And just like that, there it was, the title of his dad's show, in bright red lettering.

The Fighting Dragons

Then, *boom*, a purple sailing ship appeared, thundering across Lake Mead, America's largest reservoir.

"Wow," Ike whispered.

He hadn't watched an episode for years; it felt odd to see it again. As the ship plowed across the water, orange wings sprouted out of its sides. Then it took flight, so realistically Ike found it hard to believe that it was only a TV show, filmed in a fancy studio. As the purple boat sailed into a pale blue sky, a deep bass voice recited the familiar opening.

In the days of King Arthur, wizard Merlin concocted a magic spell that changed the course of history.

With a flash of lightning, a portal opened, revealing a passageway to a strange unknown world.

On screen, the mighty ship swooped behind a cloud, then reappeared on the other side.

From that world the locusts came. Giant locusts that ravaged the land and defeated Arthur's most famous knights of the round table.

As the camera began to pan in on the ship, the distant image of his father stood at the helm.

Finally, the desperate king formed The Royal Order of Fighting Dragons—a society of four courageous men and women who bravely mounted the last dragons of England and defeated the locust scourge, saving the United Kingdom for centuries to come.

Ike couldn't help smiling. Hearing the premise again brought home its utter absurdity. Elmira thought all of this had happened? *Really?*

And it wasn't even quite over. A moment later, the narration came to its stirring conclusion, the solemn voice trembling with importance.

Now with the return of the terrifying locusts, once considered defeated, Earth has fallen on dark times. Thankfully, the royal order has a new leader. He and his brave crew of warriors have taken a solemn vow. As long as they are on the job, our planet's future remains secure.

As the theme music grew into a triumphant fanfare of

trumpets, the camera finally swooped down to the great flying ship itself and focused on the crew. First, of course, there was Ike's father. Though Ike had seen his Facebook page earlier that day, a light shiver still ran up his neck when he came on screen. Wearing the light body armor of the Fighting Dragons, his dad looked even handsomer than Ike remembered. His thick, handlebar mustache, grown especially for the show, flapped gently in the breeze. He flashed a charismatic smile and winked as the credits rolled.

Cameron Rupert Hollingsberry is the Head Dragon Fighter

Ike smiled. His dad's name was so ridiculously British. Then again, his own formal name, Isaac Rupert Hollingsberry, wasn't much better. Thank God everyone at school called him plain old "Ike."

The camera swooped across the deck and came to rest on a hefty older man with dark hair and a giant orange earring. He gave the camera a gap-toothed grin and thumbs up.

Antonio Cortesi is the First Mate

Then the camera swooped up, up, up to the crow's nest where a young woman with light hair and an eye patch kept look out.

Clara Carrington is the Ship Navigator

After that, the camera angled back down to the deck where a man in a white cook's cap did a strange sort of jig and belly dance.

Phillip O'Leary Smith is the Ship Cook

Finally, the camera moved to the stalls. And suddenly there they were, four statuesque dragons. Like any child, Ike had grown up seeing pictures of dragons in storybooks, giant scaly lizards with large, sloping backs, wings, and an extra wide mouth. And that description was largely true. But what the creators of *The Fighting Dragons* had added were the colors. Instead of plain greens and browns, these dragons' skin was a rich blend of light lavenders, dark maroons, sea-greens, pale oranges, pinks, yellows, and blues. Even so, the creatures looked so real it was hard to believe they were no more than artistic creations of a TV studio. One by one, the beasts flapped their wings and breathed fire for the camera. Ike had always found it amusing how each had been named for a different English Park.

Dartmoor.

Loch Lomond.

Northumberland.

Snowdonia.

Then suddenly, there was Ike's father again, climbing onto Dartmoor, the largest of them all, a beautiful, terrifying creature with a silver body, golden wings, and a red stripe down the middle of his forehead. As the music grew, they soared into the sky. With a gentle tug on the reins, Ike's dad moved Dartmoor in a slow arc around the boat. It was a beautiful day, only a single cloud in the blue sky. Even though his father's flight was with wires, computers, and green screens in a TV studio, he was thrilled. His dad's bright smile filled the screen. This was the kind of day where nothing could possibly go wrong.

But then it did.

Ike had heard that it had happened fast, but he still wasn't prepared for just how soon and quickly the giant locust thundered into view. It was a great black flying thing, fully twenty feet long with round yellow eyes. On its hard forehead, between its two swooping antennae, was a small blue splotch. Not wasting a second, the mighty locust dove straight for Ike's father, who reacted immediately, pulling sharply on the reins. Dartmoor craned his neck in preparation. But when the dragon opened his mouth to deliver the death shot ... there was no fire. Not a spark. Not even a wisp of smoke.

Ike gasped.

And the locust was still coming strong. If Ike's dad was

worried, he didn't show it. Quickly, he reached to his waist and pulled a sword out of its sheath. Without a second's hesitation, he parried for the locust's body.

"Yes!" Ike shouted.

His father's sword found its mark, plunging deep into the bug's midsection. But unfortunately, the locust's stinger was already rocketing forward. In its dying gasp, the giant insect caught Ike's dad in the chest and pierced his armor. It happened just that fast. One second, Ike's dad  seemed to be in control of a perilous situation, the next he was mortally wounded, clawing at Dartmoor's left wing, trying desperately to stay on. As the locust fell out of the sky, Dartmoor contorted himself, frantically trying to catch Ike's father with his teeth. But Cameron Rupert Hollingsberry was unable to hang on and he fell, holding his sword, looking up to the sky.

Teary eyed, Ike watched his father fall down, down, down …

But then he heard it, the last thing he expected.

"Ikey," his father called.

What? Had his father called his name?

But wait. There was more, but the words had gotten lost in the wind.

Ike restarted the video. Heart pounding, he fast forwarded past the commercial, the entrance of the purple Viking ship, the pictures of his dad, Antonio Cortesi, Clara Carrington, and Phillip O'Leary Smith, and the dragons. Only when his father got on Dartmoor's back did Ike slow the film back down. Once again, he watched his dad swoop through the sky. Even now, there was a second when Ike thought his father was going to win. But as before, the locust plunged its fierce stinger into his father's chest. Then there was Dartmoor's desperate attempt to grab Ike's dad with his teeth as he fell, gazing up at the camera.

Then came the anguished cry. "Ikey."

And then ...

He had been right. There *was* more. A shout. A few words, perhaps a warning.

"Ikey, you're—a slur of words he didn't understand—dine."

Ike shook. *"Ikey, you're ... dine?"* Ike rewound ten seconds. It was painful to watch his father falling again and again, but he had to know. Unfortunately, this next viewing only brought more confusion. This time, Ike heard his father shout, "Ikey, your text is ... dine."

"*Text?*"

That couldn't be it. Frustrated, Ike looked to the ceiling and tried to clear his mind. What was his father trying to say? That he was the next to dine? Or that his text was fine? Or maybe ...

Ike shuddered.

Could it be?

Time had stopped. No doubt about it, something exciting but dangerous was about to happen. He gave himself a moment to take it all in. Then he felt a chill travel from his big toes all the way up to the base of his neck.

"I'm the next in line," Ike whispered. "I'm the next in line."

Ike was silent for a moment, almost too excited to breathe.

Next in line for what?

To star in a remake of *The Fighting Dragons?*

Or maybe ... was Elmira right? Was the whole thing actually ... *real?* Was he next in line to fight the next wave of giant locusts?

Who really knew?

There were a million questions and not a single solid answer. Even so, Ike had a powerful feeling his life was about to change, perhaps more than he could even imagine.

Chapter Five

The next two hours passed in a blur of confusion and disbelief.

What to do next?

With no clear idea, Ike paced his room, shooting basket after basket, one minute owning the possibility that he was, indeed, the next in line—whatever that meant—and the next dismissing it all as a big joke. After all, with all the weird bloggers and Fighting Dragon misfits in the world, wasn't it possible the video was a hoax? For all Ike knew, someone—maybe even Elmira or even Harrison Opal—had doctored the footage to make it appear his father was calling out to him.

Was someone setting him up? Playing him for a fool?

Ike re-watched the video twice more—all he could stand—but found no new clues, nothing to indicate either why Dartmoor's fire had failed or whether the video was real or who sent it. On four different occasions, he picked up his cell to call Diego or Kashvi. But each time he tossed his phone back to his bed. Kashvi was almost certainly in her building's courtyard, working on her two-man flying contraption thingee while Diego was most likely trying to teach his squirrel to read. But even if Ike had been able to track his friends down, how could he possibly start the conversation? Tell them he was being summoned to join a real live dragon order? Tell them his father was speaking to him from the grave? Kashvi would listen politely, that was for sure, then gently convince him that he was letting his imagination get the better of him.

But Diego? He would laugh him off the phone.

Finally, his mother called Ike for dinner. Though she had made his favorite—spaghetti and meat sauce—Ike picked at his food and answered every question thrown his way with a grunt. After dessert, back in his room, Ike picked up his phone once again, this time to call Elmira. Sure, she was nuts, but who else would have the answers he needed?

But then he paused. Elmira was a crazy person, someone he wanted in his life less, not more. Again, he tossed the phone back on his bed.

With no clear way forward, Ike pulled his American history textbook out of his knapsack and tried to study. But any hope of clearing his mind with homework didn't work either. Still too preoccupied to focus, he read the same page over and over for fifteen minutes until he heard a knock on the door.

"It's Mom. Can I come in?"

Ike sighed. He wasn't particularly surprised. Usually chatty at dinnertime, he had been an anxious, uncommunicative mess.

"Sure," he said.

The door swung open. With a single glance, he saw that his behavior had been even worse than he had thought. His mother was in full-on "concerned mom" mode.

"What's going on, honey?"

Usually, Ike confided in his mother easily. But this was different. How could he possibly tell her what was happening without freaking her out or feeling like a complete idiot?

"Nothing," he said. "I'm good."

"That's nice," his mother said, sitting on his bed. "The trouble is, I don't believe you. So why don't you just tell me."

"Tell you what?"

His attempt to play it cool was failing miserably.

"You barely said a word at dinner. I haven't seen you look that upset in years."

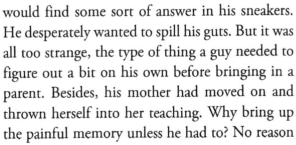

Ike looked down toward his feet, almost as if he hoped that he would find some sort of answer in his sneakers. He desperately wanted to spill his guts. But it was all too strange, the type of thing a guy needed to figure out a bit on his own before bringing in a parent. Besides, his mother had moved on and thrown herself into her teaching. Why bring up the painful memory unless he had to? No reason to upset her over nothing.

"Nothing's going on," he said, looking back up with a forced smile. "I'm fine, really."

Mom eyed him skeptically. "You seem way off. Are you having problems with Diego or Kashvi?"

Ike shook his head. "No, they're good."

"Is there trouble with one of your other classmates? Is that Harrison Opal boy bothering you?"

Ike was surprised. Parents, students, and teachers all knew Harrison was a jerk but he still hadn't expected his mother to zero in on him. Then again … maybe she had given him a way out?

"Actually," Ike said, "I missed two free throws in gym today to lose a game. Harrison was pretty obnoxious about it." He paused for dramatic effect. "He called me a height-challenged marsupial."

To Ike's surprise, instead of nodding sympathetically, his mother laughed.

"A marsupial?" she said. "I didn't know Harrison knew what that meant."

"Well, he does," Ike said, doing his best to look hurt. "And that's what he said."

His mom was too smart. She got down on a knee and took his hands.

"Ike Hollingsberry," she said, looking him square in the eye. "You will tell me this very instant what is really going on with you. I will not leave this room until you do."

Ike looked away. His mom gently turned his face back toward hers. When their eyes met, Ike swallowed hard.

"It's too weird," he blurted.

It was over. He was a goner.

"What's too weird?"

Ike paused.

"Come on, honey. Say it."

And so Ike did. Out it all came. All the events of the day, from the mysterious text in social studies, through the bizarre lunch with Elmira. As Ike spilled the news, he paced and shot baskets. Finally, he got out his phone and pressed on the link to the video itself.

"Here," he said.

His mom took the phone to the edge of his bed and watched quietly without moving a muscle.

"Did you hear that?" Ike said as his father fell from Dartmoor's back. "Dad's shouting, 'I'm the next in line.' But the next in line for what?"

Ike flopped down on his bed, close to tears. With the video finished, his mother wiped away a tear or two of her own, and rubbed a hand through his hair. Despite the grim reality of it all, Ike was hoping—praying—that she would tell him it was all a big joke. That his dad was an actor, nothing more.

Someone is messing with you, she would say. *Let it go.*

Instead, she took his hand.

"Ike," she said.

"Yeah?" he managed.

"You must listen to me very carefully. I never told you because your father made me swear not to unless it was absolutely necessary. With this video surfacing, I think it's time you knew the truth."

Ike gulped. He had never heard his mom speak with such intensity—even when she was angry. His heart was going a thousand beats a minute.

"The night before his final filming of the show, your father was crazy with worry," his mother went on. "Really losing it. So I pushed and prodded and made his life miserable until I finally got him to admit to something so bizarre I almost couldn't believe it. Sometimes, I still can't."

"What?" Ike asked.

His mother took a breath. "Ike, everything was real."

Ike felt like he was watching some other version of himself from the ceiling.

"Really? Everything?"

His mother's eyes were wide, as though she, too, couldn't quite believe it.

"The swarms of locusts were real," she went on. "His dragon was real. All the goofy stuff in the credits of the show—also real. That's what your father said."

"No," Ike said, sitting up. "It was a TV show."

His mom shook her head. "I wish that it was. But according to your dad, as a direct descendant to the first Hollingsberry—that was Sir Matthew—he had been called up to fight. The TV show was a cover-up."

"A cover-up?"

"Yes. Imagine the panic if everyone in the world saw a bunch of giant bugs and dragons flying around? The show was produced so people would see it all as entertainment."

Ike was floored. It was crazy. Insane. And yet ... it all sort of made sense.

"So wait," Ike said. "Seven years ago a swarm of giant locusts really attacked?"

His mother was still gripping his hands, as if holding on for dear life. "According to your father, they were the first swarm in three centuries. No one knew how the portal reopened, but when they came, the Order was summoned."

Ike suddenly remembered something—a scene from episode one where his dad had explained to another member why the Order was still vitally important.

"Because according to the ancient spell," Ike said, "the locusts can only be defeated by the dragons or members of the Royal Order. Is that right?"

His mom nodded. "That's what your dad told me. Conventional weapons like guns or even missiles do nothing against those giant bugs. It's part of the magic."

Ike took a moment to try and comprehend the absurd, potentially terrifying, news.

"But there is something good," his mom said, finally.

Ike blinked. "Um ... good?"

She allowed herself a small smile.

"Your father truly was a hero, Ike. The locust that got him was the last of the swarm. So that's good, isn't it?"

Ike nodded. Yes, it was good. Of course it was. But it would've been even better if his father had managed to survive.

"What about the other members of the Order?" Ike asked. "Antonio Cortesi, Clara Carrington, and Phillip O'Leary Smith?"

"They made it," his mother said. "As far as I know, they are back with their families."

"Back with their families?" Ike said. "So they aren't still on active duty?"

"That's what I'm trying to tell you," his mother exclaimed. "I don't think the Order is even necessary now. I've read blogs and followed chat-rooms every day for the past seven years. There have been no other locust sightings anywhere on Earth. We're safe."

That was good to hear. Even so, it was almost too much for one sixth-grade brain to compute in so short a time.

"Okay," he said. "But ..."

"But what?"

Ike hated to say it. "But Elmira made it seem like we were going to have to fight any day."

To his surprise, his mother blinked, then gave him a funny look.

"Did you say Elmira?"

Ike nodded. "Yeah. Elmira Hand. The weird girl from my class I told you about. Who cornered me at lunch. Why?"

His mom shook her head in disbelief. Then she grabbed his computer, called up the internet and began to type.

"What are you doing?" Ike asked.

"I can't believe I didn't put it together before."

"Put what together before?"

His mother kept typing, then pressed "Enter." Finally, she turned the screen toward him.

"This," she said.

There it was—that odd combination of light brown skin, large ears, and chapped lips that could only be one particular person.

"Why are you showing me a picture of her?"

"Because this is her website," his mom exclaimed. "Elmira Hand is *Elmira Speaks*. I read her blog every day."

"What?" Ike asked. "You read *Elmira Speaks*?"

It was almost more astonishing than anything else that had

40

happened in the previous twenty-four hours.

"I do," his mom said. "She's up there with Professor Livingston on all the dragon history."

"You've got to be kidding."

"I'm not. And she claims to be a direct descendant of the Order, too."

"She said that to me at lunch," Ike said. "I assumed she was nuts."

"Maybe not," his mother replied. "I think she said she was a distant relation to Clara Carrington."

"The navigator on dad's show?"

"Right. And Clara Carrington is a direct descendant of Sir Arthur Carrington of Pembroke who fought in the first Royal Order."

"Elmira wrote all that in her blog?" Ike asked.

"Yes."

"And you actually believe her?"

His mother shrugged. "It's possible. Lots of people who are related have different last names. Wait a second."

"What?" Ike asked.

"If Elmira Hand says there's trouble coming, that's something to consider. She hasn't blogged about that yet. It must be recent news."

"Wait a second?" Ike said. "Because Elmira said it, now you're worried?"

"Hold on," his mother said.

Just like that, she was on her feet.

"Wait," Ike called. "Where are you going?"

She was already out the door. Confused, Ike looked down the hallway just in time to see her disappear into her bedroom.

"Mom."

"Just a second," she called.

Ike had an irrational fear that his mother was going to reappear with Elmira herself, as though she had the girl waiting in her closet. But when his mom emerged a few moments later, she was alone.

"What was that about?" he called, as his mother strode back up the hall toward him.

Then he saw what she was holding. Across her shoulder was a knapsack.

"What's in there?" Ike asked.

His mom pulled him back into his room and sat next to him on the bed. Then she reached inside the knapsack and pulled out something small and gold.

"What's that?" Ike asked.

Before his mother had a chance to answer, he knew. It was a handle to a weapon. Though it had obviously been cleaned and shined, there were remnants of grainy dirt in its nooks and crannies.

"Oh, my gosh," Ike whispered. He had never felt more excited and terrified in his life. "Is that Dad's *sword*?"

His mother nodded. "They retrieved it after his death. I've been holding it for you."

Ike looked to the weapon. The handle was engraved with the face of a dragon, flaring its nostrils and baring its jaws. On its bottom was a single word, etched in bold capital letters: ORDER. Underneath, in print almost too tiny to read were initials: S.M.H.

"Sir Matthew Hollingsberry," Ike whispered.

"Yes," his mother said. "The founder of the Order. This sword was made especially for him. You release the blade by pressing this button."

Ike looked more closely. Indeed, there was a small button on the grip next to his thumb.

"So the sword is ... inside?"

His mother nodded.

Still too awed to hold it, Ike brushed a finger against the engraving of the dragon. "You don't think I'm going to need it, do you?"

His mother closed her eyes. When she opened them again, she forced a smile. "This is probably a big mess over nothing, Ike. I mean, just to say it, I agree with you about Elmira. She's a smart girl but she's a little bit out of her mind about these dragons. Even so, who knows what to believe? I don't want you to worry. Like I said, I check the blogs every single day. There are no more locusts. None. Your father defeated them. But something else is also true. If they do come back ... well, as a direct descendant of the original Order, they'll find you, Ike, wherever you are. Just like they found your dad. I know it sounds crazy but I've studied this for years now. So I'd still feel better if you took this. I know your father would want you to have it. The night before he died, he told me he wanted you to be ready."

Ike could feel his voice trembling. "You mean ... to *fight*?"

His mom nodded gravely. "If you have to." She held the sword toward him. "Here. Try it."

Finally, Ike let his right hand slip onto the dull gold handle. It had a comfortable grip and nice solidity to it, substantial but not too heavy to swing.

"Go ahead," his mom said. "Try it out."

It was hard to feel brave in the middle of his small bedroom, with a Nerf basketball at his feet. Even so, Ike stood, gripping the handle of the sword. When he extended his right arm, his thumb fell naturally over the release button. He gave it a nudge ... *Whoosh.* Out blazed the blade from the sheath, fully three feet long.

Ike gasped. Was he really holding ... a *sword*? In the middle of his bedroom? It seemed too absurd to believe. But then, something about the fierce steel hypnotized him. Standing still, he held the sword toward the ceiling and allowed himself to gain control of his breathing. Slowly, carefully, he moved the gleaming weapon to the right, then the left, watching the metal reflect against his overhead light. Then *bam*. He whipped his arm hard, sawing at the air.

"Not bad," his mother said.

Ike laughed and lunged forward with all his might, stabbing an imaginary adversary. Then he stabbed another and another after that. Finally, on a whim, he kicked the Nerf ball into the air and lunged again …

"Yaaaa," he cried.

To Ike's amazement, the Nerf ball was suddenly six inches down from the tip of the sword, skewered like a shish kebab. He wheeled around to face his mom.

"Did you see that? Did you see what I did?"

His mother laughed and wiped away a tear—out of pride or fear, Ike couldn't tell—maybe both.

"Yes, I did," she said. "Come here." She spread her arms wide.

Ike hesitated, but only for a second. As "the next in line," he was probably getting too old for such things. But the way he saw it, even heroes needed a good hug every now and then.

Chapter Six

Though Ike had graduated to walking to and from school by himself a year earlier, the next morning, his mother wanted to tag along.

"Just to make sure you're okay," she said over breakfast.

They were at the small kitchen table with Josie.

"I'll be fine," Ike assured her, pouring milk in his cereal.

"Really?" she asked.

Ike could tell from her tone she hadn't told Josie what had happened—the sword and his father's death were to be their secret.

"Sure, I'm sure. I even slept well."

It was strange, but true. Exhausted from the day's events, Ike had gone out moments after hitting the pillow.

"You slept?" his mother asked.

Josie frowned. "What's so strange about that?"

Ike smiled. His mom had no choice but to shrug.

But Ike wasn't free quite yet. Later on, when they reached the elevator, it took a little bit more than the customary mother-son back and forth before he could convince her he was really all right.

"You're sure you don't feel too weird?" she asked.

"Weird, sure," Ike said. "But not *too* weird. You said yourself the locusts were gone."

She nodded. "Yes, at least I haven't seen anything that leads me to think differently."

"Good," Ike said. "I'll be fine, Mom. Seriously."

Ike could see her looking for a million reasons to keep him home and then reject each one. "Okay, then." She gave him a quick kiss. "Have a good day. See you this afternoon."

Soon, Ike was walking down Broadway to school with his  knapsack perched on his back. Though always a substantial load to tote, today it was even heavier—and not because Ike had packed extra books. That morning, before coming out for breakfast, he had collapsed his father's sword back into its handle, wrapped it in an old New York Mets T-shirt and tucked it at the bottom of the knapsack. Yes, Branford had strict rules prohibiting any kind of weapons in school. Little kids weren't even allowed to bring toy guns. Even so, now that his mother had backed up Elmira's story, Ike had to tell Diego and Kashvi what was going on. Rather than do it over the phone the night before, he had elected to find them in the playground before the opening bell. The sword would be proof that he wasn't losing his mind.

Cutting down Broadway, Ike discovered that bearing the weight of an ancient weapon, not to mention a huge new secret, did a number on his appetite. At 90th Street, he popped into a deli for a quick bagel, but the minute he set foot back into the busy morning whirl, he nearly choked. Cruising up Broadway, directly in front of him, was a street sweeper. Ike shuddered. Was Elmira stalking him? Following him to school?

As the sweeper accelerated through the light, Ike glanced

47

inside the front cab. Not only was the driver an older man—definitely not Elmira—but the passenger seat was empty.

"Relax," Ike thought. "Chill."

It was easier said than done.

Elmira. Should he share what he had found out with her? The last thing he wanted was a closer friendship with someone everyone in his class thought was crazy. But how could he ignore the girl his mother heralded as one of the world's greatest dragon scholars? Someone his mother claimed might be related to the Royal Order, too? And hadn't Elmira said that they both had to be ready to fight? Fight what? More locusts? Did she know something his mother didn't? Was there a gang of killer bugs gathering in Yonkers, ready to attack the city?

It would sure be nice to know. On the other hand, if Ike took Elmira into his confidence, she would stick to him like a slobbery dog to an old blanket. So why show her the sword now when the overwhelming odds were that the locusts were gone forever anyway? He could always catch her up later if it was necessary.

"Later," he said to himself. "Much later."

His mind made up, Ike took another bite of his bagel and hurried the rest of the way to school.

Most mornings, Ike liked to take a minute in the playground to burn off some energy before classes. But today, he parked himself by a small crowd of students and parents who were lingering by the Branford main gate and peered down the block.

"Come on, Diego and Kashvi," he said to himself. "Anytime now."

Unfortunately, neither friend had gotten the memo that he had big news. A shaggy-haired boy who Ike briefly thought was Diego turned out to be another sloppy kid. Then Ike was distracted by a long limo that idled up the block and stopped in front of the school. Though most Branford Students arrived by foot or public bus, some of the wealthier kids were driven. And Ike knew who was about to get out of this particular vehicle long before the chauffeur jogged around to open the back passenger door— Harrison Opal.

Along with being the Branford sixth grade's most notorious jerk, Harrison held the dubious honor of being the son of Theodore Opal, the famous real estate developer who had made his fortune by knocking down old buildings then building monstrous, gleaming new ones in their place. Recently, his company had finished The Opal Plaza, a two hundred room luxury hotel north of Times Square that required the destruction of two restaurants, a toy store, a florist, and a rare record shop. Also under construction were The Opal Towers, a one hundred and three story apartment complex, and Broadway's newest theatre, The Opal.

As he did every morning, Harrison pushed out the limo door and looked up the block like he owned it. Though Ike tried to avert his eyes, he was too slow. Harrison caught him looking.

"Hey, hey," he called. "How's the basketball star of the Branford School?"

Ike grimaced. The two air-balled free throws in gym class. Over the years, he had found the best method for dealing with Harrison was either total silence or extreme sarcasm. This time, he opted for the latter.

"Thanks, Harrison. I *so* appreciate that."

Harrison flashed back his own fake grin.

"Anytime, little man. You got it."

Ike was fully prepared for Harrison to take it further, perhaps perform a dramatic reenactment of his failure at the free throw line. But with parents nearby, the larger boy didn't push it.

Or maybe there was another reason for Harrison's restraint? A moment later, an enormous man in a tightly fitted three-piece suit and a pair of navy blue loafers ballooned out of the car. It was Theodore Opal himself. With brightly dyed red hair, the elder Opal resembled a flabbier replica of his son, as though Harrison had been set on the beach to wrinkle then inflated with a bicycle pump. To Ike's surprise, Theodore was holding a silver handled cane that was studded with a dozen or more actual opals. Had he hurt himself or was he showing off an expensive new play-thing?

Though no one was saying hello, Theodore used the ornate cane to wave to the other parents like the politician he had once briefly been. Seven years earlier, Opal had run for mayor, promising "A new building for every block," and been soundly thrashed by the current mayor, the popular John Andretti. After a few 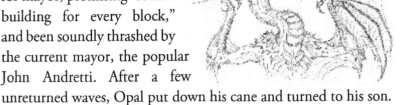 unreturned waves, Opal put down his cane and turned to his son.

"Timothy will pick you up after school," he said.

"Got it, Dad."

"And don't forget to do your homework early. We're going to the Mets game tonight."

Harrison grinned. "Front row, field level?"

"Sorry, kiddo," Theodore said. "My ticket guy could only get first row mezzanine this time. But it's going to be great. Just fantastic."

Harrison looked like he had taken a kick to the gut. "The mezzanine? Doesn't sound fantastic to me."

"Field level next time," Theodore said with a quick smile. "Behind the dugout. I'll pay someone to arrange a meeting with the players afterwards. Promise. You'll love it. It's gonna be so great."

Theodore Opal patted his son on the shoulder, waved the cane once more to his imaginary admirers and moved back to the limo. But before Opal could maneuver his cumbersome body inside, Ike was surprised by a loud voice from near the school door.

"Hey, wait a minute. Is it true?"

Opal spun around and squinted.

The voice called again, growing in intensity. "Are the papers right? Are you trying to get zoning rights to build a hotel in the middle of Central Park?"

Ike looked to his right as a middle-aged lady, obviously someone's mom, strode fearlessly toward the limo.

"What was that?" he asked.

"The luxury hotel in Central Park," the lady continued. "The Opal Palace. It was in the *Times*."

"Yes," Opal said. "And people are going to adore it."

"Adore it?" the lady cried. "You'll have to tear down the Central Park Zoo." The woman had marched all the way to the man himself. Though no more than five feet, she stood as tall as she could and met his eyes directly.

"Well?" she said, sharply. "Won't you?"

"Tear down the zoo?" Opal stammered. "I used to visit the seals there as a little boy. Polar bears, too. Animals are terrific. No one likes zoos more than me."

The woman wasn't satisfied. "So *are* you trying to build the hotel or not?"

Opal forced a smile. "Discussions with the mayor and city council are ongoing." He tossed his cane through the door of the limo and ducked quickly back inside. But in his hurry to get away, he hit his foot against the doorjamb, knocking loose his right loafer. While stretching to pull it back on, his shoe fell off completely and dropped to the pavement. The woman picked it up.

"Seriously?" she asked with a growing smile. "Navy blue

loafers?"

Opal grabbed his shoe, visibly shaken. "My clothes are custom made. Magnificent cuts. The best natural fibers. Fantastic stuff. Now, if you don't mind."

Ike bit back a laugh. He must be used to questions about his business practices, but the remarks about his appearance had touched a nerve.

Opal slammed the door. Seconds later, the limo took off down the street, leaving the irate mom choking on a mouthful of exhaust. Coughing, she wheeled around to face Harrison.

"I'm sorry to have done that in front of you," she said. "But I do not approve of what your father is doing to this city."

With that, she huffed back down the street. To his surprise, Ike found himself feeling almost sorry for Harrison. After all, he knew better than maybe anyone how hard it could be to live in the shadow of a famous father. Even so, Harrison didn't seem particularly fazed.

"Maybe you didn't hear, but no one loves zoos as much as my dad," he said. "We've got a pet vulture at home."

Ike watched the red-haired boy saunter past the school gate to join his two sidekicks. Only then did he finally hear a familiar voice echo down the street.

"Hey, Ike."

He wheeled around. Kashvi was trotting his way with her dogs, Brooklyn and Hudson, pulling hard on their leashes.

"Easy, boys," she said.

Ike reached down to scratch their chins.

"You good?" Kashvi asked.

"Yeah, great," Ike said.

In truth, seeing Kashvi made him so eager to spill what had been going on, he decided not to wait for Diego. But before he could get out a single word, a lanky man strolled up, holding a giant cup of Starbucks coffee. It was Kashvi's dad. Ike forced a smile. The gut-spilling would have to wait.

"Hey, Mr. Changar," Ike said. "How's your two-man flying contraption thingee coming along?"

"Good," he said. "We're using an 8.4 liter V-10 engine."

"From a Dodge Viper, right?" Ike said.

Kashvi pulled on the leash to hold Brooklyn and Hudson still. "Last night, I recalibrated the carburetor and experimented with liquid hydrogen to give some extra lift."

Mr. Changar beamed. "What can I say? This girl has serious skills."

Kashvi smiled at her dad then leaned close to Ike.

"You okay?" she whispered. "You look a little, I don't know, stunned."

"I'm fine," Ike said. "But listen, something's happened."

Before he could say more, Brooklyn and Hudson yanked on their leashes, yapping wildly. Glancing down the sidewalk, Ike saw

who they were so interested in: Diego. Though it looked as though he had actually combed his hair, or someone had tried, anyway, his shirt was on backwards and his red sneakers were untied.

"He's the greatest," Kashvi said. "But that kid is in desperate need of a make-over."

"Yeah," Ike said. "But maybe that's why animals love him so much?"

Kashvi let go so the dogs could run into Diego's arms. Moments later, he led them back, smiling. Now that Diego had arrived, Ike was eager for Kashvi's dad to take the dogs and scram. Instead, he took a step toward Diego.

"You know," he said. "I was killing time the other day when I decided to see what your family has been posting on Snarl.com. This Dr. Bernie J. Wong has some interesting ideas."

To Ike's chagrin, Diego's eyes lit up. Worse, Mr. Changar's question led to a head-on discussion of the possibility of animal-human languages then segued to a debate on New York City's best pets.

Ike was dying. With school about to start he'd never have the chance to tell Diego and Kashvi what was going on now. Why hadn't he called last night?

"Well," Mr. Changar said, "looks like it's time to say goodbye."

Ike looked toward the gate. In keeping with Branford tradition, Headmistress Bergman, a trim elderly woman, had come out to greet the students as they entered the school. He sighed.

"Yep," he said. "That's how it looks."

He shook his head, deeply annoyed but unable to say anything. Out of the corner of his eye, he saw Kashvi give her father a quick hug.

But then as Mr. Changar let his daughter go, he squinted into the distance. "Well, well," he said. "That's certainly interesting."

"What?" Kashvi said.

Mr. Changar pointed down 89th Street.

"That."

Ike turned and looked. On the far horizon, over the Hudson River, was a large black dot. It *was* interesting—also strange.

"What is it?" Ike asked.

"Don't know," Kashvi said.

Diego brushed his hair out of the way and squinted. "It's a black dot," he said. "What's the big deal? Nothing to worry about."

Ike wasn't so sure. To his alarm, the dot was picking up speed and growing larger and larger by the second. It wasn't making enough noise to be a helicopter and it didn't look wide enough to be a plane.

But whatever it was, it was certainly *something*. In fact, the dot was coming so fast now most everyone else in the vicinity had noticed it, too.

"Yo," someone cried, "is that a giant dirt ball?"

"No, it's a tornado."

"In New York? Not a chance."

Ike didn't think so either. It wasn't tall or thin enough to be a tornado. But as the dot grew bigger, he did notice two longish spires curling off its top. And the closer the dot came, the taller the spires grew until Ike suddenly knew what they were.

"*Antennae*," he whispered with a shiver.

What else could they be? Worse, it wasn't long before Ike noticed the dot had a mouth. And atop its back was a barely discernable blur, the rapid fluttering of two powerful wings. Then all the disparate elements—the antennae, the mouth, and wings— seemed to meld together, revealing its unquestionable identity.

"It's a bug," Ike cried. "A locust."

"Is it real?" Diego asked.

A day earlier, Ike would've said the bug was a giant robot or a clever special effect. But that was a day earlier.

"I think so," Ike said.

"Who cares if it's real?" a parent yelled. "It's bigger than a subway car."

"Cripes," somebody else said. "We've gotta move."

With the locust two blocks away, the sidewalk exploded into a cacophony of terrified shrieks and shouts as parents and kids alike ran for it, scattering lunchboxes and knapsacks as they went.

"Come on," Diego said, tearing for the street. "We're out of here."

But Ike was frozen with equal parts terror and disbelief. The bug was a block away, thundering ten feet over the sidewalk as though it had been shot out of a cannon. And now that it was closer, Ike could finally make out its body in more detail—its four small front legs and two giant back ones. Its scaly, light green skin and, worst of all, its eyes. Two giant black circles, one on each side of its head—focused directly on him.

"Ike?" Diego called from behind a parked car. "Come on. Hide."

Ike wheeled around, looking frantically up and down the sidewalk. Hide? Suddenly, there wasn't enough time. The school door was too far away and the cars were all locked. With the raging bug seconds away, Ike knew there was only one thing that could save him ...

His father's sword.

Chapter Seven

Yes. Easy.

All he had to do was take the sword out of his knapsack and slice the locust in two.

Except, there was a problem. At the rate the bug was moving, he would be chomped to pieces before he could get a finger on the knapsack's zipper.

"Over here, Ike."

It was Kashvi, crouched with her dad behind a parked car. With the locust upon him, Ike sprang wildly toward them, cutting it so close he felt the wind from the bug's wings on his back as it swooped by. Tripping on a discarded lunchbox, Ike came up next to Kashvi's dad with a badly skinned knee.

"It's after you," Mr. Changar cried.

"Run for it," Kashvi cried.

Brooklyn and Hudson were cowering in her arms.

"No," Ike said. "I have to fight."

But how? With the mighty bug already turning for a counter-attack, there was still no time to take off his knapsack, let alone grab the sword. With nothing else to do, Ike grabbed Mr. Changar's cup of Starbucks.

Mr. Changar's eyes bugged out as wide as they could go. "What are you doing?"

Standing, Ike took the cap off of the coffee. It was crazy, yes. But what other choice did he have? Wasn't the sign of a great warrior the ability to improvise on the battlefield? Wasn't that what his father would have done?

Just like that, the locust came at him, its mouth open so wide Ike could see the back of its throat.

Shaking, Ike stood in the middle of the sidewalk and cocked his arm.

The bug was ten feet away.

Five.

Ike threw as hard as he could.

Splat.

Bullseye.

Hot coffee to the face.

Hovering a few feet above the sidewalk, the giant bug shuddered, frantically rubbing its eyes with its antennae. Now to get the sword.

But the locust recovered more quickly than Ike thought possible. Before he could get the knapsack straps off, it sprung again, forcing Ike to lurch backwards then run full out for the playground. With the bug hot on his heels, Ike saw it—a city trash can. *Boom.* He kicked it on its side, spilling garbage all over the sidewalk. Then he picked up the whole can and wheeled back around, holding it in front of him like a shield.

"Okay," Ike shouted. "See if you can get me now."

The locust stopped short, temporarily confused by Ike's strange choice of weapon, but then it rose to its hind legs, growing taller and taller, suddenly looming over him like a mighty tree. Ike swallowed hard. There was a certain freedom in the knowledge he was about to die. After all, what was there to lose? He could either die terrified or finding the will to be brave.

"Come on," Ike shouted. "Show me what you've got."

The trash can was getting heavy but he didn't dare lower it. The locust waved its antennae to the right, then once to his left, like an expert boxer sizing up his opponent, waiting for the exact moment to attack. Then it lunged.

"Check this," Ike cried and threw the trash can with all his might.

Another direct hit. Right in the mouth. Eyes watering, the locust pulled wildly at his face with his antennae.

Ike calculated he had three more seconds, if he was lucky, to plan his next move. Three precious seconds, but still not nearly enough time to get his knapsack off his back and grab the sword. Should he tackle the bug's legs?

"Here," Kashvi cried.

Brooklyn and Hudson's leashes came flying through the air. Ike caught the first in his right hand and the second in his left. By the time the locust spat out the garbage can, Ike was snapping them like nunchucks.

Thwack. Snap.

Leash number one hit the attacking bug in the nose; the next thwacked the beast's forehead.

Furious, the locust went on the offensive, lashing out with its antennae, slapping Ike on either side of the face, pushing him back up the sidewalk and against the school gate. Just like that, Ike was hemmed in with nowhere to run. Though he continued to desperately flick the leashes, the locust took every blow and kept on coming. Ike swallowed hard. He was about to die, just like his dad. He needed a miracle.

Or maybe just a street sweeper ...

Ike heard the groan of the engine before he saw it, a glimpse of white that morphed into a truck jumping the curb, its circular brushes spinning like mad on the sidewalk. And who was behind the wheel? Elmira. Ike blinked. How she had gotten control of the vehicle, he didn't know—but hadn't she said that they might do battle together?

"I got you covered," she shouted.

Ike knew one thing. He had to keep the locust facing forward.

"Yo. Bug. Try and get me."

He flicked one of the leashes again, but this time the beast caught it in its mouth and pulled it out of Ike's hand. Then the locust moved to its back legs, rising a good twenty feet in the air, rubbing its antennae together, savoring the kill. Its eyes glinted. With pleasure? With hunger?

"Come on, Elmira," Ike whispered to himself. "Step on it." Then a final taunt to the locust. "Yo, bug. Bet you can't eat me in one gulp."

The locust lunged, mouth wide. Hitting the pavement hard, Ike rolled right, slithered underneath the insect's back two legs, and scrambled down the sidewalk. When the locust turned to pursue him, the sweeper was there, going all out.

"Greetings, bug," Elmira yelled.

Crunch.

Boom.

The sweeper flattened the locust against the school gate. As Elmira kept her foot hard on the gas, the giant bug twitched twice, then went still.

Ike rose from the pavement, heart pounding, light-headed.

"It's dead," Elmira called out the window, finally taking her foot off the pedal. "I told you we were going to be a team."

Classmates and parents peeked up from behind cars and rose

nervously from the street. Some students were crying, others shaking. By the school door, a group of moms were lying in a tangled heap atop of Headmistress Bergman.

Stunned, Ike stared at the enormous dead insect, almost as though it was a figment of his imagination. As he finally slid his knapsack off his back, he heard an unfamiliar sound. Cheering— *for him.*

Dazed, Ike scanned the crowd. It was true. Parents, students and teachers were on their feet clapping. The next few minutes passed in a blur of weeping, hugs, and relief. Sirens filled the air and a police car arrived, then another and another after that. Then came a fire truck and a van bearing the logo *Channel 8 - Eyewitness News.* Reporters were suddenly shouting questions into microphones and talking to cameras.

Then Elmira was there, jabbering wildly.

"Oh, my gosh, can you get a load of that bug? It's even bigger than I imagined. But we did it, Ike. Like I said we would. We killed it."

The giant insect slid from the sweeper's windshield and hit the pavement with a shiver. Again, the crowd cheered. Ike allowed himself a small smile. He had done it. Won the first real fight in his life. And against a giant monster.

But then …

He looked more closely at the bug.

"Wait, did you see that?" he asked Elmira.

"See what?" she said.

"It twitched."

"Twitched? Really?"

"Yes. I'm sure of it."

The bug lifted a shaky leg and planted it on the sidewalk, causing the crowd to scatter once again, running wildly for cars, lampposts and swing-sets. A policeman reached for his holster.

"Out of my way," he called.

"No," Ike cried. "I've got this."

As the mighty locust found its footing, Ike's hand finally found the zipper to his knapsack. He yanked out the sword handle, scattering his textbooks all over the sidewalk. Then he pressed the button.

Whoosh.

Out came the blade. The minute it saw the sword, the locust sprang with all its remaining force.

But the next in line was ready.

With a mighty lunge, he caught the bug with the blade directly in the forehead. At the moment of impact, the bug went completely still. Then as the crowd began to cheer once again, Ike pulled the sword free. The giant insect shuddered violently, teetered to its right, lurched to its left, and then ...

Like the locust who had killed his father, it happened fast—so fast that Ike saw no more than a blur.

But a searing pain exploded in his gut. With an astonished gasp, he looked to his stomach. The tip of the locust stinger slipped out of his abdomen and dropped to the sidewalk as he fell to his knees. Only then did the mighty bug's body shudder a final time and go still.

"Ike."

Was it Kashvi? Diego?

The cold, blue sky shimmered above. The sun put everyone in silhouette.

Someone shouted, "Give him room. The beast got him. He's been stabbed."

His body rose in the air. He'd been lifted ... by police or

firefighters? Someone carried him and slid him into a vehicle. An ambulance? Was he on a stretcher?

The door shut.

An engine revved up.

A siren wailed.

And everything went black.

Chapter Eight

When Ike came to, he was in a bed in a small room with gray stone walls. A single beam of light shone through a gap in the shutters of the only window.

Groggy and disoriented, he rubbed his eyes, then took stock of his surroundings. There wasn't much to see. Across the way was a bureau with three drawers. Next to that was a bare oak desk that held a picture frame with the faded photo of a young boy smiling down from a tree. At first Ike didn't recognize it. But then he did a double take. He knew that picture. In fact, he knew that kid—it was him.

Ike sat up with a start, sending a jolt of pain through his midsection. Looking down, he saw a white bandage wrapped around his torso. He remembered. The locust. The wound from the stinger. He was lucky to be alive.

But for the time being, Ike was more concerned with the picture. Slowly, he swung his feet to the stone floor, shuffled a few steps to the desk and picked it up. He remembered when it was taken, a sunny day in Central Park on one of his father's rare days off. Wearing an old *Fighting Dragons Fan Club* T-shirt, Ike was grinning down from the branch of a tree—a nice shot from a happier time.

But what was this picture doing here?

Ike took another look around the small room. Where was he, anyway?

Ike put the photo back and swung open the shutters, filling the room with light. Holding a hand out to block the sun, he blinked at a shaggy lawn that ran a good one hundred yards to the edge of what appeared to be miles of grassy swamp. To the left were two barns, one red, the other light brown. But the real surprise was down below. As Ike's eyes adjusted to the light, he made out what appeared to be a moat. And lying across the moat was a lowered drawbridge.

Ike was stunned. Was he in a castle? Had he traveled back in time to King Arthur's days? Was he dreaming?

"Where the heck am I?" he said out loud.

Just then, the door swung open with a jarring creak. More surprises. Ike wheeled around to find himself face to face with an extremely large, old man with a long, white beard and light brown eyes. Even stranger was how the man was dressed—a red tunic and boots laced up all the way to his knees. In his right hand was a dark, wooden cane.

"Well, well. You're out of bed, I see."

A British accent—one that reminded Ike of the characters on the detective shows his mother liked to watch.

Ike nodded nervously.

"Uh, yeah. I am."

"Feeling better then, I take it?" the man said.

Ike touched the bandage. His wound didn't hurt as much as he might have expected.

"I guess."

The man grinned. With every other tooth yellow, his mouth resembled a discolored piano.

"That was quite a kerfuffle you got into with that locust."

Ike blinked. "Kerfuffle?"

"Apologies. One of my British sayings. I meant fight." The man took a step forward and leaned on his cane. "But we'll have plenty of time to talk of the locusts. Tell me, Isaac Rupert Hollingsberry, what do you think of your father's room?"

"My father's ...?"

He couldn't even finish the thought. He knew what had happened. The locust had killed him. He was dead. The old man with the white beard was some sort of British St. Peter. But was this really where he was going to spend eternity? In a small room in a castle that had once belonged to his dad?

Ike collapsed onto the bed.

"What?" the man said. "It's not that bad, is it?"

"Not that bad?" It was crazy but he had to ask it. "I'm ... I'm dead, right?"

Thankfully, the man's response was perfect, a light chuckle, followed by a quick belly laugh.

"You aren't dead, boy," he said, plopping his large body next to Ike. "You're very much alive. Of course, it's lucky we were able to get you here right away. Otherwise, it would've been the end of you."

Ike felt silly to be so relieved.

"So where am I, then?"

The man looked surprised. "You mean you don't know?" he exclaimed, but then he immediately shook his head. "Of course he doesn't, you old blighter. How could he?" Then he looked back to Ike and put a well-worn hand on his shoulder. "You're at the Royal Order of Fighting Dragons."

"What?" Ike stood back up, heart pounding. "You mean,

wait—I'm at the Order? Now? For real?"

"Yes, boy," the man said, standing as well. "And this was your father's room. If you'll allow me to introduce myself, they call me Thaddeus, Head of the Royal Order. I'm also the fellow who's been sending you those texts."

That got Ike's attention.

"You? Really?"

Thaddeus frowned and twirled the end of his beard with his pinky. "What's wrong? Think I'm too ancient to use the internet? Not for nothing, you could've figured out who I was all by yourself. Replace the numbers 763-372-4667 with letters on the dial from an old fashioned rotary phone and you get ROF-DRAGONS. The Royal Order of Fighting Dragons. That's me and that's where you are."

Ike's mind spun with questions.

"But how ...?"

"Did you get here?" Thaddeus asked. "That part was pretty easy, actually. Ever since we got word the locusts were returning, we've been busy reaching out to the four new direct descendants, aiming to get them ready to fight. When the locust got you outside your school, I was there already, thank goodness, and was able to get you right out."

"How did you get me here so fast?" Ike asked.

"We took the ambulance on a little detour to the Westchester Airport where we had a seaplane ready. Flew you here directly. The locust sting has poison in it, you know. No regular hospital could have cured you. But we fixed you up just fine, I think."

Still stunned, Ike looked down at his bandage. Yes, he seemed pretty well fixed.

"But where are we?" he said. "Upstate New York?"

Thaddeus grinned, once again exposing those discolored teeth. "Somewhere warmer. The dragons like it that way."

"Then where?" Ike asked. "Florida?"

"Yes, boy," Thaddeus said. "Hidden smack in the middle of the Everglades, the largest stretch of untamed wilderness in the States."

Ike looked back out the window. Again, he saw the great, uneven lawn, the two barns and the moat. Beyond that were miles of tall grass and marsh. Was it really the Everglades? He couldn't be sure. But given the craziness of the past couple of days and his near-death experience, Ike felt in no position to dispute anything.

"Does my mom know where I am?"

Thaddeus nodded. "She does. Given what happened with that devilish locust, she knew it was for the best that you finally take your rightful place in your father's footsteps. She also knew that the Order is the only place where we could save your life."

It was a lot to take in. Luckily, Thaddeus seemed to understand that.

"Listen. I brought along someone who might help make you feel more at home." He called over his shoulder. "You can come on in, now."

The door creaked open a second time. Thaddeus was so large Ike had to peek around him to see who was entering. For an instant, he hoped it would be Diego and Kashvi. Even so, he never thought he would be so happy to see—Elmira. Indeed, there she was—and wearing the same kind of tunic and boots as Thaddeus—apparently some sort of uniform of the Order.

"What are you ... I mean, how did you ...?"

Ike was too discombobulated to finish a thought.

"I'm a direct descendant, too," Elmira said. "I told you yesterday in the lunchroom, remember?"

"Yeah," Ike said. "And my mom told me you wrote about it on your blog. You're related to Clara Carrington?"

"I'm her second cousin once removed," Elmira said. "I've known that for years. But what I didn't know for sure until Thaddeus confirmed it yesterday is that I'm her closest living relation."

"Correct," Thaddeus said. "And since Clara Carrington is a direct descendant of Sir Arthur Carrington of Pembroke, a member of the first Royal Order, Elmira is the next in line from her family to join us."

Elmira nodded. "Nice, huh?"

Ike wasn't sure just how nice it was. What other choice did he have?

"Yeah," he said. "Nice." Then he had to ask. "But what about Diego and Kashvi? They aren't …?"

"Direct descendants, too?" Thaddeus asked.

Ike nodded. He knew it was a longshot but maybe they were distant relations of his father's other co-stars, Antonio Cortesi and Phillip O'Leary Smith?

"Sorry, but no," Thaddeus said, "Diego and Kashvi are still in New York. Your mom will let them know what's happened to you when the time is right."

Ike nodded. He wished they were here, too. Then again, events such as these were bigger than friendship.

"So?" Elmira said, turning to Thaddeus. "Can I show him already?"

"Show me what?" Ike asked.

Elmira didn't wait for permission. She pulled a newspaper out of the back of her tunic and tossed it on Ike's lap.

"This."

Ike recognized it immediately. *The New York Times.* And the front page held a familiar picture. A giant locust. The headline read, "Giant Bug: Fact or Fiction?"

"Where did you get this?" Ike asked.

71

"Some of the guards keep us apprised of goings on in the outside world," Thaddeus said. "This story has gone viral. Go ahead. Read it."

With trembling fingers, Ike picked up the paper.

There were strange doings on New York City's Upper West Side yesterday morning outside the prestigious Branford School at 8:00 AM. While waiting for classes to begin, a giant bug—some say it was a locust—measuring some fifteen or twenty feet attacked a group of students.

Though details are sketchy, witnesses say a boy named Ike Hollingsberry fought off the locust with dog leashes and a mysterious sword while another child flattened the insect with a street sweeper. But it was sixth grader Harrison Opal, son of the famed real estate developer and ex-mayoral candidate, who claimed to have delivered the knock-out blow.

"It was pretty easy," the student said. "I clanged it on the head with a trash can. I had to think fast."

Ike looked up. "What? Was the reporter even there?"

"I guess not," Elmira said. "But forget Harrison. After we take care of the locusts, we'll make him regret he lied." She sat on the bed next to him. "Go ahead. Keep reading."

Police and fire departments arrived quickly to block off the street and clean up the remains of the giant bug.

"It was pretty grizzly," Sergeant Rufus Coleman stated. "Like something out of science fiction."

Questions remain. Was the bug real or a skillfully made robot? Was the bug related somehow to the fake locusts on the cult children's TV show, The Fighting Dragons? Is it a coincidence that Ike Hollingsberry, one of the children who fought the giant insect, is the son of Cameron Hollingsberry, the late star of that same show?

At this point, no one knows for sure. Late last night, Mayor John Andretti's office released a short statement. "The unfortunate occurrence at the Branford School is being fully investigated. Right now, we are working on the assumption that the bug was an elaborately constructed hoax, probably used to advertise a new film or television program. We will release the results of our investigation as soon as we know more."

"Is that cool or what?" Elmira said. "We're famous."

"I guess," Ike said. He looked to Thaddeus. "So the city is calming people down by saying it was fake. Is that it?"

"Exactly," Thaddeus said.

"Are people buying it?"

"Our sources think so," Thaddeus said. "Which is good for us. The more people think the bug is a phony, the less panic there will be. That'll allow us to do the job more easily."

Ike nodded. It all sounded strangely good. And exciting. Or as strangely good and exciting as things could be, under the circumstances. But there was one major piece missing.

"So about these dragons ..."

"Yes?" Thaddeus asked.

Ike nodded toward the window. "All of this would be easier

to believe if I saw one."

Thaddeus smiled. "Ready to see for yourself, are you?" He looked sideways to Elmira. "Shall we take the boy to the main yard for the evening feed, fire, and fly?"

Elmira nodded. "Works for me."

"The feed, fire, and fly?" Ike asked.

Elmira was already pulling him toward the door. "You heard the man. The feed, fire, and fly. Come on. It's almost time."

Chapter Nine

Amoment later, Ike was hurrying after Elmira and Thaddeus
down a circular, stone stairway.

"Watch your step," Thaddeus called over his shoulder. He was
surprisingly quick for someone so large and old, taking the steep
stairs two or three at a time, steadying himself with his cane as his
fat boots clomped on the cold stone. "Some of these are slippery."

Some were also loose. The only way Ike was able to get to the
bottom without flipping head over heels was by gripping the walls
with his palms for support. Once he was on sturdier ground, Ike
followed Thaddeus and Elmira across a banquet hall with red brick
floors. Hanging above a long oak table was a tapestry of a sturdy-
looking man with a closely trimmed black beard, sitting atop a
white horse.

"That's King Arthur," Thaddeus said. "A great rendering of a
bloody brilliant man."

Ike stopped for a quick look. Though Arthur was no better or
worse looking than any knight, he radiated an overwhelming sense
of goodness and fair play—just as one would expect from the king
who had founded the Knights of the Round Table.

"There will be plenty of time to look later," Thaddeus called over his shoulder. "Come this way. Hurry."

Ike soon found himself hustling down another circular stair, this one wider, then into an entrance hall, a spacious room covered wall to wall with tapestries of dragons and knights.

"These are some of the finest members of the Order throughout history," Elmira said as they ran past.

This time, Ike didn't stop, but made a mental note to look more closely later.

"And down that hall is the Order library," Elmira said.

Though she had only been there for a single day, Ike wouldn't have been surprised if Elmira had already read and memorized every book. But again, he didn't have time to ask questions. Not with dragons to be seen. Soon he was outside, hurrying across the drawbridge.

"Be sure not to fall in," Thaddeus called, nodding toward the moat. "We keep some alligators down there to keep things interesting."

Somehow the idea of a giant alligator didn't seem particularly worrisome to Ike—not when he was about to meet an entire Order of giant, flying lizards.

"Don't worry about us going into the moat, Thaddeus," Elmira said. "We're city kids, remember? Walkers, not swimmers."

On the far side of the drawbridge, Thaddeus finally took a breather. Winded, he leaned heavily on his cane.

"Can't run like I used to." He glanced toward the barns which stood two hundred feet away, down a dirt path that cut through a grassy field. "Looks like we have another minute before the dragons are out, anyway."

Ike was happy to take a break, too.

"How's that cut of yours, by the way?" Thaddeus asked, looking down at Ike's bandage. "Good as new, right?"

Ike patted his stomach. Yes, the wound throbbed a little bit, but it didn't really hurt. In truth, he had been so concerned with keeping up he hadn't even thought of it.

"It's good. Whatever you did worked."

Thaddeus looked pleased. "I told your mom we would tape you up. We have ancient cures here for those locust stings. Things modern medicine has never heard of. Well, what do you say? Mosey to the barns?"

"Yep," Elmira said. "Follow me."

Ike took in his new surroundings. Beyond the barns were a series of grassy meadows, separated by stone fences that curved this way and that with no apparent rhyme or reason. To the other side was the castle, complete with two turrets, a drawbridge and a moat, all of it bathed in the orange glow of the just setting sun. Taken as a whole it felt as though a little piece of Medieval England had been plopped down in the middle of a Florida swamp. And the swamp stretched around them for miles and miles.

"Say, how big are the Everglades anyway?" Ike called.

"Four thousand and three hundred square miles," Elmira yelled back from up front.

Ike had meant the question for Thaddeus, but he should have known Elmira would know.

"That's huge," Ike said.

"Which is why we picked it," Thaddeus said. "To be in the middle of nowhere. But don't worry. We're well protected by a team of Navy SEALS. One of the best military squadrons in the country."

Ike squinted into the far away weeds. Navy SEALS? Aside from an occasional coo and hiss, the swamp was completely still.

"There are soldiers out there?"

"Yep," Thaddeus said. "Disguised as swamp people and fishermen, of course. Good thing, too. Could you imagine the fuss if people found out there were dragons living right under their noses?"

"Yeah," Elmira said. "This place'd be a tourist trap in seconds."

Ike could easily imagine a line of people in Bermuda shorts stretching all the way to Miami, eager and willing to pay whatever it took to see an Order of actual live dragons. There would probably be vendors, too, hawking everything from dragon T-shirts to dragon masks, hats, and socks. Maybe even dragon underwear. And then there would be the explosion of illegal YouTube videos, capturing the dragons in flight. There might even be a documentary or two about King Arthur and the Royal Order.

"Hey," Ike asked. "Come to think of it, why is this place in America, anyway? Shouldn't it be in England?"

"It was," Elmira said.

Ike didn't even bother to ask how she knew—the girl just knew things.

"What happened?"

"World War Two happened."

"Okay, but what'd that have to do with anything?"

Thaddeus took over. "In 1941, England was getting bombed to the dickens by Germany. So Winston Churchill figured the dragons would be safer elsewhere. So they were moved here through an agreement with the American government."

Ike frowned. This was getting stranger and more complicated by the second. "So wait?" He stopped in his tracks. "The government is involved? Like the *President of the United States* knows the Order is here?"

"Cool, huh?" Elmira said, turning around. "Also the Vice President, the Secretary of State, the Undersecretary for Medieval

Affairs, and the British Ambassador. I'd love to blog about it but it's top secret."

"That's right," Thaddeus said. "But the government set up a radar-free no-fly zone that makes it safe for the dragons to fly undetected in a six-mile radius around the Order."

Ike wanted to know more. How many Navy SEALS were guarding them? How did they ship in supplies? What did the dragons eat? But then a loud creak pierced the quiet of the Order and the main door of the first barn swung halfway open. Before Ike had time to be scared or stunned or even to laugh in amazement, a dragon's foot, complete with scaly lizard-skin, four bony toes and claws, appeared out of the barn. Then the entire dragon lumbered into the open, stretching its long neck toward the setting sun.

"Oh ... my ... *gosh*." Ike said.

"Amazing, isn't it?" Elmira said.

Ike was more than amazed, really. He was flabbergasted, stunned practically speechless. Like any child, he had seen many pictures of dragons in storybooks—enormous scaly lizards with large, sloping backs, wings, and an extra wide mouth. And that description was largely true. But this particular creature was light lavender with a deep maroon stomach and yellowish-orange wings. Stepping into the open field, he shook himself and yawned, exposing a massive mouth of brilliantly white teeth. The dragon craned its neck and blew a whoosh of fire high into the air, as if clearing his throat. Then he shook himself again and ambled slowly toward a giant pile of hay.

"That's Kansas City," Thaddeus whispered. "He's always the first out to eat."

"Kansas City?" Ike asked. "That's his name?"

Thaddeus nodded. "Four dragons have been born since the Order moved to America. Remember how the older dragons your father flew were named after English parks? Well, these new ones were named after American cities."

"Look," Elmira said.

While Kansas City had strolled to the hay bales, a second door had swung open. Out stepped another enormous dragon, this one light blue with purplish wings and a greenish-blue face.

"Seattle," Elmira said.

"Seattle, huh?" Ike asked.

The dragon craned his neck and blew a plume of fire into the air.

"They like to do that before they eat," Thaddeus explained. "Something about helping the digestion. Dragons have three stomach chambers, you know."

"Right," Ike said vaguely. "Three stomachs."

A third dragon was out now, this one taller and leaner than the other two, dark red with one golden wing and a light blue right leg.

"That's Pittsburgh," Thaddeus said.

"He's beautiful," Ike said.

"You mean, *she's* beautiful," Elmira said. "Pittsburgh's a girl. You can tell by the golden dot on her forehead."

Clearly, the girl dragon had as much need to clear her throat before a meal as the boys. Again, there was the shake and the whoosh of fire into the sky. And as Pittsburgh moseyed over to the hay, a final dragon appeared, the largest of them all. His body was pure silver, his wings gold, with a thick red stripe that slashed down his forehead. When he craned his neck, the flame whooshed so high the tippy top of the plume of fire seemed to brush against the orange clouds.

"Whoa," Ike said. "What's his name?"

"Detroit," Elmira said.

"He's Dartmoor's son," Thaddeus said.

"Of course," Ike said. "He has the same silver and gold coloring."

"Right," Thaddeus said. "And he's the one you're going to ride."

Ike swallowed hard. It was exciting. Incredible. But the idea of getting on the creature's back and flying was more than a little bit daunting.

"Well, he's beautiful," Ike managed. "They all are."

"True," Thaddeus said. "And wait for it. We aren't done yet. Here come the dragons from your father's Order. Along with Dartmoor, we have Loch Lomond, Northumberland, and Snowdonia."

The four dragons of the Ninth Order came out en masse, preening as though they were contestants in a beauty pageant.

Ike recognized them all from his father's show.

Like Detroit, Dartmoor was silver with golden wings and a red stripe down his forehead.

Loch Lomond was dark green with purple wings and a yellow face.

Northumberland was the color of a pale blue sky. His wings were milky white.

Snowdonia's front legs were yellow then blended into an orange body. Her head was sea green.

"They're so big, aren't they?" Elmira said. "I mean, they looked large on TV, but this is something else. Each one has to be twenty feet long."

"And what?" Ike said. "Fifteen feet high."

"As big as dinosaurs," Elmira said.

"No disrespect to dinosaurs," Thaddeus said, "but dragons are in another league. Could a dinosaur breathe fire? Did dinosaurs survive? Sadly, no. But the dragons lived on. These have, anyway."

"Are these all that's left?" Ike asked.

Thaddeus nodded. "Snowdonia's father and Loch Lomond's mom died about ten years ago. Of course, the dragons from your dad's Order are retired from combat."

"Retired?" Ike asked. "Why?"

Thaddeus placed his hand on Ike's shoulder. "The problem that led to your father's death, I'm afraid. Dartmoor, Loch Lomond, Northumberland, and Snowdonia can't make fire."

Ike blinked. "Really?" Ike looked to the four mighty dragons. They each looked perfectly healthy. "None of them?"

Thaddeus shook his head. "It happens sometimes. There have been a couple of instances in the Order's history when dragons have lost that ability—usually, the older ones. But the good news is that the four youngsters blaze with the best of them. You'll be in good hands, trust me."

All eight dragons were in the field now, enjoying the late afternoon sun, grazing quietly.

"Let's take a closer look," Thaddeus said. "But not too close, Ike. Trust me, you don't want a case of burned kneecaps on your first day."

Ike got the point. He liked his kneecaps the way there were, room temperature.

"Don't worry. I'll be careful."

As the trio made their way closer to the dragons, Ike noticed a short man with a thick mustache bustle out a side door of the barn. He was almost as wide as he was tall.

"That's Sussex," Thaddeus explained. "He and his wife are the Dragon Keepers."

As if on cue, a woman stepped out of another side door. To Ike's surprise, she was almost a foot taller than her husband, as narrow as he was wide. But before Thaddeus could make introductions, Sussex picked up a ladder and began to walk toward one of the dragons. At first, Ike thought nothing of it—after all, wasn't Sussex a Dragon Keeper? He was probably off to do a chore. But Thaddeus? He twirled his long beard with his pinky and shook his head.

"Oh, no," he muttered. "Not again."

"What?" Ike asked.

The old man's total focus was on what was happening across the field.

"No, Sussex," he called over. "We've discussed this."

Sussex smiled, exposing a row of uneven teeth that shone out of a mouth so large it utterly dominated his smallish head.

"Oh, come now, Thaddeus." He had a deep voice for a man so small and a British brogue so thick Ike had to tune his ears to catch every word. "Just going to give it another little try. No harm in it, is there?"

"What's he doing?" Ike whispered to Elmira.

"Trying to fly one of the dragons," she replied. "Watch."

"No harm in it?" Thaddeus called back to Sussex. "We've been through this a million times. You aren't a direct descendant."

"True enough," Sussex said, stopping to stand the ladder next to him. "But why shouldn't these dragons let me on their backs? After all, I'm the fellow what feeds them every morning, clips their forepaws every night, and nurses them back to health when they've got the sneezes so bad they can't exhale a decent plume of smoke."

"True," Thaddeus began. "But that doesn't mean—"

Sussex cut him off. "After all I does for them, is it too much to ask that I take one out for a short spin? And today, Kansas City—he's the friendliest of the lot, in my opinion—gave me a nice little wink, he did, and nudge just before feeding time, which I take to mean he wants to be my tour guide around the Order."

Thaddeus looked exasperated. "But you don't know what

Kansas City meant. You can't speak to dragons."

"No, but I'm working on it," Sussex said with a laugh. "I come from a long line of Dragon Keepers, if you'll remember. And the Keepers of the First Royal Order could speak *Dragonish*."

Thaddeus looked sideways to Ike.

"Forgive Sussex. He's a good man but has some queer ideas."

Ike smiled. Perhaps so, but the small man was instantly likable.

"I'm sorry to disappoint you," Thaddeus called back to Sussex. "But if *Dragonish* was ever spoken, it's certainly not anymore."

Undeterred, the short man propped the ladder into the ground next to Kansas City then began to climb, rung by rung. For his part, the dragon continued to nibble peacefully on the hay, seemingly undisturbed.

"You know him, Mr. Thaddeus, sir," Mrs. Sussex said, walking toward them. Like her husband, she had a British accent, just as strong and thick. "Once my man Sussex gets an idea in his noggin', there's no getting it out. He thinks he can talk to the creatures. He thinks he can ride 'em. I tell him that's crazy, of course. But does he listen? Nope. And if he won't listen to his own wife what loves him despite his ample girth and limited brain capacity, then he's not going to listen to nobody."

With Mrs. Sussex's words still echoing across the field, her husband reached the top rung of the ladder. At this point, Ike could see Sussex was going to jump on the dragon no matter what anyone said.

"All right, Kansas City. Ready for a wee spin around the swamp?"

"Sussex," Thaddeus called, a final time. "Please."

But the Dragon Keeper was on a mission. He bent his knees then launched himself off the top rung of the ladder, springing high into the air. Ike held his breath. Though Kansas City had ignored the ladder leaning against his side, the instant Sussex's rear end hit his lavender back, the creature bucked like he had been zapped with a cattle prod.

"Whoaaaaaa," Sussex cried. He grabbed desperately at the dragon's neck. "Easy boy."

But Kansas City was in no mood to take it easy. In a flash, he snapped his tail and smacked Sussex high in the air.

"Aaaahhhhh!"

Up, up, up Sussex went—a good fifty feet.

Mrs. Sussex shook her head. "I told you. There's no talking sense to that man."

But the worst wasn't over. As Sussex twirled back to Earth, the dragon glanced casually over his shoulder and whooshed him with a quick blast of fire—enough to singe but not kill. By the time Sussex smashed back to the ground—luckily landing in the middle of a hay pile—the dragon was already back grazing.

"Serves you right," Mrs. Sussex called as she hustled to help her shaken husband back to his feet. "There's the next in line," she continued, gesturing to Ike and Elmira. "They will be our riders. Not you."

"Are you all right?" Ike called over.

He half expected Sussex to never move again. But despite the fact his mustache and eyebrows were partially singed and he had hay sticking out of his ears and mouth, he was in surprisingly good spirits.

"Fine, my boy," he called, spitting out the hay. "Just a little bruised ego to go with a bruised rear end."

Then to Ike's astonishment, as his wife dragged him to his

feet, the small man turned to the other grazing dragons.

"Maybe I'll have better luck with Seattle."

Mrs. Sussex was aghast. "Have I married a complete idiot? Don't you remember what happened the last time you tried that? Seattle and Pittsburgh used you as a volleyball. They played catch with you, they did."

"True enough," Sussex said, wagging his head. Again, he seemed more amused than upset by his failed attempts at dragon-flying. "But I got an awfully nice view of the Order while being swatted around up there."

"Everyone has his role," Thaddeus said, finally stepping forward. "Yours is to feed and care for the dragons so the direct descendants can kill the locusts. Come on, my good man. You've already met Elmira Hand from the brave line of Carrington's, but say hello to Isaac Rupert Hollingsberry."

"Yes," Mrs. Sussex said. "Like I said, these are two of the children who are going to ride, not you."

Given his obvious obsession with riding the dragons, Ike half expected Sussex to take him down with a running tackle. Instead, he flashed him a wide smile then marched over and clasped his hand.

"Nice to meet you, boy. You're going to work out fine, I can tell it. I have an instinct about these things, don't I, Mrs. Sussex?"

She rolled her eyes. "You have an instinct for many things, most of 'em not all that intelligent." She looked to Ike. "Do you know what happened the last time my husband clipped Detroit's toenails?"

Thaddeus cleared his throat. "I'm sure Ike is interested, but let's save that for another time."

"Evening chores?" Sussex asked.

"I'm afraid so," Thaddeus said.

"Yes, sir," Sussex said. "Right away."

"Make me a promise," Thaddeus said. "No more ladders."

Laughing, Sussex waved a hand. "Of course not, sir. Not until tomorrow anyway. Goodbye, children. Goodbye, Isaac Rupert Hollingsberry. We'll talk more soon."

With that, husband and wife strolled back to the barns.

"Don't you kids worry about what you just saw, by the way," Thaddeus said.

"What?" Elmira asked.

"Sussex's little rocket launch into space. The dragons should let you on their backs."

"*Should* let us on their backs?" Ike said.

The old man patted Ike's shoulder. "Don't get panicky on me, son. It's all going to be okay. Let me show you."

Thaddeus waved his cane in the air, once to the right, back to the left—clearly a signal of some kind. But for who? Or what? Ike soon saw. The moment Thaddeus lowered his arm, Detroit spread his golden wings and took to the sky. He soared, then dive-bombed Thaddeus, Ike, and Elmira before landing softly by their side. The old man scratched the beast under the chin.

"So Detroit, old boy," he said, glancing to Ike, "meet Isaac Rupert Hollingsberry. You're Dartmoor's son and he's the son of Dartmoor's last rider. Go ahead. Say hello."

Ike stood stone still, barely able to breathe as Detroit took him in with his pale green eyes. He worried he was about to be given the Sussex treatment, swatted into the air, then torched on the way down. Instead, the creature studied him, then nuzzled his face. Ike worked up his nerve to stroke his chin.

"Whoa," he said. "Soft."

Thaddeus patted Detroit's silver cheek. "Dragon skin is one of the softest things in all the world." He turned to Elmira. "Go ahead. Take a pat."

Detroit patiently waited while Elmira stroked his cheek. Then he grunted, craned his neck and let loose another towering plume of flame into the sky.

Thaddeus smiled to Ike. "He likes you. I knew he would."

Detroit spread his wings. With a light snort, he lifted off, flew lazily back to the center of field and continued to graze.

"What about me?" Elmira said. "Which dragon goes with Lord Pembroke of Carrington?"

"Oh, sorry," Thaddeus said. "Of course. That's Seattle."

This time, Thaddeus didn't even need to summon the beast. The blue dragon lifted off, took a quick spin around the Order, then whooshed ten feet over Elmira's head.

"See?" Thaddeus went on. "Rarin' to go."

As Ike followed his flight, the great creature circled back over the swamp and let out another whoosh of flame, before pulling up at the edge of the Order.

"Looks like he's spotted something," Elmira said.

"An alligator, maybe?" Ike asked.

"Could be," Thaddeus said.

But it was no alligator. Seconds later, Thaddeus and the two children heard what the dragon saw, the whirr of an engine cutting through the faraway weeds.

"Ah, yes," Thaddeus said. "Much better than an alligator."

"What is it?" Elmira asked.

The man was already walking quickly toward the edge of the swamp. "That, my friends, is an airboat."

"An airboat?" Ike said. "Are you expecting anyone?"

"I know who it is," Elmira said. "Other direct descendants, right?"

Thaddeus nodded. "That's my hope."

Ike smiled. Of course. The next in line from the families of Antonio Cortesi and Phillip O'Leary Smith.

"Come on," Elmira said to Ike, already running. "Let's say hi."

Chapter Ten

By the time Ike ran the one hundred or so yards down to the swamp, the airboat—an unusual looking contraption, powered by a giant circular engine—had skimmed through the weeds to the edge of the Order. Standing at the controls was a burly man dressed as a fisherman and wearing a holster and firearm around his waist. He must be one of the Navy SEALS assigned to keep guard. But even more intriguing was the blonde girl standing expectantly at the boat's prow. Dressed for adventure, she wore knee high boots, a safari coat, and a wide brimmed hunter's hat. Most intriguing of all was what was in her arms—a six-foot-long alligator.

"I told her not to pick him up," the Navy SEAL called to Thaddeus, "but the girl wouldn't listen."

Just then, the alligator snapped its jaws and furiously flashed its tail. Though the girl looked no more than twelve, Ike was surprised at how easily she was able to keep the great reptile in her arms.

"Ay there, everyone," she called, hopping off the boat to shore. Like Thaddeus and Mr. and Mrs. Sussex, she had an accent, but hers was Australian. "Check out what I found in the swamp."

Thaddeus looked momentarily alarmed, but Ike was beginning to see he was a hard man to faze.

"That's some gator, you've got there, Lucinda," he said calmly.

"It tried to snap at my feet on the boat," the girl explained. "I told him to rack off, but he kept on snapping. Didn't bloody well know who it was dealing with."

Again, the alligator made a move for freedom, lashing its tail. Again, the girl held on.

"Quiet, mate," she called. "I've got you now, you see?"

"Clearly you do," Thaddeus said. "But come. Let that poor bugger go and say hi to your new friends."

Lucinda frowned. "What? I can't keep him in my room?"

"Afraid not," Thaddeus said.

"But I'll make him a little pond in the corner."

"I do think he'd be happier in the swamp."

Lucinda sighed heavily. "You and me were gonna have such fun," she whispered to the gator. "But all right then. Back you go. Next time you see an airboat, keep your trap to yourself, okay?"

With seemingly little effort, Lucinda heaved the reptile toward the swamp. Clearly, the gator had learned its lesson. The minute it hit the ground, it scurried back into the muck without so much as a backward glance.

"Whoa," Elmira said. "That was impressive."

Lucinda shrugged. "He was on the small side compared to the ones near my family's farm."

"Maybe so," Elmira went on, "but Ike and I are New Yorkers. The primary animals near to us are pigeons, mice, rats, and a few raccoons."

"One of my friends keeps a pet squirrel, though," Ike said.

"A squirrel, eh?" Lucinda said. She wrinkled her brow. "A Fox Squirrel or a Red?"

Ike had no idea—all he knew was that Diego was crazy enough to keep him as a pet.

"A New York squirrel," he said finally.

Lucinda smiled. "I'll accept that. By the way, I know you two blokes." She nodded to Elmira. "I read your blog when we get internet at the farm, which isn't too often, because the kangas chew our wiring. But I loved your piece on King Arthur's pajamas. Pictures of unicorns? Who'd have thought it? Hilarious."

Ike didn't know if he had ever seen Elmira look so pleased.

"Really? You read that?"

"Course, I did. And you," Lucinda continued, turning to Ike. "You're Isaac Rupert Hollingsberry. I'm a big fan of your dad. Loved episode six, in particular. *The Wrath of Dartmoor*. That was television. Your pap stabbed that locust right between the eyes. Right over the Grand Canyon. Then he did a backward flip into the rapids for a swim. Talk about a beaut."

Ike felt embarrassed he didn't know his father's episodes as well as his fans. Even so, he knew when to shut up and accept a compliment.

"Thanks. That *was* pretty cool."

"It was," Thaddeus said, stepping forward. "By the way, let me officially do the honors. Ike and Elmira, meet Lucinda O'Leary Smith. Her father Phillip was a member of the last Order. I recruited her on a trip to the Australian outback."

Ike whistled. "That's a long way to travel."

"It is," Thaddeus said. "You next-in-liners can be hard to track down."

"Old Thaddeus had to hike a hundred miles through the desert to find me," Lucinda said with a laugh. "By the time he reached our place, he had a scorpion attached to both his feet and another hanging off his rear. Didn't know what he wanted at first. What was this geezer doing at our farm? But I'm a direct descendant, sure enough, just like my dad. Related by generations to an old British knight named The Earl of North Humbridge."

"The Earl of North Humbridge?" Elmira said. "The historical texts say he killed one of the original locusts by shimmying up one of its antennae and stabbing it in the eye. I've blogged about it."

"Really now?" Lucinda said. "That's excellent." She looked toward the field to where the dragons were still grazing. "So when's our turn to fly? Let me give one of these dragons a quick spin."

She held her fingers to her mouth and let loose a wild, piercing whistle so loud Ike had to hold his hands over his ears.

"No, no," Thaddeus said. "Sorry, but the dragons are resting. Training starts tomorrow. Right now, we're going to get you to the castle for some dinner."

That seemed like a great idea to Ike. Now that he thought of it, he hadn't eaten since breakfast the day before. He was famished. But Ike saw that Thaddeus had a final bit of business.

"Hey, Andre?" the old man called to the Navy SEAL. "I was hoping another descendant was coming in tonight, as well. Wasn't he at the assigned spot?"

The SEAL shook his head. "We waited for an hour on the other edge of the Everglades right where you said, sir. Lucinda was the only one who showed. But we assigned a helicopter to scout the swamp in case someone got lost. And I'll go back and look again."

"Please do," Thaddeus said.

Andre nodded. When he flipped the switch, the engine revved loudly and he maneuvered the boat back into the weeds. By the time the boat had disappeared, the enormity of what Thaddeus had asked had Ike thoroughly shaken.

"So wait. There's only the three of us to fight off the locusts?

That's *it?*"

"For now," the old man said casually. "But don't get in a tizzy, son. There'll be one more. At least, there should be. Each Order has four members."

Ike shuddered, remembering his fight with the giant locust. That had been one enormous, scary insect.

"Only one more?"

"Relax," Lucinda said. She slapped his back hard. "I heard you held off that first bug with hot coffee and a trash can. Keep thinking fast like that and we'll be fine."

"I agree," Elmira said. "The historical record is full of instances where troops are hopelessly outnumbered only to defy the odds and win."

"I'll take the three of us against a horde of stupid bugs any day," Lucinda said. "Especially if I can get a little dinner before the battle." She turned to Thaddeus. "You don't mind if I add something to the menu, do you?"

"Add something?" he said. He gave his beard a quick chew. "What did you have in mind? Not another alligator, I hope?"

"Nope, not a gator."

Lucinda smiled mischievously, then reached to her waist. Then to Ike's amazement, she peeled something off—a three foot long snake.

"You're wearing a ... snake?" he asked.

Lucinda held him high for all to see. "He's a looker, ain't he?"

"Oh, my Lord," Elmira said. "I cannot wait to blog about this."

"We have them for snacks all the time at home," Lucinda said. "Makes a darned good appetizer."

Ike was liking Lucinda more and more. If she could wrestle alligators and use snakes as articles of clothing, imagine what she could do to a swarm of locusts. Maybe the three of them really would be enough to save the day.

"I'm sure the snakes are delicious," Thaddeus said with a light chuckle. "But some of them are poisonous."

"Same thing in Australia," Lucinda said. "But I'm not concerned." She looked her snake in the eye. "He doesn't look poisonous to me."

"He might be anyway," Thaddeus said. "Better throw him back."

Lucinda scowled. "You mean I can't keep this one as a pet, either?"

Ike smiled to himself. Too bad Diego wasn't there. Lucinda was a kindred spirit.

"Sorry," Thaddeus said. "No snakes in the castle."

Lucinda sighed. "Well, if you're going to be that way about it ..."

With a flick of her arm and wrist, she twirled the snake over her head and launched him over her shoulder. Like the alligator before it, it didn't linger, slithering quickly back into the water.

"Do tell me," Thaddeus asked, "are you wearing any more wild animals?"

Lucinda patted her pockets and the top of her head. "None that I know of."

"All right then," Thaddeus said. "Let's eat, shall we?"

Soon, the small group was seated at an oak table in the banquet hall underneath the giant tapestry of King Arthur. There they dined on a meal notably less exotic than snake—fried chicken, rice, string beans, and salad. By the time chocolate cake was served, Thaddeus had caught the three children up on some basic facts.

For the most part, the opening credits on *The Fighting Dragons* were correct. The Order had been in existence since Arthur's days, formed when Merlin, for reasons still unknown, had cast a spell that brought the first scourge of giant locusts to the Dark, Dank

Woods. What *The Fighting Dragons'* credits didn't say was that these killer locusts had appeared only nine other times since the days of King Arthur. With each new locust attack, a new Royal Order was called.

Over dessert, Thaddeus showed Ike, Elmira, and Lucinda a scroll that contained the dates and locations of the previous nine attacks.

515—the First Royal Order, the Dark, Dank Woods

545—the Second Royal Order, Northeast Shropshire, England

630—the Third Royal Order, London

715—the Fourth Royal Order, South Wales

1100—the Fifth Royal Order, Ireland

1305—the Sixth Royal Order, Scotland

1315—the Seventh Royal Order, Kensington

1709—the Eighth Royal Order, London

2009—the Ninth Royal Order, Nevada

"Whoa," Ike said. "The dates are so spread out."

"True," Thaddeus said. "And I wish I could tell you exactly why that is. Our thought is that someone has to actually say the spell to make the portal open."

"Makes sense. But who's been behind it all these years?" Ike asked.

Thaddeus raised an eyebrow. "If I knew that, I'd be the happiest man in the State of Florida. Unfortunately, we know virtually nothing about the people who have been behind these attacks."

"Maybe the spell was lost and rediscovered?" Elmira suggested.

"Makes sense to me," Lucinda said. "Probably by some bad bloke looking to do some serious damage."

"That's quite possible," Thaddeus replied. "Another strange

thing about the last Order is the sheer number of times the locusts came. There were sixteen separate appearances, always a week apart."

Elmira nodded. "Of course. Which is why there were sixteen episodes of *The Fighting Dragons*."

"Correct," Thaddeus said. "Thankfully, only one or two locusts came each time."

"Is that what you expect this time?" Ike asked hopefully. "One or two locusts spaced a week apart?"

In truth, that didn't sound so bad. Four fire-breathing dragons could kill a couple of locusts a week. But Thaddeus wasn't entirely reassuring.

"I wish I knew the answer," the old man said. "In the year of 812, the second Royal Order had to face over two hundred locusts at once."

"Over two hundred?" Ike asked.

Thaddeus held up a hand. "Don't get panicky. Remember, yesterday outside your school there was only one. So that's what we're expecting this time. One or two at a time."

Ike exhaled, momentarily relieved.

"Okay," he said. "So if the first locust came yesterday, we have six more days until the next ones come, right?"

Thaddeus smiled. "If the attacks are spaced every week like they were for your father. But we aren't sure about that either. Each time the locusts come, it's different. If I remember correctly, when your dad was called to duty, they only had three days to prepare."

Ike vaguely remembered it. His dad had been starring in a Broadway production of Shakespeare's *Hamlet* when he'd suddenly quit to join the cast of *The Fighting Dragons*.

"Really?" Ike said. "My dad only had three days to get ready to fight?"

Thaddeus nodded. "Same with Lucinda's dad and Elmira's

second cousin. They trained here then took the Flying Purple Viking Ship to Nevada. That's where the locusts appeared last time."

"That's all good," Lucinda said. "But why do you even need the flying boat? Can't the dragons fly themselves where they're going?"

"They could," Thaddeus said. "But a dragons' lungs and wingspan are built for sprints. Short, fast attacks. If our dragons had had to fly the hundreds of miles to Nevada, they would have been too exhausted to do any real fighting by the time they got there. So we built the flying boat."

"I get it," Elmira said. "And the boat also made the whole thing seem more like a kids' TV show."

"Right," Thaddeus said. "We knew those locusts would be on the evening news the minute they showed their wings and stingers, so we had to find a way to keep people from panicking."

"Is that what you're going to do with us then?" Ike asked. "Present us like it's a new version of the show?"

"That's the plan," Thaddeus said. He took another bite of cake. "Of course, there is a small problem with the boat. The last time we tried, it wouldn't take off. Something about the left wing. Not enough air-lift."

Ike exchanged a concerned glance with the others.

"Then how are we going to get the dragons to New York?" he asked.

"Sussex has a group of Navy SEALS on it," Thaddeus replied. "Don't worry. They'll have that boat fixed."

Ike nodded. It all made sense. Except he couldn't shake one overwhelming question—could they really learn everything they needed to know about dragon-fighting in six days? Then again, he was one of the next in line, wasn't he? Fate didn't usually hand jobs to people who weren't up to the task.

"To tell the honest truth," Lucinda said between bites of cake, "I don't see the big deal about a bunch of stupid insects. On our farm, we have dragonflies as big as hawks."

"I'm sure that's accurate," Elmira said. "But the locust that attacked Ike at school was prehistoric with antennae that were two stories high."

"Whatever," Lucinda said. "A bug is a bug is a bug." She popped a final piece of cake in her mouth for emphasis. But before anyone could say another word, she stopped chewing and cocked her head toward the window.

"Did you hear that?" Lucinda asked.

"Hear what?" Thaddeus replied.

Lucinda washed down her cake with a glass of milk.

"Listen," she said.

Thaddeus, Ike and Elmira were dead silent. At first, they heard nothing. But then, emerging from the eerie stillness of the swamp was the hum of another engine.

"Another airboat?" Ike asked.

"Shouldn't be," Thaddeus said. "Andre has the one we use back at the mainland."

The sound had already grown quickly into the *thunk-thunka-thunk* of something larger than an airboat anyway.

"A helicopter then?" Ike asked.

"That's what I was about to say." Elmira said.

"That's what it is all right," Thaddeus said. "Don't forget, we're a military installation. We're resupplied by air. Just not usually at night."

"Then who is it?" Lucinda said.

By that time the *thunk-thunka-thunk* had grown so loud they had to shout to hear one another. Then a spotlight shone so brightly through the window that the group shielded their eyes.

And then ... a boy with a thick mop of jet black hair swung through the window on a rope.

"Greetings, *miei amici*," he cried in a brilliant Italian accent. "Never you fear. Alexandro Lafcadio Cortesi, he has arrived."

Letting go of the rope, Alexandro slid across the banquet table like he had been shot out of a cannon, pulling the tablecloth and everything on it along with him.

Smash. A plate of half eaten chicken flipped into Elmira's lap.

Thunk. A piece of chocolate cake flew directly into Ike's mouth.

Boom. Lucinda teetered back and forth in her chair then fell backwards to the floor. Meanwhile, Alexandro kept sliding, first on his back then on his stomach, picking up speed, until *bang*—he smashed feet first into Thaddeus's belly.

"Ooof!" Thaddeus crashed backward to the floor.

"My apologies," Alexandro shouted. He rolled off the table and helped Thaddeus to his feet. "Your stomach is okay, eh? Sorry that I missed the airboat. I pick up a ride on a military helicopter instead. Time is of the essence, eh?"

"Alexandro," Thaddeus said, finally managing to speak. He sank back into his chair. "That was quite an entrance."

He shrugged. "I do what I can."

Ike had managed to spit out the chocolate cake while Elmira finished picking clumps of chicken and bits of rice from her hair. Lucinda sprang quickly back to her feet.

"Who is this?" she asked.

"Say hi to the fourth member of the Order," Thaddeus said.

The boy bowed. "Sorry for my late arrival. But I am here. So when do we ride these dragons?"

Ike admired this new kid's enthusiasm and fighting spirit.

Mostly, he was relieved to have more help.

"Tomorrow morning," he said. "I'm Ike, by the way."

"Of course, you are. I read about you in the paper. You killed the first locust with your pappi's sword. Superb. And look who we also have here—the author of *Elmira Speaks*."

"Really?" Elmira said. "You read it, too? I never knew I had an audience outside of the United States and England."

Alexandro smiled—a big, winning grin that showed off a row of perfectly straight, white teeth.

"You have readers everywhere, *mio amori*," he said. "I bet there is an old lady in a Chinese fishing village reading you right now. And an Inuit on vacation atop the Andes Mountains—also reading. I use it to keep up on dragons and practice my English."

"Wow," Elmira said. "That's ... great."

Ike thought she might faint. Now Alexandro was ready to meet the final member of the team, bowing low to Lucinda.

"*Bongiorno, mio forte* lady. What a pleasure it is to ..."

Before he could finish the sentence, Lucinda had him on the table helplessly wrapped in a wrestling hold.

"Hey," Alexandro cried. "What did I do?"

"What did you do?" Lucinda cried. "You wrecked my dessert, you bloody idiot."

"I'm sorry. I'll bake you a new cake. Promise."

In response, Lucinda tightened her grip, maneuvering Alexandro's legs over his head.

"Please," he said. "I don't think my knee is meant to bend in this direction."

"Come now, Lucinda," Thaddeus said. "Alexandro can't fly a dragon with a broken foot."

"He could manage," Lucinda said.

Even so, she released him, but not without giving Alexandro a cuff on the head for good measure. Only then did she finally smile.

"Nice entrance, mate."

Alexandro rubbed his knee, then hopped off the table.

"I'll get you more cake. I promise." Then he got Lucinda's hat from the table and placed it back on her head. "Again, apologies for the dramatic entrance," he went on to the group, "but I want to meet you all as soon as I could. Ever since Thaddeus tracked me down, I've been itching to join the action." He winked at Elmira. "Even though my momma was a little bit unhappy to be reminded my family has English blood."

Ike couldn't believe what he saw. Was Elmira blushing?

"My grandmother once told me I'm one eighth Cherokee Indian," she said.

That was a new one. Ike knew Elmira was bi-racial but not Native American.

"Really?" Ike asked. "You're one eighth Cherokee?"

"I haven't been able to substantiate it," Elmira snapped. "But that's what grandma says, okay?"

"No matter," Alexandro said. "I'm only one sixteenth British but that little bit dates all the way back to the first Order. So here I am. Life is so funny."

"I guess it is," Ike said. A lot had happened in a short period of time. "Three days ago I was this kid in New York."

"Tell me about it, mate," Lucinda said. "I was a farm girl who went on vacation once a year to wrestle bull sharks."

"And I was a girl who rode around New York on a street sweeper."

"Yes, I read about that," Alexandro said. "Did you drive the sweeper down here? Is that how you came to Florida?"

"I wish," Elmira said. "No, we took a plane."

"How about you?" Lucinda asked Alexandro. "Did your parents allow you to come or did you have to slip off?"

"Well, at first my momma and poppa don't want me to go," Alexandro said. "Yes, my father fought in the last calling of the Order. Even so, he was worried. 'How's a kid with the bad English going to get along in America?' he say. Then my mother asks, 'What kind of food are they going to feed you at that Order? Will there be fresh pasta? What if these dragons decide they want an Italian boy for breakfast?'"

"So how did you convince them?" Elmira asked.

"I get an idea, that's how. See, in Roma, my family live by the old Coliseum. So I try to convince my parents by comparing myself to the gladiators who used to do mighty combat with the lions."

"That's when they said it was okay for you to come?" Elmira asked.

Alexandro shook his head. "No, that make them more nervous. But I don't give up, eh? I get down on one knee and say I have been called to ride the dragons by Mars, the Roman God of War."

"And then they said yes?" Ike asked.

Alexandro shook his head again. "I have to sneak. My grandmother—what a *fantastico* lady and a great cook, by the way—she give me money for a plane ticket to Miami." He smiled broadly. "First class."

"First class?" Lucinda said. "Sounds plush. I got here by three buses, a boat, two trains, and another bus. But at least my parents let me come, no questions asked."

"Really?" Ike asked. "How'd that work?"

"I may live on a farm but my parents are crazy about adventure stories," Lucinda said. "My father, Phillip, loved fighting with the last Order. So when they heard it was my turn, he practically kicked me out the door. 'Move it, sweetheart,' my dad cried.

'Anyone can sheer sheep. But you, my dear, can save the world.' So he gave me a few quid for travelling expenses and here I am."

Ike looked to Thaddeus. The old man seemed happy the group was hitting it off. But as soon as Lucinda finished recounting her trip to Florida, with particular emphasis on a bus ride from Bolivia to Mexico City filled with a convention of toreadors, Thaddeus brought the conversation back to the issue at hand.

"I know this has all been surprising and strange," he said, "but however you managed to make it here, you're a team now—the Tenth Royal Order of Fighting Dragons."

"Excellent," Lucinda said.

"It certainly is," Alexandro said. "But one quick question, if you please. Why didn't you ask the members of the Ninth Order to continue? After all, my poppa is still alive."

"So is my second cousin once removed," Elmira said.

"My father, too," Lucinda said. She caught Ike's eye. "Sorry, mate."

"No, it's okay," Ike said. He turned to Thaddeus. "I was wondering the same thing. Do the young dragons need young riders? Is that why?"

"Precisely," Thaddeus said. "Once an Order member rides a dragon, no one else can. If you recall, Dartmoor and the rest can't make fire anymore. So we needed to call up a new set of fighters— all of you—to take Detroit, Seattle, Kansas City, and Pittsburgh."

Ike nodded. That made sense. Young fighters for young dragons.

"As for the members of the Ninth Order," Thaddeus went on, "there's no need to involve them now. You'll find almost all of your training is on the dragons themselves and Sussex and I can show you what to do." Thaddeus turned to Alexandro. "As I told the others, we hope to have six days to train. Based on how the locusts behaved the last time, that's when we anticipate the next bugs will hit New York City."

Alexandro whistled. "Six days, eh? I like it. When do we start?"

"Tomorrow, directly after breakfast, we'll meet outside the barns to learn how to fly."

"Works for me," Alexandro said. "What do we do until then?"

"What do we do?" Thaddeus indicated the plates, silverware, chicken, rice, salad, and chocolate cake all over the floor. "We clean up."

"Hold on, bronco," Lucinda said. "This is Alexandro's mess."

"We're a team, remember?" Thaddeus said. "So if one of you swings by a rope from a helicopter and turns our dining room table into a catastrophe, everyone pitches in."

Ike had the feeling Lucinda would have objected to anyone else in the world. But even though Thaddeus was gentle by nature, his enormous size and furrowed brow enabled him to play the part of the tough commander with ease.

"After the banquet hall is spic and span, I'll take you on a quick tour of the castle before bed. So come, members of the Tenth Royal Order. Get cracking."

Chapter Eleven

Ike and the other members of the Tenth Order got the banquet hall in shape, then followed Thaddeus down a long hallway, lined with doors of solid oak.

"This place is really quite small for a castle," the old man said. "Then again, we don't need much room, do we? My chambers are up the circular stairs at the end of the hall. Next to yours, actually. Mr. and Mrs. Sussex have a room off the first barn. These rooms down here are of mostly historical interest."

He used his cane to point at the first door. "That's the old armor room. You see, back in olden times, the knights of the Order liked to wear heavy metal mail."

Hustling to keep up, Ike was once again amazed at how quickly Thaddeus could move.

"And see that door there? The orange one? That's where we keep the dragon saddles. Don't know why we still have them. It was Alistair Hollingsberry of the Fifth Order who decided that the warriors would be better off flying bareback."

108

"And that's been better?" Elmira asked.

"It's been brilliant," the old man said. "The Fourth Order was always getting their boots caught in the stirrups. Ah, and see that down there? That's the infirmary where we patched up Ike from that beastly locust sting."

"You did?" Ike said. "I don't remember that."

"Of course you don't. You were half dead," Thaddeus said. "See that door there? That's where we keep a giant bathtub. Then again, most people around here wash in the moat while someone watches the alligators."

Ike thought he might prefer the bath. Before he had much time to think about it, Thaddeus stopped outside the last door in the hallway. He twirled his beard with his pinky and smiled brightly.

"This, my friends, is the game room."

"Do they have billiards?" Lucinda asked. "I'm killer at billiards."

Thaddeus laughed. "Sorry. This room is mostly filled with strange pastimes from the days of King Arthur. Games like Blister-ball, Round Table Tag, and Shufflericketts."

"Shufflericketts?" Elmira said. "I never heard any mention of it in the historical texts."

"Not everything made the texts, my dear. It's a cross between horseshoes, high jump, and tag."

"Sounds impossible," Lucinda said. "I can't picture it."

"Perhaps you teach us, yes?" Alexandro asked.

"Tomorrow, if there's time," Thaddeus replied. "Right now, we need to see to an important Order tradition."

With that, the old man turned and moved as quickly as ever back down the hallway. Ike and his cohorts exchanged an amused glance and followed. What else was there to do?

Back in the banquet hall, someone had set five brass mugs on the table.

"Very good. They already put it out. Dragon Ale."

"Dragon Ale?" Alexandro asked. "Like beer?"

Thaddeus laughed. "No, no. Not beer. It has its own special flavor. Magical, I think. And utterly non-alcoholic. As I said, it's an Order tradition. Before the first day of training, the new members take a drink together. So go ahead. Grab a mug."

The mug was heavier than Ike expected. The drink itself was light brown and carbonated with an exotic scent he couldn't quite place.

"Here's to the Tenth Order," Thaddeus said. "All right then. Bottom's up."

Ike had expected more of a toast. But when Thaddeus brought his mug to his lips, he and the others did the same. With a single sip, Ike tasted bits of ginger, cinnamon, mint, and even bitter dark chocolate.

"What's in this exactly, anyway?" he asked.

"It's brewed from over thirty different spices and herbs," Thaddeus replied, "most of them only available in England."

"What do you do then?" Alexandro asked. "Have the spices imported to the Order from overseas?"

Thaddeus nodded. "We get a shipment every fortnight."

"Fortnight?" Ike asked.

"There I go again," Thaddeus said. "Every two weeks."

"But didn't you say this was a military installation?" Elmira asked. "Do American tax dollars pay for everything?"

Thaddeus grinned widely. "Precisely."

"It's worth every penny," Lucinda said. She had finished hers in a single gulp. "You know what this reminds me of? The drink my dad got me in a pub on the day I caught my first funnel-web spider and fed him to a wolf. That was when I was three, I think."

"A funnel-web spider, eh?" Alexandro said. "Doesn't sound so scary to me."

"Don't be so sure," Elmira said. "Funnel-webs are big and hairy and poisonous. A bad bite left untreated can prove fatal."

"She's right," Lucinda said. "A person can barely go outside where I live without stepping on two or three of them. That's why I wear these."

She lifted a foot, allowing the kids to take a closer look at her hunting boots, which laced all the way up to her knees.

"Cool," Ike said. "Do you wear your hat for protection, too?"

Lucinda nodded. "Right. Keeps the sun out of my eyes and the goliath Goshawks off my head."

"Yes, nice clothing," Alexandro said. "But I know a thing or two about wild animals, too, eh? A year ago, my family travel to Africa for a Safari. And a lion breaks into our camp. A big one. So do I run? No, I hop on its back and ride him out of there like an American cowboy. Yee haw!"

"You? Ride a lion?" Lucinda said. "That's a laugh."

Alexandro looked stunned. Clearly, he wasn't used to anyone speaking back to him.

"You don't believe me, eh? Well, it's true. I even rode him backwards."

Ike and Elmira exchanged a glance. Perhaps the ease with which Lucinda had wrapped him in a wrestling hold bothered Alexandro more than he had let on.

"That's enough," Thaddeus cut in before Lucinda could answer. "Let's save all this emotion for the battlefield, okay?"

Ike guessed that the old man didn't think a fight between new members would be good for morale the day before the first training session. Also, it was getting late. As Ike drained his bottle, Thaddeus let loose a giant yawn, making him look a bit like a lion himself, albeit one with a white mane.

"Big day tomorrow, friends," Thaddeus said. "I don't know

about you, but I'm completely knackered. Lucinda and Alexandro, you'd better follow me on up and I'll show you your rooms."

Ike felt certain Alexandro and Lucinda would insist upon staying downstairs to share stories and arguments until dawn, but to his surprise Lucinda yawned, too.

"I am pretty bushed," she said. "In Australia, it's tomorrow already."

"And in Rome it's tomorrow morning," Alexandro said. "A good night's rest before my first dragon ride. This is a smart idea."

Though he wasn't sleepy yet, Ike was ready to follow everyone up. But Elmira had different ideas.

"There's something I want to show you in the library," she whispered. Then before Ike could respond, she looked to the old man. "I presume it's all right to take Ike to the library?"

Thaddeus turned for the circular stairs.

"Fine with me," he called over his shoulder. "The castle is perfectly safe. Guarded well. Don't be up too late."

To Ike's dismay, Alexandro and Lucinda were following Thaddeus up, leaving him alone with Elmira.

"Goodnight, *mi amici*," Alexandro called.

"Yeah, night, mates."

Thaddeus, Alexandro, and Lucinda disappeared up the stairway.

"So?" Elmira asked. "The library?"

Ike sighed. For all he knew, she had found a book on *Table Manners in the Middle Ages* or an article on King Arthur's left elbow.

"Listen," he began, "I don't know if I ..."

Before he could complete the thought, Alexandro's voice echoed sharply down the stairwell.

"*Mamma*. These stairs are slippery."

Then there was a loud crash.

"I told you to hold on," Thaddeus called.

"Hold to what?" Lucinda called. "There's no bloody bannister."

"If I can do it, you can do it," Thaddeus said.

"*Ai. Mamma.*"

Elmira met Ike's eyes. What else was there to do but smile?

"Interesting pair, huh?" he said.

"Raring to fight, that's for sure," Elmira said.

"So do you believe the story about the lion?" Ike asked.

He realized a bit guiltily that it was one of the first genuine questions he had asked Elmira in his entire life.

"I've never done any research on man's ability to ride wild cats," the girl replied. "But anything is possible, I suppose. Don't forget, we did kill a giant locust yesterday."

Yes. Anything was possible.

"So, what is it you want to show me? We really have to go to the library?"

Despite Thaddeus's reassurances, walking through the castle at night felt creepy.

"We do," Elmira said. "Trust me on this, okay?"

Moments later, Ike was following Elmira down the stairs to the castle's first floor. With the sun nearly set, the main entrance was shrouded in an eerie half-light, just bright enough for Ike to see where he was going but too dim to make out the faces in the portraits that adorned the walls. Nervously, he scurried after Elmira down a short hallway. There, she pushed open an oak door and flicked a switch on the wall.

A lone light revealed the library, a smaller room than Ike had expected, but one where not an inch of space was wasted. With the exception of a window that overlooked the main grounds, bookshelves rose from the floor to ceiling, filled with row after row of weighty tomes, all related to dragons. With a single glance, Ike saw books on dragon history, dragon physiology, dragon psychology, and dragon eating habits. There were also tomes on dragon dentistry, dragon skin conditions, and his favorite, a five hundred page hardcover entitled *Dragon Throat Conditions: The Downside of Breathing Fire.*

"Amazing, huh?" Elmira asked.

"It is," Ike said. "So what did you want me to see?"

"This."

The girl pulled a thick hardcover off a lower shelf. Then she lugged it to the center of the room and dropped it on a small desk. Ike looked at the faded red cover. The full title read:

By-Laws of The Royal Order
And Sundry Necessary Information
On Basic Dragon Care

"Whoa," Ike said. "There are by-laws for this organization?"

"Yes, from King Arthur's times," Elmira said.

Ike flipped a thumb across the pages.

"This thing is huge," he said. "Have you read it all?"

"I've only been here a day, remember?" Elmira said. "But I've browsed through enough of it to see they thought of pretty much everything." She pushed Ike onto the wooden desk chair. "Check this out. Rule 14, Paragraph A, Section C."

With Elmira leaning anxiously over his shoulder, Ike flipped through the old manuscript, skipping over pages on everything from suggested dragon feeding schedules to preferred methods for cleaning stalls. Finally, at Rule 14, he skimmed down the page for Paragraph A, then further on to Section C.

"Read it," Elmira said.

Ike cleared his throat.

Rule 14, Para A, Sec. C.

Dragon Toenails. Whereas a dragon has feet which produce toenails of unusual length, thickness, and sensitivity, said nails shall be cut by a specially sharpened dragon-toenail-clipper no less than every other week. To wait longer might cause a longish nail to infect the dragon's tender foot, making it difficult for said creature to move with enough forward motion to achieve proper lift-off. Warning: Dragon toenail clipping should never be practiced by an amateur, but only by an expert Dragon-Keeper, fully proficient in any and all dragon arts.

"Isn't that great?" Elmira said when Ike was finished. "Look at the years of care that have gone into keeping these dragons healthy and safe."

"Yeah, it's cool," Ike said. "I get it. But I thought you were going to show me something, well … something more important."

Elmira's eyes went wide. "More important? Didn't you get what you were reading? If a dragon's nails are left uncut for too long, it inhibits their ability to take-off."

Ike sighed. For the past few hours Elmira had seemed almost normal. On the other hand, it was almost reassuring to be reminded that some things would never change.

"I hear you, okay?" he said. "It's important."

Elmira shoved herself next to Ike, taking half the chair. "There are lists of plants from the Middle Ages, really strange things you've never heard of like Wurstrot and Firebane. And look here at Rule 16, Section 9. Did you know that every two members of the First Royal Order had an assistant called a Dragonfly? Not the bug either, but a person who was responsible for helping the Order members get ready for battle. They even shined their armor. Not bad, huh?"

Try as he might, Ike couldn't get as excited about the details as Elmira. In fact, the sudden return of her usual annoyingly frantic energy was exhausting. Suddenly, all he wanted to do was get himself up the castle steps and collapse.

"This is cool, Elmira," Ike said, yawning. "But I'm wiped."

Elmira frowned. "You really want to head up?"

"Yeah," Ike said. "Like Alexandro said, we need a good night's sleep before flying the dragons, right?"

Elmira sighed. "Okay, be that way. I'll stay here and read some more."

Ike expected nothing less.

"Good," he said, making for the library door. "Have fun."

"But I guess that means you don't want to see the prophecy."

Ike stopped short. A prophecy? It was unlike Elmira to hold back news. Usually, she shrieked whatever she had to say so all the world could hear. Was she joking?

"Prophecy?" he said. "Of what?"

Elmira flipped to a page in the beginning of the Bylaws. "Thaddeus probably knows about this. He has to. But he probably didn't want us to get too freaked out."

Now Ike was seriously nervous.

"What do you mean freaked out?"

"You'd better just read it," she said. "Section One, Chapter 8, paragraph 3a: The Prophecy."

In the dim light, she flipped to a page near the front then turned the musty tome to face Ike. Trembling, he sat back at the desk.

Section One

Chapter 8
Paragraph 3a)

The Prophecy. It is still unclear why the famous wizard, Merlin, a great man by all accounts and King Arthur's most trusted aide and advisor, enacted a magic spell that introduced the world to a scourge of giant killer locusts. Before King Arthur died, it was written that the great king mentioned a prophecy to his cousin, The Earl of Cumbrington, in which Arthur foresaw what a future of these enormous and terrifying insects might entail. According to Arthur, the tenth in line to the house of Hollingsberry must successfully and categorically defeat the final locust scourge. If said Hollingsberry the Tenth is unsuccessful—if a single locust is left alive—then, according to the spell, portals will open in every city and town and hamlet in the land, permitting the creatures to appear at will throughout the world, dominating the planet for centuries to come.

Ike looked up to Elmira, too stunned to speak.

"So, wait?" He gulped. "Is this true?"

"I think so," Elmira said. "I don't see why not."

"What if this book is a hoax?" Ike said. "How do we know it comes from Arthur's time?"

"I ran some quick tests on one of the pages. From everything I could figure, it dated from the year 550."

Ike shuddered. Why couldn't Elmira be wrong—just for once?

"So the fate of the world is riding ... on us?"

"Yes," Elmira said. "You, me, Lucinda, and Alexandro. If we don't kill them all, the giant locusts will come like a plague and

117

destroy the planet."

Ike felt like he had taken a kick in the stomach. He had known the stakes were high, but this was something entirely different. The fate of the world? In his hands? It was almost too much to bear.

A moment later, a distant whinny and snort echoed into the room through the window, followed by the *whoosh-whoosh* of flapping wings. A dragon or two going out for an evening fly.

"Man," Ike said, nodding outside. "I hope they know what we're up against."

"Don't worry," Elmira said. "The dragons'll come through for us."

Ike wished he could be more certain. Hadn't his father depended on Dartmoor to flame the locust that had killed him?

"Anyway," Elmira went on, "we should tell Alexandro and Lucinda, right?"

"Right," Ike said, forcing himself to focus. "But let's wait until tomorrow. We might as well let them have a good night's sleep, don't you think?"

Before Elmira had a chance to reply, a positively enormous *BANG* shook the room. And even though the stone of the castle muted the sound, it was thunderous enough to shock Ike into lurching backward into one of the shelves and knocking a copy of *Introduction to Dragon Tooth Decay* to the floor with a loud thwack. If he had been nervous about the prophecy before, now he was terrified. Was the castle under attack?

"What was that?" he cried.

"I don't know," Elmira said. "But if anyone was asleep, they're sure awake now."

"It sounded like it came from upstairs," Ike said. "Let's move."

Chapter Twelve

Ike followed Elmira at a mad sprint through the main entranceway and up the stairs to the banquet hall. That's where they saw it, a thin line of bluish smoke wafting down the circular stairway.

"Up there," Ike cried.

They struggled up the treacherous stairs as quickly as they could, each falling once, and soon found themselves on the landing by their rooms. By that point, Ike was half worried that Alexandro and Lucinda were dead. Or at least buried under a pile of rubble. To his relief, his two new friends appeared to be fine. In fact, they were standing in the hallway with Thaddeus, directly in front of the old man's doorway. To Ike's surprise, the smoke was coming from inside his room.

"What's going on?" Ike was sucking air, winded from the sprint. "Is everything okay?"

"Yes, yes," Thaddeus said. "Sorry to alarm you. It was just a little accident."

"It didn't sound so little," Elmira said. "Did something explode?"

"It sure did," Lucinda said. "Scared me clean out of my pajamas."

"It knocked my Italian-English Dictionary off my nightstand," Alexandro said.

"What were you doing?" Elmira asked.

The four children had formed a small circle around the old man.

"You're all looking rightly surprised," he began. "But it's really quite simple. All this talk of Merlin and King Arthur has gotten me interested in magic. The other week, I got an old book of spells from the Order library. But I guess I've gotten ahead of myself. I nearly blew up my night table."

Ike and his friends exchanged a surprised glance. Thaddeus seemed like a man more likely to use his spare time to get ready for the next day's training than to fool around with ancient magic.

"What sort of a spells were you trying?" Ike asked.

"A little bit of this and that," Thaddeus said. "Trying to turn a toad into a frog. Trying to move my desk chair across the room without touching it. That sort of thing."

"Did they work?" Alexandro asked.

Thaddeus smiled. "Did it sound like it? I nearly blew up my room."

"You didn't blow up a toad, did you?" Lucinda asked.

"No," Thaddeus said. "No dead toads. The spell that backfired on me was one that would have restored the fire to the dragons of the last Order."

Ike thought that sounded worthwhile. But Elmira seemed skeptical.

121

"That condition was caused by old age. Isn't that what you said?"

"I did," Thaddeus said with a nod. "But I felt it couldn't hurt to see if magic can reverse the process."

"*Si, si,*" Alexandro said. "This makes good sense."

Ike agreed. Why not do everything they could to make all the dragons battle ready?

"But don't worry," the old man went on. "No more spells for tonight. No more explosions. You children go to sleep. You need your rest for tomorrow."

Alexandro stretched. "*Si. Buonanotte,* my friends."

"That means, 'Goodnight, mates,'" Lucinda said. "Works for me."

But Elmira wasn't quite ready to let things go.

"You know, Thaddeus," she said. "I've never seen an actual book of spells."

The old man raised his eyebrows. "You haven't? Well, perhaps we can arrange that."

Of course, Thaddeus hadn't meant at that precise instant. But Elmira was already moving toward his door. She should have asked permission—Ike knew that—but he was still surprised by how quickly the old man moved to block the entranceway. Clearly, he didn't want her poking around. But before he could stop her, Elmira managed to give the door a push. As it swung open, something inside crashed to the floor. To Ike's surprise, a wild array of sparks shot into the hall with a loud hiss.

"Oh, my gosh," Ike called, jumping back. "What is that?"

He blinked. As a second wave of smoke cleared, this one smaller than the first, Ike saw Thaddeus's cane spinning in the entranceway. The old man quickly gathered it up.

"*Fantastico,*" Alexandro said. "Did your cane explode?"

"It didn't explode," Lucinda said. "It shot sparks."

"Still pretty weird behavior for a cane," Elmira said.

"It is, I admit it," Thaddeus said. "The last spell called for reciting an incantation using a stick of some sort. With nothing else around, I grabbed my cane. But see?" He held it out for their inspection. Though the end was slightly charred, the rest was unharmed. "It's all fine now. Not even smoking. All is well that ends well, right? Sorry to have disturbed. No more loud explosions, I promise. We have a big day tomorrow. Sleep well."

With that, Thaddeus took a step back into his room and firmly closed his door. As the blue smoke cleared from the hallway, they were silent for a moment.

"That was one nervous guy," Elmira said, finally. "What's he got in there?"

Alexandro shrugged. "Maybe he left a pair of underwear on a chair? It's happened to me."

"Righto," Lucinda said. "A man is entitled to his privacy."

"Sure," Elmira agreed. "But did you see how fast he blocked the door?"

"We all did," Ike said. "But we also saw you try to barge in without asking."

"Don't make this about me," Elmira said. "He was acting suspicious, right?"

"Yeah, maybe a little bit," Ike admitted. "But a really, really little." He shot Elmira a curious look. "What? You can't think Thaddeus is the guy behind the locusts."

Elmira shook her head. "No, no. Not that. But maybe he knows more about this magic than he's letting on."

"Knows *more* about magic?" Lucinda said. "Perhaps you didn't see what just happened? The bloke nearly blew up his room. He knows *nothing* about magic."

"*Si*," Alexandro said. "My ears are still ringing from the giant boom."

123

"But someone is behind the portal re-opening, right?" Elmira said. "Look, I'm not saying it's Thaddeus. All I'm saying is that we've got to be thinking about it."

"All right," Ike said. "So here's what we'll do. Everyone will keep his or her eyes and ears open during training tomorrow. Maybe we'll find some things out. Sound good?"

"Works for me," Lucinda said.

"*Si*," Alexandro agreed.

"Elmira?" Ike asked.

The girl shrugged. "Sure. Eyes and ears. Open."

Thankfully, that was all Ike had to say on the subject—for the time being, anyway—because suddenly he was blindsided by another wave of exhaustion. This one there was no fighting.

Moments later, Ike was lying in bed, listening to the quiet coos and hisses of the swamp. Though the room was strange, he felt more at home than he could have reasonably expected. Why not? His father had slept on the same soft pillow and mattress.

Before drifting off, Ike took a short moment to revisit what had just happened. Had Thaddeus really just been fooling around with an ancient book of spells, trying to find a way to restore Dartmoor's flame? Or was Elmira right? Was there something to be suspicious about? Ike wished he knew. But further speculation would have to wait.

In the distance, Ike heard a snort echo up from the main grounds, perhaps one of the four younger dragons thinking about the coming battle.

"Goodnight, Detroit," Ike murmured. "Goodnight Seattle, Kansas City, and Pittsburgh. You'd better be ready. We're going to need you."

Chapter Thirteen

Ike was jolted awake the next morning by a knock so loud it sounded as though the door had been kicked.

"Up you go," Thaddeus called. "Breakfast. Ten minutes."

Ike sat up and rubbed his eyes, all sense of peace and ease gone. *Bam. Bam. Bam.* Thaddeus pounded on the doors of his compatriots. "Hop to, you blighters. Big day ahead."

Clearly, the old man wasn't messing around. No more laid back meals, no more late night magic hours.

"Time to get to work."

Ike jumped out of bed and found a clean tunic in his dresser drawer. He dressed quickly, laced his boots and made for the banquet hall. But just before reaching the treacherous circular stairway, he stepped back into his room, pulled his dad's sword from the bottom dresser drawer and tucked it in his tunic. Ready, he hurried down to breakfast.

"First things first," Thaddeus said once they had assembled at the banquet hall. "Once again, I apologize for last night's little explosion. Chalk it up to the strange customs of an old man who should know better than to try to learn a new skill in the last years of his life. I am the current leader of the Royal Order, not a wizard.

From now on, I won't forget that. Now. Let's talk about armor."

"Armor?" Alexandro asked. "I thought you said the last few Orders didn't wear any."

"Not the metal kind anyway," Thaddeus said. "But this is different. It slips on over your tunics."

The old man tossed them each a plastic bag. Like most kids, Ike associated the word "armor" with the heavy metal outfits worn by knights of old. What he pulled out of his bag resembled a black long sleeved T-shirt.

"What?" Alexandro said with a laugh. "This couldn't protect me from a baby goldfish."

"It does seem thin, doesn't it?" Elmira said, holding the shirt close to her eyes. "The fabric doesn't appear to be reinforced."

"Hard to know how this thing is going to hold up against a locust stinger," Lucinda said.

Thaddeus raised a single eyebrow. "Do me a favor and put them on."

Once again, Ike was struck at how changed Thaddeus was from the night before. Gone was the befuddled man with the exploding cane. In his place stood a firm, no nonsense leader, a man able to control a room.

With no further discussion, all four children slipped the light "armor" over their tunics. At first, Ike's armor felt exactly as he expected, like a long-sleeved T-shirt. But after a few seconds, he began to feel the smooth, cold material lining its inside.

"Ah ha," Elmira said. "Reinforced with special fabric, I see. Something cutting edge. Probably developed by the government, right?"

Thaddeus nodded. "From a rare alloy that comes from a National Park in Utah. Trust me, this armor is your best chance at survival if one of the locusts gets a shot at you."

"All right then," Lucinda said. "We've got our armor. So when do we fly?" The second she stopped talking, a dragon punctuated the morning stillness with a giant snort, followed by an even louder roar. "That one sounds good to go."

"That's Kansas City," Thaddeus said. "And I'm sure he is. But I have something to show you first. After shelving my book of spells, I was up half the night working on it. The new opening credit sequence."

The four children exchanged a confused glance.

"Opening credits?" Ike asked.

"Yes." Thaddeus said. "Of the new version of the show. *The Return of the Royal Order*. Come. Look."

As Thaddeus got a laptop out on the edge of the banquet table, the kids grabbed toast, waffles, and pieces of bacon and pushed close.

"I used some of the footage from your father's credit sequence," Thaddeus told Ike. Then he allowed himself a small smile, his first of the morning. "Nothing beats opening the show with a picture of that flying boat, am I right?"

Ike looked to his three Order-mates. He could tell they were all thinking the same thing. Yes, the flying boat was amazing—but wasn't it in the barn in a state of disrepair? Would the Navy SEALS be able to get it airborne in six days?

But that was a concern for another time. Thaddeus pushed the "Return" key with his thumb. As the monitor filled with the image of the purple ship soaring into the sky, the new title scrolled across the screen—*The Return of the Royal Order*. Then the low and powerful voice of the narrator resonated throughout the room.

"In the days of King Arthur, wizard Merlin concocted a magic spell that changed the course of history. A portal opened, revealing a passageway to

a strange unknown world."

As before, the mighty ship swooped behind a cloud, then reappeared on the other side. But then the visuals changed. Suddenly, a picture of a giant locust filled the screen—the same one Ike had fought outside the Branford School. Ike gasped. Because there he was, too, standing up before the giant bug, holding Mr. Changar's cup of Starbuck's coffee, primed to throw it in the bug's face.

"What a clever move, *il mio amico*," Alexandro said.

Ike looked to Thaddeus, amazed. "You had a camera there?"

"We got it off of someone's cellphone. You'll find that we're a pretty well run operation."

"Shhh," Elmira said. "Watch."

Ike turned back to the screen as the credits continued.

"And the locusts came. Giant locusts that ravaged the land and defeated Arthur's most famous knights of the round table.

Finally, the desperate king formed The Royal Order of Fighting Dragons, a society of courageous men and women who bravely mounted the last dragons of England and defeated the locust scourge, saving the United Kingdom for centuries to come."

Now the four dragons named for American cities strutted out of the barns, as they had the evening before.

"Seven years ago, Cameron Rupert Hollingsberry was summoned to defeat the last locust uprising in a dramatic showdown over the sands of Nevada. Now the locusts are back and they are after New York City. Thankfully, The Royal Order has a new team."

Again, Ike saw himself—except now he was stroking Detroit's

cheek.

"Wow," Ike said. "Did you film us brushing our teeth, too?"

"Not that," Thaddeus said. "And sorry for the hidden cameras. We needed to get this credit sequence finished."

"How about the rest of us?" Lucinda asked. "You got us, too, I figure?"

Thaddeus nodded. "You figure right."

The rest of the cast was introduced. Elmira came first, watching Seattle whoosh through the sky. Then there was Lucinda, wrestling the alligator over her head, followed by Alexandro sliding down the banquet table. Meanwhile, the narration continued.

"Isaac Rupert Hollingsberry and a new team of knights are on the job. And according to the ancient prophecy, delivered by King Arthur himself on his deathbed, this is it. If The Royal Order does not defeat the locust scourge once and for all, the mighty bugs will destroy the Earth."

As the theme music grew into a final fanfare of trumpets, the camera focused on Ike, stabbing the locust outside his school and pulling his sword out of its eye. Then the screen went blank.

"So?" Thaddeus said, flipping off the computer. "What do you think?"

Ike glanced to Elmira. She looked as confused as he felt.

"You know about the prophecy?" he asked Thaddeus.

The old man nodded. "Of course I do."

"But I discovered it in the bylaws yesterday," Elmira said. "Why didn't you mention it to us?"

"Why didn't I mention it?" Thaddeus replied. He seemed genuinely surprised. "Wasn't it enough for one day to learn you had to prepare to fight an entire portal full of bugs? I thought it was best to let you know the full severity of our situation bit by bit."

Ike understood, but it didn't make him feel any better. What else hadn't Thaddeus told them?

As for Alexandro, he seemed almost amused. "This is wild, eh? Now on top of everything, we have a prophecy. The fate of the world is in our hands. I like it."

"Works for me," Lucinda said. "Pressure is good for the reflexes. That's what the croc hunters say."

"It's true," Elmira admitted. "Sometimes groups of otherwise uncourageous people have been known to respond more bravely when the stakes are higher. I've blogged about it."

Elmira had a point. Ike couldn't know whether Thaddeus had done it on purpose, but seeing the footage of his heroics at the school had given his confidence a boost. Whatever the future held, he had never felt more ready.

"All right, then," the old man said. "So it's all on us. Which means we'd better get down to it. What do you say we ride those dragons?"

Ike and the others wolfed down their breakfasts then followed Thaddeus out the castle entrance. With a single glance from the drawbridge, Ike could tell that Mr. and Mrs. Sussex had been working since before dawn to get everything ready for the first training session. Outside the main barn, Detroit, Seattle, Kansas City, and Pittsburgh were already standing in a row, ready to be taken on a test flight. And to Ike's surprise, there was a woman—in army fatigues and now fully visible—standing by the moat, filming with a handheld camera.

"Ah," Alexandro said, indicating the woman as they crossed the drawbridge. "More footage, eh?"

"From now on, most of your training will be recorded,"

131

Thaddeus informed them. "Remember, only we and a few people in the American government know what's at stake. Everyone else in New York City, not to mention around the world, has to think this is just another crazy kids' show. We need video of you in training, understood?"

The kids nodded.

"All right, then," Thaddeus said. "Follow me. Time to make some history."

Approaching the dragons, Ike was overcome by a terrible excitement and an equally terrible terror. Yes, facing down the locust at Branford had been brave, but he had taken up the fight on solid ground. Now he would be airborne. And the dragons were big—a good twenty feet tall.

Even more intimidating, Detroit was the largest. Getting onto his back would be tricky enough. How would it feel to soar through the sky? What happened if he fell off?

Heart pounding, Ike willed himself forward, one step, then another, until Thaddeus stopped ten feet from the giant creatures. They stood in a row—Detroit, Kansas City, Pittsburgh, and Seattle.

"There they are," the old man said. "Ready to go."

Detroit glanced back and met Ike's eyes. Ike's first thought was to run for the swamp and swim for home. Yes, Detroit was beautiful—his golden wings and silver body glinted magically in the morning light—but even more striking was his mammoth size and strength. Then again, the dragon seemed friendly enough. At least he wasn't tossing him into the air with his tail. Not yet, anyway.

"I think he likes you, eh?" Alexandro said.

Ike forced a nod. "Maybe, yeah."

But then, as if he sensed that Ike was taking his cooperation too much for granted, the dragon lifted his head to the sky and let loose a mighty whoosh of flame. Ike jumped back. It was so sudden, so powerful.

"Don't worry, son," Thaddeus said, gripping his shoulder and leaning close. "That's just how they get ready to fly."

Ike swallowed hard, calming himself as Sussex hustled out of the main barn, wearing the exact same outfit as the evening before. For all Ike knew, he had been up all night making preparations and hadn't had time to change.

"What're you doing now, Detroit?" the Dragon-Keeper said, calling up to the giant creature. "Scaring off Isaac Rupert Hollingsberry? You two are going to get along just fine."

The dragon shook himself then nibbled at some hay.

"See?" Sussex called. "I told you I could speak to these creatures."

Before Ike or Thaddeus had a chance to answer, Mrs. Sussex was striding toward her husband so quickly she appeared to be leaping. "Speak to them? Detroit just happened to shake himself and take a bite to eat. It had nothing to do with anything you were saying." She looked to Thaddeus and the four children. "Is my husband's head full of Shufflericketts' balls? Because that's what I'm thinking. Shufflericketts' balls."

"He means no harm, Mrs. Sussex," Thaddeus said. "Go easy on him, hmmm?"

"If you insist." She cuffed her husband affectionately on the head. "But my goodness, it's hard sometimes. Anyway, you'll find the dragons fully prepared, sir. They've been washed down, brushed, and fed. We also took the big scrubber to their throats and washed away any residual ash. No coughing fits today, if we can help it. Followed all the usual procedures."

"Very good," Thaddeus said with a nod.

"And don't forget the toenails," Sussex said. "I spent the night on me hands and knees filing them down. Won't be any problems taking off, I'm certain."

Elmira shot Ike a glance. Again, she had been right. Apparently the section in the bylaws about toenail care was of critical importance.

"Excellent," Thaddeus said. "Do the honors, Sussex, and tell our new Order-mates how this all works."

Sussex nodded vigorously. "Don't mind if I do," he said. "There's not that much to know, actually, that's the good part. It's mostly trial and error. You have to get a feel for your beast. Your dragon needs to trust you. That's what Sir John Smith of Humbridge always said."

"From the First Order, right?" Elmira asked.

"Indeed!" Sussex exclaimed. "Now listen up. Just because these dragons are enormous, powerful creatures, doesn't mean they don't have feelings. Be gentle with them and they'll be gentle with you."

"Got it," Ike said.

"How do we get on them?" Lucinda asked. "Is there some sort of vine connected to the barn that we swing off?"

"Vine?" Mrs. Sussex said with a cackle. "Where do you think you are, girl? In the middle of the jungle? There are no vines here." She batted Sussex on the shoulder. "Go ahead, husband. Tell them how to mount."

"Of course," Sussex said. "Mounting the dragons. Important stuff. We're going to start you off with a ladder, much like the one I used yesterday. Couldn't be easier really. You prop it by the dragon's side and climb aboard. As you get better, you'll learn how to shimmy up the beast's tail. But however you get there, once you're on the creature's back, all you need is a little nudge with your heels in their sides to get him flying. No more mind you. And look at the reins. Be gentle with them, will you? When you want to go to the left, pull a bit on the left rein. To go right, you pull on the right."

"What about when we want the dragon to shoot flame?" Elmira called.

"*Si*," Alexandro said. "How do we do that?"

Sussex nodded. "Dragons have got an extra set of lungs, like a blacksmith's forge, where they generate their fire. And they know precisely how far they can shoot it, too. They hate the locusts as much as we do, so if they see one of those bugs in range in the heat of battle, they'll shoot it down, mark my meanings. But you can prod them along by giving them a slight pinch right at the base of the neck. Again, a little bit will do."

"And one last thing," Thaddeus said. "Under no circumstances will you fly the dragons beyond a six mile radius. That's our no-radar zone. After that, these dragons will be spotted by everyone from foreign governments to kids on spring break."

"Fine," Elmira said. "But how will we know when we've hit six miles?"

"Military helicopters will fly alongside and show you how far you can go," Thaddeus said. "They'll also have cameras to collect footage we can use in the show. So how about it, Isaac Rupert Hollingsberry? You're the leader. Come on then. Up you go."

By that point, Sussex was already leaning a ladder against Detroit's side. Before Ike could take a single step, Alexandro tapped his shoulder.

"No disrespect, *mio amico*. The way you fought the locust with the cup of coffee and the doggie leashes? That was *eccellente*. But why do you automatically get to be our leader? Isn't it a little bit unfair?"

Ike blinked. "What?"

"Truth to tell, I'm wondering the same thing," Lucinda said.

"I can degut a scorpion with a spoon then go four days with nothing to drink but the marrow from a wallaby bone. I've got serious skills. I should be in charge."

Ike shuddered. The last thing he expected on the first day of training was a power struggle. But a power struggle it was. Before he could reply, Alexandro turned to Lucinda.

"I'm sure we are all glad about your wallaby bone," he said, forcing a smile. "But don't forget, I come from a long line of Roman warriors. I'm a born leader."

Lucinda laughed. "Right. Who I put in a headlock yesterday."

Ike looked to Thaddeus, but the old man held his tongue. Was he waiting to see how the "next in line" would handle the situation? Probably.

"Hey," Ike said, "let's dial it—"

"Forget that silly headlock," Alexandro said, cutting Ike off. "You forget that I had just leapt out of a helicopter."

Now Elmira got in the act.

"Yeah," she said with a smirk, "into a chocolate cake."

Alexandro was clearly losing his sense of humor. "In Europe, we call it making the dramatic entrance."

"In Australia, we call it showing-off."

"At last something *you* know something about," Elmira said, turning to Lucinda.

"What?"

"You showed up here wrestling an alligator and wearing a snake. If that's not showing off, I don't know what is. Besides, shouldn't the smartest lead? That's me."

"Who says you're smartest?" Alexandro said.

Elmira pointed at her head. "This awesome brain does."

Lucinda reached for her belt. "Well, this whip says I'm the toughest."

"You don't scare me," Elmira said.

"Me neither," Alexandro cried. He clenched a fist. "How do you Americans say it? Game on."

"*Settle down and shut up.*"

Ike swallowed hard. Had he just yelled louder than a drill sergeant? And had it ... *worked?* Stunned, Alexandro and Lucinda looked at him blankly with something bordering on respect. Even Elmira held her tongue. And Thaddeus? He was still standing back, giving Ike room to sort things out for himself. With all eyes cast his way, Ike knew he had about two seconds to take full control of the group or cede his authority.

"I may not be able to wrestle an alligator or jump out of a helicopter or recite every fact about the history of the Royal Order," he said. "I know that, okay? But I also know this. Hollingsberrys have led each Order since the beginning for a reason. My dad defeated the final locust seven years ago. And you watch. When our last locust is soaring out of the sky, I'll be there to kill it for us. Because that's what Hollingsberrys do."

Ike had spoken more forcefully than ever before in his life. There was only one thing left to do.

"Sussex," he cried. "My dragon."

"Yes, sir," Sussex said, gripping the ladder. "Whenever you're ready."

Heart thumping, Ike looked straight up the dragon's side. The beast seemed almost too large to fathom, like the giant dinosaurs he had seen on display at the Natural History Museum in New York. But there was no turning back—especially not after making such an impassioned speech. With a breath for courage, he stepped on the first rung and began to climb. One rung after the next he went, forcing himself to keep his nerve until he reached the top and swung himself aboard. Looking down to his friends, he half expected them to be racing to their own mounts. But his speech had hit home. Alexandro, Lucinda, and Elmira seemed to have forgotten their spat and were looking up at him, waiting their turn.

"How's it feel?" Thaddeus yelled.

Surprisingly comfortable, actually. The dragon's silver back was smooth and fit snugly with his legs.

"Good," Ike replied.

Once again, the dragon turned his head lazily and looked him in the eye. Then he looked back ahead and stood still, poised, waiting. Yes, Ike felt steady enough, but would the dragon fly for him? He still couldn't be sure. Half expecting to be bucked off any second, Ike looked back down.

"Okay, then," he called, as he grabbed hold of the reins. "What next?"

"Give the beast a little nudge with your feet," Mrs. Sussex said.

"That'll get him walking," Sussex went on. "Then once he's out a ways in the field, give him another nudge. That's all you'll need."

"And don't forget to hold on," Thaddeus said.

It was good advice. For as Ike cocked his heels, Detroit's whole body went tense. When Ike gave a single brush of his heels against the dragon's side, the creature took off—and not at a slow trot or canter, either, but fast, like a racehorse at the starting bell. Then with no further prodding whatsoever—not so much as a single kick or tap on the neck—the dragon flapped his golden wings and up he went. It happened just that fast.

In seconds, the Order spread out below Ike like a picture postcard. There were the two barns ... and the castle ... the two turrets—he saw that one of them had a flag flying from it, emblazoned with the Order's insignia—The Royal Order of FD. As Detroit swerved over the Order, Ike held on for dear life. But mingled with the fear was a wild, irrepressible thrill.

He had done it. He was flying a dragon. The first one of the

Tenth Order. All he had to do was hold the reins and steer. And then, as Detroit soared higher, Ike remembered the directions. He pulled gently on the right rein. The dragon swooped back over his friends. By now, the power tussle was forgotten. Caught up in the thrill of the moment, they were cheering like mad.

"Way to go, *il mio amici*," Alexandro called.

"Nice, mate."

"I knew you could do it," Elmira called. "I told you these dragons were real."

Ike laughed. Leave it to Elmira to get in the last word. For soon, Ike had the great creature back in the sky. When he looked over his shoulder, Ike saw his three Order-mates finally sprinting toward their respective dragons, climbing three separate ladders. Alexandro was the next to get his into the air, zooming straight up on Kansas City. A moment later, Elmira on Seattle, and Lucinda on Pittsburgh, took off at the exactly same time. Soon the four dragons were flying in formation, close enough for the kids to shout back and forth.

"I love this," Alexandro cried. "Even easier than riding a lion."

"You never rode that lion," Lucinda said.

"Did too. I'll show you the pictures later."

"I never realized the force of the wind would be so strong," Elmira yelled. "The G forces must be close to five hundred and forty."

The best was yet to come. To his left, Ike saw Alexandro give Kansas City a small pinch. The dragon released a blast of fire that left a trail of smoke one hundred feet long. Ike smiled. What was he waiting for? He gave Detroit a pinch of his own and the dragon let loose a whoosh of flame that spiraled a good two hundred feet into the sky. As the fire blew out of his mouth, the beast jolted forward so powerfully Ike had to squeeze hard with his legs to keep from falling off.

"Yee-haw," Ike cried.

"Quite a kickback, eh?" Alexandro yelled.

"Sure is," Ike called.

"Take that, locusts!" Lucinda exclaimed.

Again, Pittsburgh proved female dragons were every bit as powerful as their male counterparts, letting fly a gust of flame that spiraled out a good two hundred feet in no more than two seconds.

Finally, it was Seattle's turn.

"Death to the bugs," Elmira called.

With a powerful whoosh, her dragon proved that he had the goods as well.

"Who is the best Order, eh?" Alexandro cried, whooshing by Ike.

"The Tenth Order," Ike replied.

"You're bloody well right it is."

Ike laughed. The next thing he knew, the dragons were swooping this way and that, weaving in and out and around each other, flaming at anything and everything.

Suddenly there was a stealth military helicopter flying soundlessly by their side. A soldier was at the controls and another was leaning out the side with a camera.

"Hey," he called to Ike. "Over here."

Ike grinned widely. Holding the reins with one hand, he reached for his sword and pressed the button, exposing the blade and waving it over his head.

"I love it," the photographer yelled.

Suddenly, Ike loved it, too. All of it. The dragons. His new friends. The thrill of standing up for himself as the rightful leader. Even the prospect of being on TV. Being "the next in line" wasn't half bad. He retracted the sword's blade, tucked it back in his belt, and swooped below the helicopter as the dragon let loose a thunderous blast of fire. Once he had gotten his shot, the cameraman gave Ike a thumbs up but then pointed back toward the Order.

Ike looked back over his shoulder. These dragons were even faster than he thought. After what had felt like a short ride, the Order was already a distant dot of green in the middle of a vast swath of brown. The cameraman held up six fingers. Ike understood. At the six mile radius of the no-radar zone, he tugged on the left rein, bringing the dragon on a slow arc back toward the Order.

But there was a problem. Kansas City and Pittsburgh hadn't gotten the message. Instead of slowing down to turn back, the two dragons thundered forward, gaining speed.

"You think you can outrace me, *mi compadre*, eh?"

"Sure do, mate," Lucinda cried. She was holding onto her hat with one hand and the reins with the other. "This dragon of mine's got raw power."

"Raw power? Your dragon? He is slower than my nonna—and she uses a walker."

"Pittsburgh is a *she*. And she'll destroy your mangy beast any day of the week."

"Hey," Ike yelled. "Stop."

In a blur of light lavender and dark red, Kansas City and then Pittsburgh rocketed by.

"Wait. The no-radar zone."

It was too late. Before Ike could stop him, Detroit had wheeled around. Flapping his mighty wings like mad, he accelerated rapidly away from the Order.

The race was on.

Chapter Fourteen

Detroit stretched his neck and flew, his wings a blur. Though Ike pulled like mad on the reins, it wasn't long before he realized a horrible fact. Though their routine exercise regimen included two daily flights, the six-mile flying limit made it all but impossible for dragons so young to burn off the energy they needed. With a new crop of riders on their backs, they were raring to fly fast—none more than their leader, Detroit.

"Come on," Ike called. "Whoa, boy."

If the dragon heard or understood, he gave no sign of it. In moments, he had caught and passed Kansas City and Pittsburgh. Though Alexandro and Lucinda frowned, Ike was too busy trying to get Detroit to stop to take pleasure in the fact his dragon was wasting the competition. And not just the other dragons. Detroit was so powerful he was out-flying the helicopter.

And once Detroit got out front, he stretched his hind legs and beat his wings even faster, opening up an even larger lead. Ike looked down. Thankfully, the swamp was still below him. Maybe he could get Detroit turned around before being spotted?

But then, the endless brown of reeds, weeds, and muck began to change to the green and brown of grass and roads. And then the landscape was dotted with an occasional home and a building or two. Then more country roads … then a highway with cars.

Panicking, Ike looked over his shoulder. The helicopter and the other two dragons were a good fifty yards behind—all completely exposed.

"Stop," he cried to Detroit. "Please."

Boom.

A passing bird glanced against Ike's head. Looking to his left, Ike gasped. A small plane was flying no more than one hundred feet away. And the pilot was looking at him, eyes wide, mouth agape.

Ike looked down again. To his horror, he was over all-out civilization, rows of homes, roads, stores, and what looked to be a school. And was that a church? Was that a fast food joint?

And people were looking up, horrified, pointing. Ike could only imagine what they were saying. Were they imagining the end of the world? An interstellar alien invasion? Ike glanced over his shoulder. The helicopter and the two other dragons were still giving chase.

Three dragons out in broad daylight? Was there any way the Order would be able to cover this up?

If only he could get Detroit to turn around.

He pulled desperately on the reins. He shouted, "Whoa." He even tried kicking. But not until the dragon had burned off all his excess energy and satisfied his competitive nature did he cut the speed. Still moving fast, the dragon rested his wings and glided for a bit. Looking over his shoulder, Ike saw Kansas City and Pittsburgh push hard to catch up. In moments, the three dragons were flying side by side, all winded.

"How do you stop these guys?" Ike called.

"I don't know," Alexandro said.

"Pulling their reins sure doesn't work," Lucinda said.

"Oh, man," Ike shouted. "Look."

On the far horizon was a beach. Next to the beach was a resort hotel. And not just any hotel either. A giant neon sign read, *The Miami Opal Grand.* Ike was so surprised he nearly fell off Detroit's back. He knew Theodore Opal's real estate empire stretched across the country, but he'd never thought he would see one of his buildings while on dragon back in Florida.

Then Ike noticed something else. In between the beach and the hotel was a gleaming amusement park. There was a roller coaster, a Ferris wheel, a water slide, another roller coaster, and too many other rides and games to count. And people—many people—were lining up at the entrance gates waiting for it to open. Ike felt weak. This was getting worse by the second. It seemed as though half of the state of Florida had seen them now.

Finally, the helicopter caught up. The photographer leaned out, holding a megaphone.

"Pat their necks three times."

"What?" Ike yelled.

The photographer made a patting motion with one of his hands. "Three times, do you hear?"

Finally. A way to get the dragon to stop and turn back.

"Got it," Ike called and all but banged on Detroit's neck—one, two, three. But to his horror, the dragon didn't turn around at all. And he didn't stop either. Instead, the creature began a speedy descent, straight for the amusement park. By now, the crowd had swelled to hundreds of people, kept at bay by a hastily constructed police line. Everyone was looking at the three arriving dragons, pointing, yelling, and taking video on their phones. The next thing he knew, Ike was holding on tight as Detroit touched down by the roller coaster to gasps, cheers, and finally, wild applause. And then, before Ike could catch his breath, Alexandro and Kansas City were on ground next to him. And then Lucinda and Pittsburgh, followed closely by the helicopter, *thunking* loudly before the pilot cut its engine. Finally, to Ike's utter surprise, came Seattle and Elmira.

"Amazing, right?" Elmira shouted. "I told you these dragons would fly, Ike. I told you."

Ike was too terrified to answer. What was going to happen? Would the dragons be taken to the zoo? Would they be shot? Would the crowd turn on them? Or maybe even worse, would the dragons flame everyone in sight to cinders?

Only then did Ike discover the true power of the Order. Before he or his three friends could say another word, the photographer was out of the helicopter and jumping onto a hastily constructed platform.

"Yes, here they are, ladies and gentlemen," he said into a microphone. "Our fake flying dragons. Don't you think these robotic beasts look like the real thing? Well, I do. It's for the new TV show you've all been waiting for—*The Return of the Royal Order*. Now let's meet our stars."

To Ike's delight, everyone in the crowd cheered wildly. The four Order-mates exchanged a quick series of glances. Immediately, they all realized what had happened. In the time it had taken them to fly toward *The Miami Opal Grand*—no more than ten minutes—Thaddeus and the higher-ups at the Order had created a face-saving publicity event.

"First up, atop a gorgeous silver and golden dragon is none other than Isaac Rupert Hollingsberry."

Ike smiled as a resounding wave of applause swept over him. Getting into the spirit of the event, Ike stood on Detroit's back, waved to the crowd, and pumped his fists. Then he got an idea. He reached back into his belt and took out the sword. Then he released the blade.

Whoosh.

"Whoa," a little boy near the front cried over the applause. "That's the dude who smoked the locust outside his school in New York."

"I saw it on the news," a woman said. "Nice going, Hollingsberry."

More shouts quickly followed.

"Remember Episode Eight where Ike's dad destroyed the queen locust with a spear shot and the entrails exploded all over his face?"

"Sure do. I've got it on a poster on my wall."

"Your wall? I've got that poster on my living room ceiling."

"What's a stupid poster? I've watched all sixteen episodes start to finish one hundred and two times."

"I've watched it one hundred and nine times—in Danish."

The shouts grew and blended together into one massive cacophony of adoration. Taking it all in, Ike kept on waving, liking his new role more and more. How many other kids could claim to be a TV star and an earth-saving hero at the same time?

Soon the photographer-turned-host was back at the microphone.

"Let's meet our other stars, shall we?"

Now it was the other children's turns. While they stood atop their dragons, the photographer introduced them, each followed by raucous applause and cheers.

"Here's a new Order member by way of Rome. The son of

Antonio Cortesi of the Ninth Order, this fine young man has been known to eat gnocchi off the backs of lions while quoting verses of Horace's famous Odes. Say hello to Alexandro Lafcadio Cortesi.

"Say hi to the roughest, toughest young lady in the seven continents. Have an alligator you need removed from your basement? Is there a southern blue lined octopus stuck in your daughter's Easy-Bake Oven? This is your girl. Give it up for Phillip O'Leary Smith's daughter, Lucinda O'Leary Smith.

"Finally, this girl may not look strong but what she lacks in size she makes up for in smarts. Who else races street sweepers by day and memorizes dragon history by night? Need to know something about anything? Here is Clara Carrington's second cousin once removed. Speak to *Elmira Speaks.*"

The cheers following the introductions were thunderous—and then all four dragons craned their necks and unleashed towering plumes of fire.

"Can you believe how life-like these dragons seem?" the photographer went on over the whoops and hollers. "That's because we at the Royal Order Studios have developed the latest in cutting-edge robotics technology. But don't touch. These fake dragons are delicate, friends. Their claws are made of a non-flammable synthetic fiber used only on certain high-security Chinese space stations. Their flaming throats are constructed out of a rare steel alloy forged in the mountains of Southern Peru. Their whiskers are constructed from the quills of three different species of rare porcupine, delicately knitted together by gypsies in a high-end mill in Bavaria. Sadly, this is all the time we have for today. But we'll see you soon. Check your local listings for our first show. Locusts are coming to New York and *The Return of the Royal Order* will be there to kill every last one of them."

The applause was explosive. To Ike's delight, a few kids began a chant, *"Holl-Ings-Ber-Ry. Holl-Ings-Ber-Ry."*

With a flair for the dramatic, Detroit let loose another blast of flame, then took off with two mighty wing-flaps. Looking down, Ike waved back to the cheering crowd as Kansas City, Pittsburgh, and Seattle followed. Ike couldn't help but take a certain satisfaction that Harrison Opal would almost certainly see video footage of him being treated like royalty at his father's resort.

But it wasn't long before the resort was far behind him. In seconds, the helicopter was leading the four dragons back to the Order. Soon the stores, homes and roads of civilization had faded from view, replaced by the sprawling swampland of the Everglades. And then, after minutes of nothing but brown, Ike saw the dot of green in the distance. The Order. They were nearly home.

Yes, Thaddeus would probably be furious. On the other hand, though Alexandro and Lucinda should not have tried to race, Ike knew that it wasn't their fault the dragons were so under-exercised. And it seemed as though the fake publicity event had worked. From what Ike could tell, everyone at the amusement park had bought the fact that he, Alexandro, Lucinda, and Elmira were actors and the dragons nothing more than technologically beautiful robots.

Even so, by the time the dragons swooped over the main meadow, Ike could see the Order had already responded. Thaddeus was there to greet them, as expected, but now a team of Navy SEALS—maybe thirty—were keeping visible guard around the Order edges.

After the dragons touched down by the barns, Sussex and three Navy SEALS were at their sides with ladders. Ike descended as fast as he could and hurried to Thaddeus. Over time, he had learned that when something went wrong, it was better to own up to it right away and get whatever punishment was coming over with.

"I'm really sorry," he said.

To his surprise, the old man wasn't as angry as he'd thought.

"That didn't go as we would have liked, but what's done is

done."

"Why all the security?" Elmira asked, running over.

"A precaution," Thaddeus said. "We think the publicity stunt at the Opal Grand worked, but we don't doubt for a second that whoever is behind the reappearance of the locusts is following our every move. Once the sighting of the four dragons goes viral, whoever it is will know the Order is near Miami. Don't forget, according to the spell, only the dragons and Order members, you four kids, can stop the locusts. So there might be a pre-emptive attack to stop us. We have to be ready."

Ike nodded. It all made sense. In fact, the speed with which the Order had responded was extraordinary.

"Now then," the old man went on, turning to Alexandro and Lucinda. "I hope you two have gotten that competitive nonsense out of your systems. When we go to New York, there will be no room for that."

"Sorry," Lucinda said.

Alexandro bowed. "*Mi dispiace.*"

"We are a team," Thaddeus went on. "A team that works together. Like every Hollingsberry since the First Order, Ike is your leader. It would also appear he's the only one of you with good sense."

Ike looked to his shoes, pleased but embarrassed. He wasn't used to getting compliments—especially about his leadership capacity. To his relief, Alexandro and Lucinda nodded. Most likely, they still didn't like that he was in charge but they also knew the matter had been settled. Ike hoped he could live up to Thaddeus's expectations.

"All right, then," the old man said, turning to Elmira. "It's time, don't you think?"

She nodded firmly. "The timing is ideal."

Ike blinked. "Time for what?"

Thaddeus smiled, a bit mischievously, and leaned hard on his cane. "What would you say to meeting a couple of new Order members?"

Ike blinked. Alexandro and Lucinda looked as shocked as he felt.

"What?" Ike said. "New members?"

Without another word, Thaddeus waved to Sussex, who called out to Mrs. Sussex to knock on the barn. Seconds later, a side door opened.

Ike had never been more surprised—or happy—in his life.

Out stepped Diego and Kashvi.

Chapter Fifteen

At first, Ike thought he was hallucinating. Had the stress of the last three days affected him to the point where he was seeing things?

"Diego?" he stammered. "Kashvi?"

In seconds, his friends were running toward him in what seemed like a dream.

"Yo, Ike," Diego said. His shoelaces were untied, trailing behind him as though streamers had been taped to his sneakers. "Cool Order you've got here. Mr. Sussex let me check out Dartmoor and the other dragons of the Ninth Order. I'm gonna transcribe their conversations for Snarl.com."

Before Ike had time to respond—Dragon *conversations?*—Kashvi's arms were around him. Covered with fresh grease stains, she had apparently already found something to tinker with.

"Hey, you," she said. "I'm so glad you're okay."

For a moment Ike wasn't sure what she was talking about. Then he remembered—his wound.

"Yeah, I'm fine," he said. "But how ...?"

"Thank Elmira," Thaddeus said.

Ike blinked. Of course, Elmira. Who else? Suddenly, she was there, circling Ike like an over-wrought mosquito.

"Remember last night when I showed you the bylaws? That thing about the First Order members having assistants called Dragonflies, right? Well, after everyone went to bed, I realized what we needed to do so I woke Thaddeus. He thought I was coming back to search his room. But I wasn't. I told him we needed to get Kashvi and Diego here on the double. I figured Diego could help with the dragons. And I had a feeling we could use Kashvi's know-how to fix the purple boat."

"I think I can do it, by the way," Kashvi said, turning to Thaddeus. "There's a mechanism in the rear rudder shaft that's  catching on the left circular sprocket. The engine is built like a classic 1969 Triumph Spitfire. When I get it going, I'm going to juice the horse power."

Ike laughed. Yeah, it was Kashvi all right. No wonder she was covered in grease.

"Good news," Thaddeus said.

"This girl is good," Sussex said, walking over. "I'm not sure if the Navy SEALS would've gotten it working."

"It's not fixed yet," Kashvi said. "But I'm hoping."

"I hope so, too," Mrs. Sussex called over from where she was laying out buckets of water for the dragons. "You can see how tired these poor creatures get after a workout. No way are they going to make it all the way to New York without it."

"She'll have it ready," Ike called over.

He had no idea if that was true. But Ike was so happy to see his two best friends that anything seemed possible.

"To finish Elmira's story," Thaddeus said, "after she woke me up, I reviewed the bylaws and saw she was right. If the original Order members had a Dragonfly for every two members, why shouldn't we? So I contacted Diego and Kashvi in New York late last night and arranged for immediate transport."

"Military helicopter," Diego said. "Wasn't half bad."

"Glad you approved of the ride," Thaddeus said.

"But wait," Ike said. He turned to his friends. "What about your parents?"

Kashvi and Diego exchanged an uncomfortable glance.

"Well," Diego said. "We sort of left them a note."

"A note?" Elmira said.

Kashvi nodded. "We each said we were sleeping at the other's house to work on a school project."

For two smart kids, that seemed like a pretty dumb solution.

"You think they're going to believe that?"

"Maybe for a day or two anyway," Diego said defensively. "But what else could we do? This is important, right? I mean, the fate of the world is at stake. That locust nearly ripped your face off."

Diego had a point. The stakes were plenty high.

"I'm sorry my last minute invitation led to a little, shall we say, purposeful parental misinformation," Thaddeus said. "But you're right, Diego. This couldn't be more important. And when you get credit for saving the city, I have a feeling they'll be more proud than angry."

"That's what I was hoping," Kashvi said.

"Anyway," Thaddeus went on, looking over the whole group, "the good news is now your merry little band is six."

With that, Alexandro stepped up to Kashvi and flashed his customary winning smile.

"Alexandro Lafcadio Cortesi," he announced with a bow. "Welcome to the Order, *mio amori*. Wonderful to make your acquaintance."

Ike blinked. Was Alexandro laying it on extra thick? Did he like Kashvi? Or was that how he was with everyone? If so, she didn't seem to care. He had never known Kashvi to show interest in a boy and she didn't seem ready to start.

"Nice to meet you, too," she said, shaking his hand. "Pardon the grease. That purple boat's spark plugs were dripping oil like a broken faucet."

"Ah, *si*," Alexandro said. "Thank you for fixing it." He turned to Diego. "And you are an animal expert, eh? You communicate with them a bit? We could use someone like that."

"Wait a second, mate," Lucinda said. "We already have an animal person on this team. That person is me." Narrowing her eyes, she took a giant step toward Diego and looked him over. Then she turned back to Ike. "This is the friend of yours with the pet squirrel?"

"That's right," Ike said.

"Named him Scruff," Diego said. "I have him eating acorns and glazed donuts. The little dude loves it."

If Diego expected a recitation of his pet's diet to win Lucinda over, he had another think coming.

"A donut-chomping squirrel?" she said derisively. "That's crackers. At my farm, we've got real animals. I've got a pet gator and kanga." She stepped closer until the brim of her hunting hat was nearly hitting Diego's forehead. "I wrestle pandas for fun. When I'm bored, I feed poisonous spiders to wild boar."

"Wild boar?" Elmira said. "I thought you said wolves."

"Wolves, too," Lucinda exclaimed.

Diego looked to Ike, unsure what to think. Then he smiled. "You're kidding me, right?"

"Actually, Lucinda is for real," Ike said. "She showed up here wearing a snake."

Lucinda shrugged. "I wear all sorts of animals. What of it?"

"Nothing," Diego said. "Hey, I do, too."

"You do?" Ike asked.

He had plenty of memories of Diego holding animals and claiming to talk to them. But wearing them? No.

"Well, I wasn't really wearing it," Diego admitted. "But remember the time I went to school with a pigeon in my knapsack?"

"Oh, yeah," Ike said. "I remember."

"So do I," Elmira said. "Two minutes into homeroom, the bird pecked his way out, went to the bathroom on the teacher's desk and flew out the window. Then you were sent to the headmaster's office."

Lucinda laughed. In their short acquaintanceship, Ike had never seen her more amused. "You couldn't even tame a pigeon?"

"Well," Diego stammered, "maybe a pigeon doesn't sound like much to someone from the Outback, but there aren't many animals to choose from in New York City. But my mom is a vet and my dad works for the Natural History Museum. We have a website devoted to exploring human-animal communication. Snarl.com."

Ike expected Lucinda to respond with another burst of derisive laughter, but he was surprised. Suddenly, she seemed to take him more seriously.

"Snarl.com, eh? You know, my great-aunt could communicate with animals, too."

"Cool," Diego said. "What happened?"

"She got eaten by a yellow bellied sea snake."

The thought of Lucinda's great aunt being ingested by a giant snake stopped the conversation long enough for Thaddeus to move things along.

"This has been a nice start," the old man said with a slight smile. "But we'll have plenty more time to catch up and get acquainted. For now, we've got to stay busy. Kashvi, you get back to that purple boat. Diego, you help Mr. and Mrs. Sussex in the barns. The rest of you come with me."

"What are we up to now?" Elmira asked.

Thaddeus was already moving toward the castle. "Videotape," he called over his shoulder.

"Of what?" Ike called after him.

Thaddeus turned. "Of the episodes of the Ninth Order, that's what. It's time to learn to fight these locusts by studying the masters."

For the next two hours, Ike, Elmira, Alexandro, and Lucinda sat at the banquet table in front of the laptop, watching Ike's dad and the other members of the Ninth Order swoop in and around bands of locusts, incinerating them one after the other. Thaddeus ran the Order with great efficiency, but Ike soon discovered that his greatest joy seemed to come from teaching.

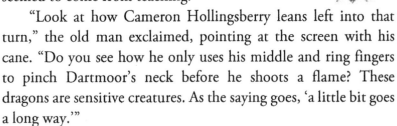

"Look at how Cameron Hollingsberry leans left into that turn," the old man exclaimed, pointing at the screen with his cane. "Do you see how he only uses his middle and ring fingers to pinch Dartmoor's neck before he shoots a flame? These dragons are sensitive creatures. As the saying goes, 'a little bit goes a long way.'"

And then, "Elmira. Look how your cousin laid her body against Loch Lomond's back until the last minute. Then *bam*. She fires the death shot. That's what I call technique."

And then, "Lucinda and Alexandro. See how your fathers grip Northumberland and Snowdonia with their thighs. That's how you stay on at high speeds when you've got one hand on the reins."

Ike was thrilled. In truth, he had been too young to see the show when it had been on the air. Then, after his father had died, it had been too upsetting to watch. Now that he was finally seeing him in action, he had greater appreciation—even awe—for what he had done, given his life to defend his country. By the time the lesson was over, Ike was shaking with pride and a certain amount of fear. Now he knew it for sure—his father had been a true hero. How could he ever live up to that?

Then Ike got some unexpected encouragement. Over lunch, Thaddeus sidled next to him.

"Hear me straight," he whispered. His shaggy beard brushed against Ike's cheek. "You're every bit as talented as your dad."

Ike swallowed hard. Was Thaddeus teasing him? He met the old man's eyes.

"You really think so?" He looked to his Order mates, who were all digging in to sandwiches and chips. "Alexandro and Lucinda are so confident. And Elmira? She's brilliant."

Thaddeus placed a big, wrinkled hand on Ike's shoulder. "They all have their special talents, but you have yours, too, my boy. I know what I see in you."

Ike trembled. "You do?"

Thaddeus nodded. "A leader isn't necessarily the loudest, strongest, or even the smartest. If the others feel they should be in charge, that's good—I like an Order with confidence. But you're a Hollingsberry. You'll rise to the challenge. Trust me. I've been around plenty long enough to know."

Plenty long enough to know?

Ike took a closer look at Thaddeus. The lines on his face were so deep Ike could see many of them through his thick beard. His hair was pure white. It was rude to ask an elderly man his age but after Thaddeus's suspicious behavior the previous night, Ike couldn't resist the opportunity to find out more about the man who ran their training.

"If you don't mind my asking," he began, "how long is 'plenty long enough'? I mean, how long have you been at the Order?"

Thaddeus gave him a strange look. Ike couldn't tell if he was amused or offended.

"So you want to know a little bit more about me, eh?"

Ike felt his heart begin to thump. Had he gone too far? But then the old man grinned, exhibiting his discolored teeth in all their glory.

"If you really want to know," he whispered, leaning close, "I was friends with Sir John of Carrington. He was in the Third Order. And Lady Anne Smith? She was a hoot. She was in the sixth."

Though he was looking straight at Thaddeus, Ike could sense Elmira, Alexandro, and Lucinda were listening, too. Was Thaddeus pulling their legs?

"Really?" Ike managed. "The Third Order?"

"And don't get me started on King Arthur himself," the old man blurted with a nod. "He was a corker. We used to ride bareback through the royal pastures, side by side on two white horses. And did you know he began each day in the throne room with one hundred push-ups? I used to coach him."

Ike glanced at his friends.

"Bareback with King Arthur?" Alexandro said.

"Push-ups?" Lucinda added.

"You're teasing, right?" Elmira asked. "Sure, King Arthur pulled a sword out of a rock, but I've never seen anything in the historical records to suggest he was into fitness."

Thaddeus burst out laughing—not an everyday belly laugh either, but a full-fledged guffaw.

"What?" Ike asked.

"You kids, that's what," Thaddeus managed. "You're so gullible. Knowing King Arthur? *Me*? Why that would make me one thousand and five hundred years old."

Ike had never felt so foolish. The only consolation was that he could tell his friends felt the same.

"Okay, not my finest hour, I guess," Lucinda said sheepishly.

"*Molto stupido*," Alexandro said.

"Yeah," Elmira said. "Especially considering that the oldest recorded living man in history was only one hundred and twenty."

Thaddeus waved a hand. "Don't feel badly," he said, still smiling. "I've been rude. It's wrong for an old timer like me to tease a group of well-intentioned children. I'm sorry. Of course, you want to know about me. It's perfectly reasonable."

Thaddeus took a long gulp of water. Ike and the rest of the Order slid their chairs closer.

"There really isn't much to tell," Thaddeus went on. "I guess you could say that being the Head of the Order is something of a family business. My father was the last Royal Head and his father was the one before that. I was born here in America right after the dragons moved to the Everglades during the Second World War."

"So that explains your accent," Elmira said. "Your grandfather and dad were British."

Thaddeus nodded. "Precisely. I grew up in America but was raised by Brits—which is why I talk like one." He raised a shaggy eyebrow. "Any other questions?"

Ike felt a strange chill. Was there a sudden edge in Thaddeus's voice? Was the old man telling them not to push any further?

"No, no," Ike said. "Thanks for filling us in."

"Yeah," Elmira said. "That explains a lot."

"Si," Alexandro said. "*Grazie*."

161

"What he said," Lucinda said. "Thanks."

"Then finish up your food, warriors, because after lunch we're back on the dragons for another test flight. And this time, you will stay within the six mile no-radar zone, understood?"

They nodded.

"Understood," Ike said.

"Excellent," Thaddeus said. He slapped the table with his open palm. "I'll meet you on the main grounds in ten minutes. We have locusts to fight in a week."

"A week?" a voice called out. "Try one day."

Ike wheeled around. To his surprise, there was Diego, taking the final steps of the stairway two at a time, hair flapping.

"What?" Thaddeus said. "One day?"

Before he could answer, Diego stumbled on a shoelace then staggered the rest of the way to the table.

"That's right," Diego said, planting himself on a bench next to Ike. "One day."

"What are you talking about?" Lucinda said.

"Yes," Thaddeus said. "Speak."

First, Diego grabbed Ike's water mug and took a long gulp. Then he wiped the ever-present hair out of his eyes.

"It was like this," Diego said finally. "I was working with Sussex with the dragons. Talk about amazing creatures. Dr. Bernie J. Wong would have a blast studying these dudes. Did you know that Dragon Keepers of old could talk to them?"

"Truly?" Lucinda asked.

"It's what Sussex thinks, anyway," Thaddeus said. "Evidence is inconclusive. So what's this about the locusts coming in one day?"

"I'm getting to it," Diego said. "Just as I was helping Mrs.

162

Sussex finish brushing Snowdonia's back, we hear a *bring* from the back of the barn."

"Yes," Thaddeus said. "Our computer hook-up for the Order."

"Right," Diego said. "So Sussex goes to look and it turns out the blogosphere is lighting up. I mean, dragon bloggers are going berserk."

Elmira's eyes went wide. "And I wasn't there to be part of it?"

"Relax," Alexandro told her. "You're a bigger part of it here."

"What was going on?" Ike asked.

"Just this," Diego said. "Late last night, the police began to monitor a hollow whooshing sound over the Hudson River. Like a weird echo. That's when the dragon bloggers got involved. A guy named Hugh something or other."

"Hugh Seymour Livingston," Elmira said. "Professor of Ancient Studies at Oxford in England. My mentor."

"Right, him," Diego exclaimed. "He figured out these sounds were coming from the portal that produced the locust that attacked Ike. And then it gets better. This morning, a group of schoolkids found a small colony of tiny locusts in Riverside Park."

Ike had no idea what these things meant, but Thaddeus looked stricken.

"All signs of a coming attack," the old man said. "During the battles of the Ninth Order, we would pick up strange sounds emitting from the portal before each locust appearance. We'd also see flurries of normal-sized locusts."

Ike gulped. The news was finally sinking in. "So they're really coming ... *tomorrow*?"

"That's what I've been trying to tell you guys," Diego said. "That's why Mr. and Mrs. Sussex told me to haul my butt right over here."

"Where are they?" Alexandro asked.

"Getting the dragons onto the main grounds for your afternoon training," Diego said. "In fact, I better get back to help them. See you soon."

Diego stuffed the last half of Ike's sandwich into his mouth then stumbled back to the stairs.

"Tomorrow morning?" Ike said to Thaddeus. "That fast?"

"It would appear that whoever is controlling the portal has upped his or her game," the old man replied, standing up. "So we'll have to up ours. Warriors of the Tenth Order, this afternoon we'll start with sword technique, then move on to basic reining and flaming. Finish up fast and I'll meet you there."

Thaddeus took a giant step toward the door, but then stopped and turned. To Ike's surprise, he was twirling his beard with a pinky.

"What?" Ike asked.

"Admit it," Thaddeus said. "This is bloody brilliant."

"Bloody brilliant?" Ike asked. "Why?"

"Don't you see, Isaac Rupert Hollingsberry?" the old man exclaimed. "*The Return of the Royal Order* is about to go primetime."

Chapter Sixteen

The rest of the afternoon passed in a blur. After wolfing down the rest of their lunch, Ike and his cohorts rushed back to the meadow where Mr. and Mrs. Sussex had Detroit, Kansas City, Seattle, and Pittsburgh waiting. Since Ike already had his father's weapon, Thaddeus retrieved swords for Elmira, Alexandro, and Lucinda. Like Ike's, each of theirs had been forged for the knights of the First Order. Working fast, Thaddeus showed them how to release the blades then how to parry and drive forward for the kill.

"Go for the locust's eyes," the old man said. "That's the death shot. And don't forget to hold on to your dragon when you strike. History has it that a member of the Third Order stabbed a locust between the eyes, only to slip and topple directly into another bug's jaws. The poor man was found days later half-chewed atop the Tower of London."

With a story like that, Ike vowed to always keep a hand on the reins, a technique they all practiced when taking the dragons back into the air. In between each flight, they grilled Thaddeus on topics ranging from flying technique to swordplay to basic dragon care.

By late afternoon, their legs were sore and their arms were aching. Even so, they had all had made remarkable progress, growing more and more confident as fliers and fighters.

"You've done well," Thaddeus said with a satisfied nod when practice was over. "Time to rest a bit. Get cleaned up then be in the banquet hall at seven."

"For what?" Alexandro asked.

"The traditional pre-fight banquet, right?" Elmira answered. "Every Order since the first has dined together the night before the swarm comes."

"Right. And I'm off to grab a quick rest beforehand."

By that time, any concerns Ike and the others might have had about Thaddeus had vanished. How could a man who was such a devoted trainer possibly be up to anything underhanded? So what if he did magic in his room and made jokes about being over one thousand years old? A man was allowed his quirks, and even his secrets.

"Do that," Ike called out to him. "And thanks."

As Thaddeus took a tentative step toward the drawbridge, Ike realized just how much effort he had put into getting them ready. It couldn't be easy to run up and down the castle stairs and see to their training—not at his age.

"My pleasure," the old man said.

"I don't know about you guys," Alexandro said, "but I'm going to try out that giant bath. Clean up before dinner."

"I'm going to wash in the moat," Lucinda said. "Might be able to get in a quick wrestle with one of the gators."

Their plans set, Alexandro and Lucinda followed Thaddeus back to the castle.

"So?" Elmira asked Ike. "Are you coming, too?"

Ike was as tired as anyone. His right arm ached so badly he could barely lift it over his head. Even so, he found himself glancing back toward the barns. Though he had seen Diego on and off throughout the afternoon, Kashvi had been locked away in the second barn the entire time, repairing the purple boat. Had she successfully fixed the engine? Would they have a way of flying the dragons to New York the next morning? Ike wanted to see for himself—and say hello, too.

"I'll find you later," he said to Elmira.

For a moment Ike worried she was going to invite herself along. But apparently, even Elmira needed a break sometimes. She rubbed her eyes.

"I'm going to take a sixteen minute power nap then hit the library before dinner."

Elmira turned tiredly toward the castle. Ike remembered there was something he needed to say.

"Hey, Elmira. Thanks ... I mean, for thinking of Diego and Kashvi."

Elmira smiled. "Yeah, well, I thought it'd be nice if 'the next in line' could see his two best friends."

Yes, Diego and Kashvi were his two best friends—always had been and always would be. But even though she wasn't a good friend yet—and might never be—Ike was seeing sides to Elmira he had never known. Sides he actually liked.

"Well, thanks again," he called.

"Sure thing."

Elmira turned back to the drawbridge and Ike ran past the first barn then onto a narrow pathway to the second.

"Hey, Kashvi?" he called as he approached. He knocked on the front door. "Kashvi? It's me."

No response—which he assumed meant she was hard at work

and unable to hear him. After another knock and shout, Ike turned the knob and pushed his way inside.

At first, all he could make out was the outline of a large, undefined shape, and not much more. Gradually, as his eyes adjusted to the dimness of the barn, the ship came into focus. Yes, he had expected it to be big—after all, it had to carry four dragons and their riders through the sky—but Ike gasped at its sheer enormity. Over one hundred feet long, the boat had the curved prow of a Viking Ship of old with a statue of a dragon head at the bow. Though Ike knew the ship had a powerful engine and wings that appeared just before take-off, the boat also had a towering mast and four sails. As his eyes fully adjusted, he could finally see the color—every inch of the vessel was a rich, dark purple.

"It's enormous," Ike said.

"Sure is."

Ike looked around. He knew that voice.

"Kashvi? Where are you?"

"Up here."

Another voice—Diego's.

There they were, standing on the bow. Diego was covered in even more grease than Kashvi. Clearly, he had been doing double duty.

"Come on up," she said. Her hair was back in a ponytail, a look Ike had seen before when she was in serious work-mode. "I think we've finally gotten it to work."

"Really?" Ike asked.

"Uh huh," Diego said. "Our girl has serious skills."

He pointed to a side ladder. Seconds later, Ike was on the boat, following his old friends down a set of stairs to the lower floors.

"This ship is amazing," Kashvi said. "There's a pilot's room and dragon stalls on the deck."

"And down here is a room where the Order members can

169

chill," Diego said.

Ike looked around in wonder. Here he was, walking through a flying boat he had always assumed was nothing more than a cardboard set.

"And then there's this," Kashvi said.

She stopped by a smaller door. Diego pushed it open and Ike found himself looking down a short stairway, lit by a lone bulb hanging from a wire.

"The engine room?" Ike asked.

"Exactly," Kashvi said. "Come on. I have something to show you."

"What?"

Diego nodded. "Just come, pal. You'll see."

Moments later, Kashvi and Diego led Ike into a smallish room. A toolbox was open on the middle of the floor with a wrench and screwdriver lying next to it. In one corner was a twisted array of cords, wires, and gears. The engine.

"You got it working?" Ike asked.

"Fifteen minutes ago," Kashvi replied. "There was a problem with the left sprocket wing override."

"Didn't you hear us fire up the motor?" Diego asked.

Ike shook his head. "I must have been flying at the time. So what did you want to show me? How you fixed this thing?"

Kashvi smiled. "Something better."

She reached behind the engine and pulled out a beat-up composition notebook.

"This," she said, handing it to Ike. "Take a look."

The book was old and had sustained water damage. Even so, the print on the cover was still lightly legible. So was a single word, scrawled in an uneven script across the top. It read, "Thoughts."

"Recognize that handwriting?" Diego asked.

Ike shook his head. Then he drew in a sharp breath.

"Wait. My dad?"

Kashvi nodded. "Your dad."

Ike trembled. "Where did you find it?"

"Down here," Kashvi said. "Inside the engine."

"Here's what we think," Diego jumped in. "Your dad knew the ship was breaking down, right? He knew someone would have to fix it so he hid his notebook there so someone would find it one day and get it to you."

Ike's eyes went wide. "This is for me?"

"Turn to the first page," Diego said. "Look at what it says."

Equal parts excited and nervous, Ike did as he was told, turning the thin cardboard cover to the first yellowed page. Despite more water marks, it was all fully legible.

To Isaac Rupert Hollingsberry

With a gasp, Ike looked to his friends. Indeed, it was a note—to him.

"Wow," Ike said. "Have you guys read it yet?"

"No way," Kashvi said. "It's yours."

Trembling, Ike turned the page. Why read it to himself when he was almost certainly going to share it with Kashvi and Diego anyway? And he could use the moral support.

"I'll read it out loud."

"Sure," Kashvi said.

Diego picked up a pail to sit on, stumbled over it, then kicked it aside and remained standing.

"I'm listening. Do it."

Ike took a breath then began.

"'How I hope you'll never receive this letter, Ikey. I hope the locusts are gone forever. I hope you never have to learn about this Order. Yes, it's been exciting to be a part of it and I've felt the need to serve, but the more I fight, the more I realize it's come at an enormous cost—being away from you.'"

"Hey, that's sweet," Kashvi said.

Ike swallowed hard. "Yeah."

Diego patted his back and Ike kept reading.

"'If you ever do find this notebook, Ikey, it will mean you have been called to duty. It will mean you are 'the next in line.' I know you'll rise to the challenge and finish whatever I was unable to finish. Even though you are only a little boy, I see great things in you.

"'I'm leaving you this note with the boat damaged—perhaps critically—only an hour before the sixteenth and what I hope will be the final attack of the locusts.

"'It is still unclear how and why they reappeared after three centuries. Did Merlin's original spell call for them to return? Or did some new wizard or criminal learn how to manipulate it? I still don't know for sure—but I want to tell you what I have found out. You see, for some time, I have suspected Thaddeus has some sort of double identity.'"

Ike looked to Kashvi and Diego, eyes wide.

"Double identity," Diego called. "Thaddeus? Keep reading."

Ike didn't have to be told twice.

"'Yes, he is a kindly old man and the Head of

the Royal Order. But lately I have seen him trying to do magic with a wand. Crazy as it sounds, I have come to suspect he is a wizard.'"

"A wizard?" Kashvi exclaimed. "Could that be true?"

"Maybe," Ike said with a gasp. "We found him doing spells in his room last night. And this morning at lunch, he joked he knew King Arthur."

"This is getting good," Diego said. "Go, go. Keep reading."

As his friends pushed closer, Ike turned back to the notebook.

"'So I made a decision. After our fifteenth battle against the locusts—episode fifteen of our show—I decided to stick to Thaddeus like glue to see what I could find out. That decision took me all the way to England. That's right. You see, to my surprise, Thaddeus traveled to the Dark, Dank Woods, Merlin's home and the spot where the original spell of the locusts was cast so many ages ago. Today, it is a heavily wooded National Park. On a cloudy day, just before dusk, I followed the old man to a clearing in the darkest, most secluded part of the woods. That's where something incredible happened. Thaddeus stopped, looked around, then raised his wand to the sky. Then he shouted some sort of incantation—I couldn't make out the words— but after that, he cried out in plain English, 'By the power of King Arthur, break Edward's spell.'"'"

Again, Ike looked to his friends.

"By the power of King Arthur? Wow."

"Truly intense," Kashvi said. "But who's Edward?"

"Beats me," Ike said.

Diego motioned to the notebook.

"I know," Ike said. "I'll keep reading."

"'To my astonishment, as Thaddeus thrust his wand high in the air a thunderclap shook the woods. The sky went dark. Had this Edward's spell been broken? But then, in the stillness after the great boom, I heard a rustling in the woods across the way. Someone else was there. Thaddeus heard it, too, calling out, "Who is it?" There was no answer, just the sound of someone running like mad to escape. Thaddeus dashed after the intruder. Then the rain came, fast and furious. I came out of hiding and searched around. Before the rain washed them away, I found Thaddeus's bootprints in the dirt. More important, I also discovered the footprints of a standard shoe with a marking on the heel the rain made hard to read. In any case, whoever it belongs to is somehow connected to this plot, Ikey, I am sure of it. I did my best to sketch it.'"

"'All of this leaves me confused. Who was Thaddeus speaking to? Is he himself a wizard? If so, why has he never shared his magical abilities with the Order? Clearly, he knows more about the locusts than he lets on. Why? We, those who fight against the locusts, have the right to know everything there is about them. Can someone so secretive be fully trusted? Who is Edward? Questions, questions ... and no precise answers.

"'In any case, I rushed directly from my trip to the Dark, Dank Woods back to the Purple Flying Boat for the sixteenth battle with the locusts. After we win this fight, I plan to speak to the others and confront Thaddeus. Keeping secrets of such importance from the Descendants has to stop. But in case the worst happens—if I don't make it through this battle—I wanted you, my son and the 'next in line,' to know everything that I do.

"'I wish you luck, Ikey. I wish I had known you better. I wish I could hold you right now. Please know I always loved you even if I wasn't around as much as I wanted.

Love, Dad.'"

Finishing, Ike blinked away a few tears.

The letter had overwhelmed him. But he would have to save his response for later. There was more work to be done. Collecting himself, Ike turned to his friends.

"What do you think?" he asked. "It sounds like Thaddeus might be a wizard, after all. But it's weird. In my dad's note, he has a wand. Now, he has an old cane."

"Maybe it's his new wand?" Kashvi said.

"Maybe," Diego said. "But if he is a wizard, who is he working for?"

"Sounds pretty evil to me," Kashvi said. "The sky went dark right after he held up his wand, right? There was even thunder and lightning."

"True," Ike said. "But maybe he was trying to overturn the spell of the locusts? That would make him good."

"Also true," Kashvi said.

"So what next?" Diego asked.

To his surprise, Ike realized his two friends were looking to him for guidance.

"We tell the others," Ike said. "That's first. Then we find some way to get more information on Thaddeus—and fast. Come on."

Sprinting back to the castle, Ike allowed himself a moment to think about the more personal parts of the letter. The truth was he had no memory of his dad ever telling him he loved him. Reading the actual words had touched him deeply, to the point that while crossing the moat, he briefly choked up. But by the time his boots hit the stone floor of the castle's main entranceway, Ike had collected himself. This wasn't the time for sentiment. His father had left him some valuable clues. He had to finish his work.

Chapter Seventeen

That afternoon, a team of Navy SEALS showed that their talents went beyond protecting the Order. Swapping their weapons and swamp gear for pots, pans, aprons, and tuxedos, they had gotten busy cooking and redecorating the banquet hall. By the time Ike and the rest of the Tenth Order found their way downstairs, two men and a woman, now dressed as elegant waiters, were bustling this way and that, setting out flower arrangements and laying placemats and the final pieces of silverware on the table.

"Welcome," one of the SEALS called. His freshly fitted tuxedo identified him as the headwaiter. "Good to see you. The festivities will start soon."

As the waiter hurried off, Ike turned to his friends. He shared his father's letter with Elmira, Lucinda, and Alexandro, and the six children came up with a plan. With time running short, they would do their best to enjoy the banquet. Afterwards, Diego, Kashvi, Lucinda, and Alexandro would lure Thaddeus to the game room to teach them Shufflericketts, giving Ike and Elmira a chance to search his room. Though Ike hated to snoop, no one could think of a better way to find proof of what Thaddeus was hiding.

And that wasn't the only unresolved mystery.

"What I don't understand is this," Diego said as the gang waited to take their seats, "who is Edward?"

"I was wondering, too," Elmira said. "So I did some research."

Ike exchanged a quick glance with Kashvi. Why wasn't that surprising?

"Already?" Ike asked. "When?"

"While I was changing for the banquet. I looked in the bylaws."

"The bylaws," Kashvi said. "You changed in the *library*?"

"No, no," Elmira said. "I lugged them to my room after training so I could read more before the banquet."

"Okay," Alexandro said. "So what did you find out? Any Edwards?"

"I didn't have a chance to check every page," Elmira said. "Not even close. But I did find a chapter called *Historical Figures of the Order*. It turns out that one of the first Dragon Keepers was Edward Hale of Oxford, and Edward Carrington was a member of the Seventh Order."

"Did it say anything about either of them experimenting with magic?" Ike asked.

"Nope. Afraid not."

"No other Edwards in there?" Lucinda asked.

Elmira shook her head. "None."

"So we still have no idea who Thaddeus was calling out to," Diego said.

Ike nodded. "Or if Thaddeus really is a wizard at all."

"So we're back to our plan," Kashvi said. "We sneak into his room tonight and see what we can see."

"Works for me," Diego said. "And do you know what I like best about it?"

"What?" Ike asked. "That you get to learn how to play

Shufflericketts?"

"No, we get to eat first."

Diego strode to the table, took a giant gulp of Dragon Ale, wiped his mouth with his sleeve, and shoved an entire dinner roll in his mouth—an act of defiant silliness that gave the other five children permission to laugh.

"You're right," Alexandro said. "We worry about dragons, locusts, and magic spells later, eh? Now pass me that ale."

"Me, too." Lucinda said.

"Fill me up."

"Right here."

"I'll take a glass."

Though it was non-alcoholic, something about chugging the strange and spicy concoction made Ike giddy. Yes, in less than a day, he and his friends would be the only ones standing between prehistoric-sized locusts and the possible end of modern civilization. But as terrifying as that was, it was also sort of thrilling. He was no longer the boy who had been teased after missing two foul shots in gym class. He was a full-fledged member of the world's only Dragon Order.

Soon, the six friends were spearing appetizers, talking smack, and laughing over everything and anything. And then, as Alexandro and Lucinda began to take bets on who would shoot down more locusts and from what angles, Sussex charged into the room, crashing a pair of cymbals.

"Is everyone ready for a feast?"

Bang.

"Then indulge me, if you would."

Crash. Bang.

"I will entertain you with a poetry reading later. But first, a dance."

Without waiting for a response, Sussex crashed the cymbals a final time and executed a mad jig that involved hopping from side to side while waving his arms in circles. Seconds into her husband's strange boogie, Mrs. Sussex swept into the room in a long blue dress.

"What are you trying to do, Mr. Sussex? Scare these poor children away?" She grabbed her dancing husband by the nose and pulled him into his seat. "If the children run off, who will fly the dragons then?"

"Ouch. Careful!" Sussex cried. "That's my best nostril."

"Then sit," his wife said. "First, we eat. Isn't that right, Thaddeus?"

Ike and his compadres wheeled around to the stairwell. The old man stood by the circular stairway, regal and majestic, dressed for the occasion—but not in his usual red. No, Thaddeus wore a tunic of jet black. In his right hand he held his cane. Atop his head was a hat—a wizard's hat?—also black, pointing straight to the ceiling.

"Man oh man," Diego whispered. "He looks like some sort of Dark Lord."

It was true. Ike could barely swallow, he was so scared. Then it got worse. Thaddeus spread his arms wide, holding out his cane. Ike closed his eyes. Was he about to hit them with a spell right then and there?

"Sorry to be late," the old man cried. "Welcome to the feast."

Still trembling a bit, Ike opened one eye and then the other. To his surprise, the old man was smiling, taking his seat at the head of the table with a Sussex on either side. Then the doors to the kitchen swung open. Exhibiting fine military training, six waiters stepped out in perfect unison, carrying trays of steaming food and more jugs of Dragon Ale.

"Thaddeus actually looks pretty friendly," Kashvi whispered.

"Yeah," Ike said. "He does."

"So maybe he isn't going to cast any spells," Kashvi said. "At least not now."

"Maybe not," Ike said.

"Great," Diego said. "So that means I can eat."

But as Diego reached for a serving spoon, Thaddeus rose to his feet.

"A word before we begin."

Diego looked painfully at his empty plate then dutifully placed the utensil back on the table. Then the old man reached inside his black tunic. Once again, Ike tensed, exchanging worried glances with his friends. Maybe the merry entrance had been a decoy? Maybe Thaddeus had waited to be at the head of the table before pulling out the stops?

Once again, Ike's fears proved unfounded. All Thaddeus produced from his tunic was an ancient looking scroll.

"This is what King Arthur read to the First Order the night before they flew into battle," he said.

Again, Ike relaxed, feeling more than a little silly for being quite so worried.

"King Arthur?" Elmira said. "Seriously? How come I've never read about this?"

"Because not even you know everything, Miss Hand," Thaddeus said with a smile. "This scroll has been passed down through the generations."

Thaddeus unrolled the yellowed piece of parchment adorned with elegant black script. When the entire thing was stretched out, he began to read.

"'Good men and women of the Royal Order of Fighting Dragons. You are hereby called to duty. Tomorrow you go into battle against a locust scourge of indeterminate size and strength—catastrophically large insects that first appeared in the Dark, Dank Woods and have bedeviled our land too long. But this I know, good knights. Though the battle will be difficult, though blood will be shed, in the end you and your flying dragons will defeat these dreaded creatures. So tonight let us eat. Let us celebrate the good days to come. For tomorrow, we will fight. Victory shall be ours.'"

As Arthur's words resonated throughout the hall, Ike and his friends didn't move a muscle until Thaddeus finally broke the spell with a smile.

"You heard what Arthur said," he said. "Tonight, we celebrate."

Again, Diego reached for a serving spoon.

"But one more thing," Thaddeus thundered.

Ike held his breath. By this point every time Thaddeus raised his voice, reached for something, or waved his cane, he couldn't help fearing the worst. As for Diego, Ike could tell that any apprehension his friend harbored toward the old man had vanished in a wave of extreme hunger.

"You're killing me here," Diego cried. "One more thing? When can we eat?"

"In another minute," Thaddeus replied. "First, I want you all to see something. A short commercial is playing in America this second, promoting your show. Don't forget, we fight the locusts tomorrow—it's your world premiere."

As Thaddeus brought out his laptop, the headwaiter dimmed the lights. Soon the triumphant theme-music of *The Fighting Dragons* filled the room. The words, "They Are Back" flashed on the screen.

Then came a series of images in rapid succession.

Ike soaring through the sky on Detroit ...

Alexandro waving his sword bravely through the air ...

183

Lucinda wrestling the alligator ...
Elmira studying in the library ...
Kashvi working on the purple boat ...
Diego tending to the dragons in the barns ...

Then came a picture of Ike, Elmira, Alexandro, and Lucinda, all taking to the sky atop dragons. As they flew in triumphant circles around the Order, the music swelled ... then the screen went dark, flashing text in dramatic cinematic fashion.

The Tenth Order. Coming To You Tomorrow. Watch Them Save The World.

When the short commercial was done, a Navy SEAL whisked away the computer and the headwaiter turned back up the lights.

"Whoa," Ike said. "Cool."

"I look pretty good with that sword, eh?" Alexandro asked.

"Not as good as I looked juggling that gator," Lucinda said.

"Amazing," Kashvi said. "I can't believe this is really happening."

Thaddeus nodded. "That it is. As King Arthur said, tomorrow we fight. Tonight, we feast. And I must say, the food looks scrummy."

"Means yummy," Lucinda whispered to the others.

"Okay, so we've got scrummy food and six hungry kids," Diego said. "Can we finally eat or what?"

Thaddeus waved a hand. "Yes. Eat. Go."

And so they did.

There was stew, mutton, fresh vegetables, and oat bread. There was wild fowl on sticks and plates and a delicious soup made of barley and roasted cinnamon. As everyone dug in, waiters bustled this way and that, doling out seconds and pouring more Dragon Ale. Ike took a break from worry about Thaddeus. After all, they were having too much fun to stress about unsolved mysteries. Let the scary stuff wait until after dinner when they would search his room and find out what they needed to know.

Soon the main courses were cleared. When the waiters brought out dessert, Sussex returned for round two. This time he didn't crash cymbals, but sprang onto the center of the table and whistled so loudly Ike dropped his ice cream spoon mid-bite to cover his ears.

"All right, then," Sussex announced. "Who's ready for a history lesson?"

"History?" Lucinda said. "You're kidding? At a party?"

"History of what?" Elmira asked.

"Of what?" Sussex cried. "*Your* history, of course."

"Our history?" Ike said.

"It hasn't been written yet," Alexandro said.

To that, the little man nodded toward his wife. Mrs. Sussex smashed her own set of cymbals.

"That was in case any of you were feeling sleepy," she called.

"Everyone is quite awake," Thaddeus said. "Let's have the lesson."

"Indeed," Sussex said, leaping to the floor. "Listen, children. Every Order had a bard or a minstrel, a poet of great cunning and genius, who immortalized its members the night before the first battle."

"And that's you?" Diego said with a laugh.

Sussex bowed low.

"Aside from being a Dragon Keeper extraordinaire, I am a man of letters."

"Very well," Alexandro said. "But if you are to tell our history,

185

what will you say, eh?" He flashed a grin. "That I am the best looking, of course?"

"And that I'm the bravest," Lucinda said. "Anyone else here ever worn a bull ant bracelet?"

"I'll give you that," Elmira said. "But I'm the smartest. I've blogged in Mandarin, people."

"Whoa, slow down," Thaddeus called. "You all have special talents. That's one of the reasons you're here. Listen to Sussex. This is an important Order tradition. Like Dragon Ale before the first day of training, it is said a good verse will help you in the field of battle."

The Dragon Keeper needed no other encouragement. With a final crash of the cymbals, the little man hopped back onto the table and began.

> *Since the days of King Arthur in the great Middle Ages.*
> *Ten dragon Orders have graced history's pages.*
> *And many great knights have agreed to be focused*
> *On ensuring the Earth stayed forever de-locusted.*
> *And each one of these knights, there are ample statistics,*
> *Brought to the battle unique characteristics*
> *That helped him dispatch the bugs straight to perdition.*
> *Now the Order of Ten carries on the tradition.*

Ike swallowed hard. Though obviously comic, Sussex's verse made him see himself in a new context, as the successor to a long line of great knights. Could he and his band of four children and two Dragonflies possibly measure up?

Clearly, Sussex thought so. He jumped down from the table again and put his hands on Elmira's shoulders.

> *First of all, there's Elmira, no girl is as smart.*

As insightful as Einstein. As keen as Descartes.
Watch her mind hard at work, her thoughts growing deeper,
As she blogs while she rides on her garbage street-sweeper.
With intelligence so keen, we can say without braggin'
No smarter young lady has flown on a dragon.
So watch it, oh locusts. You'll soon be a shriekin'.
When you get a strong dose of what Elmira is Speakin'.

Ike had seen Elmira blush once before—when Alexandro complimented her blog. Now she did so again. It occurred to him that with only an elderly grandmother for company, she probably didn't get much emotional support. Perhaps she needed it more than she showed?

"Nice, Elmira," he called.

"Yes," Alexandro said. "These words, they are true."

The compliment left her uncharacteristically speechless.

"Oh, yeah, well," she managed. "Whatever."

Elmira was left to blush in peace when Sussex hopped over to Diego and mussed up his hair.

Here's a boy who's unspeakably unkept and unshorn.
Has a sloppier child ever been born?
But beneath all that hair is a down to earth warder.
Who'll boost the morale of any good Order.
A sidekick unequalled, this son of a vet
Has a certified genius for chatting with pets.
Which will only be helpful with dragons, it should.
Because dragons, like people, need to be

understood.

"Thanks for that," Diego said. "But I'm not really that sloppy, am I?"

The comment was met with total silence. Only Kashvi had the heart to speak the truth.

"Um, let's put it this way ... where are your socks at this moment?"

Diego glanced down then looked up and shrugged.

"I'm only wearing one."

"Diego has personal style," Thaddeus said. "That's a good thing. A very good thing."

"Yeah," Diego said, nodding to Thaddeus. "What he said."

"Who's next, Mr. Sussex?" his wife called.

Ike watched as the Dragon Keeper did another of his spasmodic jigs and landed by Alexandro.

He's dashing, he's cultured, he's strong as a stallion.
He gives a good name to all things Italian.
Whether riding a lion or eating pasta caprese
He's a miracle in motion. He's Alexandro Cortesi.
But that isn't all. With his good looks and style,
When the bugs catch a glimpse of his glorious smile,
Their antennae will quiver, their wings fall apart.
And they'll die, the whole swarm, of a broken bug-
heart.

"It's true, eh?" Alexandro cried. "That's how we'll do it. One smile from me and boom. All the locusts. Dead."

Ike hoped so. After all, with the odds against them, the Order would need all the help they could get.

With Alexandro still reveling in the power of his good looks, Sussex moved on. This time, he planted himself by Kashvi.

Next say hello to a lady who kicks it.

*You have something broken? She's the girl who can
fix it.
She'll rebuild your computer. Repair your fake
chimp.
She'll rejigger your oven. Refurbish your blimp.
This girl is so handy she could, I suppose,
Replace your car's engine, then straighten your
nose.
The Order mechanic, she's talentedly tooled.
So watch out, oh locusts, you're about to be
schooled.*

When Sussex was finished, Diego banged his ale mug on the table and chanted, "Kashvi. Kashvi." As the other kids joined in, Kashvi smiled and looked shyly at her shoes, until Sussex finally moved on to Lucinda.

*Here's a girl who tames snakes. Rides a wild
kangaroo.
A girl so courageous she could fight a whole zoo.
Is a tiger nearby that's gnashing its jaws?
Lucinda will tie his back legs to his paws.
So listen up, locusts. You're gonna shed tears
When this girl zaps your stingers smack into your
ears.
She'll cry, "Good day mate," and smash you out of
the sky
Then wear your antennae as a belt and a tie.*

Lucinda rose to her feet, pumping her fists.

"Why didn't I think of it? An antennae belt. Love it. I'll get one for my father, too."

Now Sussex looked to Ike. He was next. And last. What would Sussex say about him? Everyone else in the Order had some sort of special talent. What was his?

Apparently, Sussex had no such questions. With no hesitation, he cleared his throat, quieted the room and launched into his final verse.

And last here's a boy who's unspeakably fine.
Could we ask any better for our next "next in line?"
Isaac Rupert he is. Some might say things look grim now.
As the prophecy states, it's all up to him now.
Yes, the fight will be tough, tomorrow looks scary
But like his father before him, he's a true Hollingsberry.
And true Hollingsberrys are leaders of men.
It's never a question of "if" but of "when"
They will pull out their swords and rise to the occasion,
Leading their troops against a locust invasion.
Like a game winning touchdown or a grand slam homerun,
No one can doubt it
Historians will shout it
If you've got it, you flout it.
The tenth is the one.

When Sussex was finished, Ike's Order mates applauded and rattled their glasses.

"Nice, Ike."

"True enough."

"*Fantastico.*"

"Good show, mate."

Ike swallowed hard, too touched to know what to say. Then to make matters worse, everyone was suddenly on their feet, cheering. Ike had no way of knowing if Alexandro and Lucinda still felt that they should be the Order's leader—most likely, they did—

but clearly they had accepted their roles and thrown their support behind him.

"You can do this, Isaac Rupert Hollingsberry," Thaddeus said, grabbing him by the shoulders. "You *will* do this."

Ike swallowed hard. But before he could think of how to respond to such a flattering vote of confidence, he noticed something. Through the glare of the setting sun, above the field next to the first barn, was a bright red dot.

"Look at Ike," Diego said. "The kid is overwhelmed."

"Don't worry, mate," Lucinda said. "You're going to kill it tomorrow."

"No," Ike stammered.

The dot had gotten even bigger.

"Yes, yes," Kashvi said. "You're our leader."

"Yeah," Ike said. "I mean, thanks. But that's not what I'm saying." He turned to Thaddeus. "Do any of your deliveries come from a ... hot air balloon?"

The old man looked surprised. "A hot air balloon? No. Why do you ask?"

Ike pointed out the window. Thaddeus's eyes went so wide they seemed to stretch over a good half of his face. Then Ike saw his lip tremble.

"What?" Ike said.

By now everyone had seen it. No more than a hundred feet in the air, the balloon was descending fast. Worse, standing in its basket was a strange man in a cape, holding some sort of a staff or wand. Next to him were four men or women—it was hard to tell—dressed entirely in black.

"That looks like a wizard," Kashvi said.

"With a team of soldiers," Diego said. "With crossbows."

"They've found out where we are." Thaddeus said.

"Who?" Ike asked.

"Whoever is behind the return of the locusts. They're here to stop us before the fight really even begins. Come on everybody. Battle stations, I say. Everyone to battle stations."

Chapter Eighteen

Once again, Ike saw that old didn't necessarily mean slow. Taking command, Thaddeus got everyone in armor and led the charge out the main entrance of the castle, moving so quickly they had to run full out to keep up. Even so, despite rushing, the team still wasn't quite fast enough. By the time Thaddeus reached the far end of the drawbridge, the hot air balloon had landed. The four soldiers were on the ground, each with a powerful crossbow. Then the strange wizard hoisted himself out of the cart, holding a long wand with a silver handle.

"What happened to the thirty guards you had around the perimeter?" Elmira asked.

The old man wheeled around, looking. "That's a good question. Where are they?"

A quick glance to the side of the moat provided the answer. There was a Navy SEAL, lying on his back, eyes closed.

"Look," Ike said.

"My gosh." Kashvi cried. "Is he dead?"

Lucinda felt his neck for a pulse.

"Not dead, just knocked out."

"It's some sort of spell," Thaddeus said. "Does everyone have their weapons?"

In unison, Ike, Elmira, Alexandro, and Lucinda drew their swords and released the blades.

"We do," Alexandro said.

"Let's bring it," Lucinda said.

"What about Kashvi and me?" Diego said. "Are we supposed to fight a wizard and a team of armed soldiers with sticks and rocks?"

"Not at all," Thaddeus replied. "Catch."

He reached into his tunic and flipped a sword to both Diego and Kashvi.

"Better now?" Thaddeus asked.

"I don't really know what I'm doing with this thing," Diego said, releasing the blade. "But sure, I'm good."

"Just keep your hair out of your eyes and stick it in the bad guys," Sussex said. "The blade will take care of the rest."

"Works for me," Kashvi said, using her sword to lunge at an imaginary adversary.

"Good!" Thaddeus bellowed. He waved his cane in the air. To Ike's utter amazement, a sword appeared out of its end. The old man winked at him then faced the troops. "Is everyone ready?"

Ike didn't know if he could ever truly be ready for something like this. Across the way, the wizard had already slipped inside the unguarded barn door. Two Navy SEALS were passed out on either side. The four soldiers had taken up defensive positions behind the stone fence. Ike's heart was beating like mad. His hands were sweaty. But he found himself nodding along with everyone else.

"Of course we're ready," Sussex cried.

The six children, the two Sussexes, and

the three waiters—eleven people in all—drew weapons and formed a line behind Thaddeus. For a moment, everything was still. Though staring straight ahead, Ike could feel the tension in the ranks. This was it. Their first real battle.

"On my command," Thaddeus cried. "Ready? Charge."

Just like that, they were off. Again no one was faster off the mark than Thaddeus. Boots smashing against the ground, beard flapping wildly in the breeze, the old man barreled forward like a giant grizzly on the hunt.

"Stay with me," he cried over his shoulder.

Running after him, Ike saw the four soldiers take out their crossbows. Then the arrows began to fly. The first whizzed by Elmira while the second went over Lucinda's head and landed in the moat. But the third found its mark—Sussex.

"Ah," the little man cried. "My big toe. An arrow got my toe."

Indeed, there it was, sticking out of his boot. Mrs. Sussex didn't seem particularly concerned. With a giant yank, she pulled the arrow free. Meanwhile, Ike and his friends stayed on the move. But the soldiers were finding their groove, proving why they had been picked for the wizard's team.

Ping. Ping. Ping.

An arrow hit Lucinda in the stomach.

"Bloody archer," she cried.

Another glanced Alexandro in the chest.

"*Mamma.*"

If it hadn't been for the armor, the damage would have been serious. As it was, the arrows made an impressive clunking sound, then bounced harmlessly to the ground, allowing the kids of the Order to keep up the charge.

"We're close," Thaddeus said.

Ping. Ping. Ping.

Three more misses.

196

Ping. Ping. Ping.

Two arrows to Elmira's chest, blocked by the armor, and another that whizzed by Diego's ear.

Then suddenly, another hit. This time it was Thaddeus with an arrow sticking out of his elbow.

"Arrggghh!" the old man cried.

"Hold on," Ike called. "I've got you."

Ping.

Ike felt as though he had been pushed hard. Then he saw the arrow that had hit him in the chest fall to the ground. The armor had saved him. Recovering quickly, Ike pulled the arrow from Thaddeus's elbow.

"There you go," he said, then looked toward the soldiers.

They were fifteen feet away, crouched behind the fence, a defensive stance Ike found cowardly.

"Come on, everyone." he shouted. "Charge."

With a renewed burst of energy, Ike raised his sword high in the air and sprinted madly for the stone fence.

Ping.

An arrow hit his shoulder and glanced off. Then another whizzed between his legs. And then, with a few more long strides, he jumped the stone fence and—*BAM*—knocked a soldier in the mouth with his elbow.

"Good one," Lucinda said.

Now that Ike had leapt the fence, the rest of the Order followed. Though skilled as archers, the soldiers were less talented at close fighting. With a couple of healthy whacks from Ike and his compadres all four ran for the balloon.

"Let them go," Thaddeus said. "We have to find that wizard."

"I'll check on the boat," Kashvi called. "If they realigned my engine, they die."

"I'm coming with you," Diego said.

"Good," Thaddeus called. "The rest of us—to the dragons."

And so the group split up. As Kashvi and Diego made for barn two, Thaddeus led Ike and everyone else into barn one. Soon, they were at the stalls, breathless, swords drawn, exchanging shouts.

"Where is he? Where's the wizard?"

"Don't see him."

"What was he here for?"

"Who knows?"

"Are the dragons okay? Have you checked their wings?"

"Yes, wings checked. No nicks or cuts."

"How about their toenails? They need to be just right for takeoff, right?"

"Toenails look good."

"Can they still breathe fire?"

To that, Sussex pressed on Pittsburgh's neck. The dragon obliged him with a small, but forceful whoosh of flame out the window.

"They sure do," Sussex called.

Indeed, the dragons seemed fine, with no bruises, scrapes, or cuts to their wings.

"This is madness," Lucinda said. "Did the wizard even come in here?"

"He sure did," Elmira said. Ike saw her drop to her hands and knees, investigating the soft dirt by Seattle's stall. "Footprints."

Indeed, there were—footprints one after another, clearly belonging to the same man.

"Those aren't mine," Sussex said. "Too big."

"Not mine either," Mrs. Sussex said.

"It's our wizard, I think," Elmira said. "And they're headed back outside."

"Good work," Thaddeus said. "That's where we're going then. Outside."

Again, Thaddeus took the lead, barreling past a line of dragon stalls to a side door. Moments later, the group burst into the main meadow. To Ike's dismay, they were too late once again. The balloon cart carrying the wizard and soldiers was already ten feet in the air, rising rapidly into the sky.

"We missed them," Ike said. He turned to Thaddeus. "What next?"

To Ike's surprise, the old man had stopped moving altogether and was staring at the balloon, eyes as wide as they could go.

"Thaddeus?" Ike repeated.

He kept his gaze fixed on the rapidly ascending balloon.

"So that's who has it," he whispered.

"Has what?" Ike asked.

Thaddeus didn't have the chance to answer—the soldiers released a final barrage of arrows.

"Duck," Sussex called.

Ping. Ping. Ping. Ping.

Ike dove for the ground, dragging Thaddeus along with him. By the time it was safe to stand, the balloon was out of range, a good seventy feet in the air.

"Should we fly the dragons after them?" Alexandro asked.

"By the time we get up there, they'll be miles out of the no-radar zone," Ike said. "Besides, it'll be fully dark in about ten minutes."

"So what do we do?" Elmira asked.

Just then, the sound of an engine, sputtering spasmodically, thunking, and backfiring, erupted from barn two.

"Is that … the boat?" Ike asked.

It was. The door to barn two swung open. A moment after

that, the purple flying ship rolled into the meadow, running smoothly, emitting a long whoosh of yellow steam from its chimney.

"Oh, my gosh," Ike cried.

There they were, Kashvi and Diego, in the pilot's cabin.

"You got it running," Elmira said, sprinting over.

"We told you that we did," Diego called down through an open window.

"Should we go after them?" Kashvi asked.

"Yes, go," Sussex called. "Bring them back here alive, if you can. We have to find out what they were up to before tomorrow's attack."

"We're on it," Diego said.

"Everyone stand back," Kashvi called. "I packed an extra two hundred horsepower into this puppy. Let's see how she runs."

With that, she flicked a switch on the dashboard, then pulled a chord that hung from the ceiling. Then Ike saw Diego yank a green lever. The ship began to rumble. Waves of green steam shot out of its sides. Then it vibrated ... and then ... it rolled, slowly at first, but then a bit faster, then a bit faster still.

"It's working," Ike said.

It certainly was. Kashvi pushed another button. Diego pulled another lever. With another whoosh two orange wings jutted out of the boat's sides.

The spectators cheered.

"That's what my grandmother would call a nice flying boat, eh?" Alexandro called.

"I love this," Lucinda said.

Soon the ecstatic shouts of Ike and his friends began to blend with the encouraging cries of Mr. and Mrs. Sussex and the Navy SEALS—and not just the three who had been assigned to waiter-duty. Whatever spell the wizard had cast was wearing off. All the

SEALS were waking up, just in time to witness a miracle.

"Here we go," Kashvi yelled. "Takeoff."

She pushed the throttle to full. The boat sputtered a final time, coughed, then began to really move, gliding across the meadow as though sliding across a sheet of ice.

"Look at that thing go," Sussex called. "Fly boat. You're going to fly."

But the little man had spoken too soon. For no sooner had the boat begun to accelerate than the engine let loose a tremendous *clunk*. Then a thin plume of black smoke spiraled up from the wings as another *clunk* filled the grounds, as loud as a cannon-shot.

And then ... the boat stopped cold.

Sussex stared straight ahead, eyes as wide as they could go. "This isn't good," he muttered. Then he shouted it, "This isn't good!"

In seconds, Ike was leading everyone in a mad sprint toward the ship. When they reached its side, Kashvi was busily pulling levers and flicking switches.

"What happened?" Ike called.

"I don't know," she said. "It just stopped."

Elmira looked to the sky. The balloon was a barely perceptible dot on the far horizon.

"Our visitor did something, after all," she said. "He wrecked the boat. We can't transport the dragons tomorrow."

"So what do we do?" Diego asked.

"Fix that boat, that's for sure," Lucinda said.

"Right," Ike said. "We have to be off in the morning. Isn't that right, Thaddeus?"

The minute the words were out of his mouth, Ike felt something was off. Thaddeus? He hadn't said a word since they had run out of the barn. Where was he?

Panicked, Ike wheeled around and surveyed the grounds.

"Thaddeus?" he called. "Hey."

Everyone was silent, exchanging glances.

"Maybe he's back with the dragons," Diego said.

"Or the castle," Alexandro said. "Went back for a rest, eh?"

Then Ike saw it.

"Oh, no."

He began running as fast as he could—running like he never had before. With the sun casting a final streak of orange across the evening sky, Ike reached the old man. He was lying by the side of the barn with an arrow sticking out of his stomach.

"They got me in that final hail of arrows," Thaddeus said calmly. He forced a pained smile. "My own fault really. If I were a little bit thinner, the armor would've covered all my giant belly."

In seconds, the other children were there. Navy SEALS appeared with a stretcher. Ike found himself choking up. Yes, he still didn't know why Thaddeus had gone to the Dark, Dank Woods or who Edward was or what he had been muttering before he'd been hit, but he was still the man who had taught him so much in one short day—a man who had just fought valiantly against a well-armed opponent and been wounded for his troubles.

"You're going to be okay," Ike said. "You'll see."

Thaddeus nodded. "They'll do their best, I'm sure. But forget me for now, Ike. Do you hear me? Your job is to get Kashvi fixing that boat. And to make sure the dragons are good to go. You're in charge now. Don't take your eye off the most important thing—preparing for tomorrow's battle."

"Get this man to the castle," Mrs. Sussex called. "The castle. Hurry."

With those words, four Navy SEALS lifted the stretcher and began to run.

Chapter Nineteen

"**H**ey. I need to show you something."

Ike had stood as still as a statue, watching the SEALS carry Thaddeus across the drawbridge and into the castle. Elmira was already tapping him on the shoulder. Didn't she have any sense of propriety? Couldn't she give him the space to worry about Thaddeus before hurrying back to business? Apparently not.

"Come on. You've got to see what I found by the dragon stalls."

Ike was still finding it hard to focus. Would the old man be all right?

"Listen up, okay?" Elmira said. "This is important."

Ike wheeled around. "Didn't you just see what happened?"

Elmira nodded. "Of course I did. Do you think I'm stupid? It's terrible. But you know what Thaddeus would want us to be doing right now? Not thinking about him, I tell you that much. He'd want us to be figuring out how to save New York City tomorrow."

Ike sighed. Once again, Elmira was right. It was growing tiresome.

"Kashvi and Diego are already back working on the boat,"

Elmira said. "Lucinda and Alexandro are helping, too."

"Okay," Ike said. "So what's up? What do you have to show me?"

Elmira smiled, something she did all too rarely. Not only that, this particular smile stretched clear across her face. Whatever she had discovered was truly momentous.

"Follow me," she said.

After giving the castle a final look, Ike turned with Elmira for the barns.

"What is it?" he asked.

"Better that I show you, okay?"

Moments later, they were inside at the dragon stalls. Elmira turned on the light.

"This way," she said.

Ike half expected something to be wrong with one of the dragons. Maybe the wizard had hit them with a spell after all. A case of wing-rash or an injured foot or two. Anything to stop the creatures from defending New York the next day. But when Ike quickly checked the stalls, the dragons appeared to be all right. Most were lazily dozing. Kansas City gnawed gently on a pile of hay. Pittsburgh lay on his side, wings over his face, fast asleep. Elmira led Ike past Detroit, busily licking his toenails clean, to Seattle's stall.

"When I first saw the footprints, I was too rushed to know for sure," Elmira said. "So while you saw to Thaddeus, I ran back to check. Look."

As before, Ike saw the trail of the wizard's footprints, headed from Seattle's stall out the side door.

"Okay," he said. "What am I looking for here?"

Elmira got down on her hands and knees. "Don't you see it? At first, we all assumed these were boot prints. But they aren't."

"They aren't?" Ike asked.

"No. Boot prints have tread on the bottom but these are smooth and slender like a shoe."

"So?" Ike said. "The guy was wearing shoes, then. I still don't get why this is important."

"Here's why. Remember the sketch your father made of the footprint he discovered in the Dark, Dank Woods? There was no tread on that either, right?"

"Okay, but that doesn't mean it's the same person."

"Hear me out," Elmira said. "What kind of shoes have no tread? Loafers, right?"

"I guess so. Still—so what?"

Elmira got down on her hands and knees to get a closer view of one of the footprints. "What else was there about the picture your dad drew? A smudge on the heel, right? He couldn't tell what it was because of the rain, remember? Well, check this out."

Ike's interest grew. Getting down on his knees next to Elmira, he looked more closely. No, there was no smudge on the heel of the footprint. Instead, there was something even more distinct outlined in the dirt.

"Oh my gosh," he said. "Are those letters?"

"Yes," Elmira said. "T and O."

Ike blinked. "I don't get it. Who would put letters on the heel of his shoes?"

"Think about it," Elmira said. "The same guy who wears custom-made loafers and carries a cane that could double as a magic wand."

Ike stood back up, slowly letting the astounding facts fully line up.

A cane that doubled as a magic wand?

Custom-made loafers?

The initials TO?

"Really?" he stammered. "*Theodore Opal?*"

"Yes!" Elmira cried.

The news was so surprising Ike needed another moment to take it in. "He's ... a wizard?"

It was staggering.

"Well, we can't be positively sure of that," Elmira said. "But he was here, it had to be him."

"But why would Theodore Opal want to destroy New York?"

"Not destroy it," Elmira said. "Control it. He ran for mayor seven years ago, right? And he lost, didn't he? Mayor Andretti mopped the floor with him. And now he's fighting to put up that hotel in Central Park, right? The Opal Plaza? Well, with a bunch of killer locusts flying around, I bet the mayor and city council would let him build whatever he wants wherever he wants."

Ike blinked. It was crazy. But somehow ... completely believable.

"But why? Theodore Opal is already so successful."

Elmira was unimpressed. "History is full of super successful people who feel like it's not enough. That's part of how they got successful to begin with. They want more and more and more. It's a sort of a sickness."

"So let's piece this together," Ike said, beginning to pace. "Opal found some way to use Merlin's spell."

"Right," Elmira said. "But the first time he tried to conjure the locusts through the portal, he messed up."

"They showed up in Nevada," Ike said.

"Exactly," Elmira said. "Which didn't help him, because at that time he wanted them to help him control New York. Don't forget, that's when he was running for mayor."

"I remember," Ike said. "But why now? I mean, why wait

seven years before calling the locusts again?"

Elmira shrugged. "That we don't know. Maybe to make sure he got the spell right?"

Ike nodded. "Or to make sure he could get the locusts to appear in New York when he needed them?"

"Which is now," Elmira said.

"To build his hotel in Central Park," Ike said.

"Or worse," Elmira said.

Ike stopped pacing. "Worse?"

"Yeah," Elmira said. "Maybe he's figured elections are too much trouble. He'll use the locusts to take over the city."

It was amazing news. Like most New Yorkers, Ike wasn't a big fan of the Opal buildings, gleaming, ostentatious high rises with the Opal Logo bursting out in glaring neon. On the other hand, Ike had always assumed Theodore Opal was an essentially honest, if loud-mouthed, businessman—not a crazy person.

But that's how it seemed to be. After discussing it for another few minutes, Ike and Elmira ran to barn two to break the news to the rest of the Order. Being foreigners with no deep knowledge of New York City, Alexandro and Lucinda were easy to convince. To them, anything could happen in the city they'd heard so much about but had never seen. Like Ike, it took Kashvi and Diego a few more minutes for the news to settle in.

"Talk about wild," Kashvi said. "I mean, Theodore Opal? The guy behind the locusts?"

"Looks that way," Ike said.

"He has a brutally obnoxious son," Diego said. "But I never marked the dad for a crook."

"More than a crook," Elmira said. "A criminally insane lunatic."

"That either," Diego said.

"So what do we do?" Kashvi asked.

"We go to New York and defend our city," Ike said. "Which means you have to fix this boat."

Kashvi picked up a wrench. "We'll have this thing blowing exhaust by midnight."

Ike was happy to hear it. But something didn't seem quite right. That Theodore Opal had traveled to Florida to put the boat out of commission made perfect sense. But why hadn't he done a better job of it? Why hadn't he set it on fire or cut down the mast? It didn't follow that it should be quite so easy to fix.

"You're sure you can get it done?" Ike asked.

"Of course she can," Diego said. "She's Kashvi Changar, remember?"

After leaving Kashvi and crew to the boat, Ike knew who he had to see next—Thaddeus. He had to see if the old man was all right. Also, there were questions that needed answering. After saying goodbye to his friends, Ike ran for the drawbridge, then took the stairs to the banquet hall two at a time. There he found Mr. and Mrs. Sussex seated at the table, waiting for news, quietly holding hands.

"Is he okay?" Ike asked nervously.

"We aren't sure yet," Mrs. Sussex said.

"Where is he?"

Mr. Sussex nodded down the hallway toward the game room. Of course, Ike remembered now. The castle had an infirmary— where he had been taken for his locust sting before being moved up to his father's old room.

"Okay," Ike said. "I'll check it out and report back."

But a few steps down the hallway, he stopped. There was one last thing he needed to do before confronting Thaddeus with everything he had discovered. Something he needed to finish. So instead of heading to the infirmary, Ike made his way back past the Sussex's and up the circular stairway. Heart pounding, he marched down the short hallway and pushed open the door to Thaddeus's chamber.

It had never occurred to Ike that the Head of the Royal Order would have a room that wasn't much bigger than his own. And furnished just as simply, too. There was a dresser, a rocking chair, a desk, and a bed. Nothing that seemed to have anything whatsoever to do with wizardry or magic.

"Weird," Ike whispered. "Why didn't he want us to come in the other night?"

But then he saw it.

Hanging on the wall by the desk was a painting.

Ike walked across the creaky floor to look more closely. Then he gasped.

For there was Thaddeus, sitting atop a sturdy white horse. But what made the picture so astonishing was the regal man with the black beard next to him on a white steed of his own—a man who Ike recognized immediately from the portrait hanging in the banquet hall.

It was King Arthur.

Chapter Twenty

Ike stood completely still, heart pounding.
Could it be?

Over lunch, Thaddeus had said that he used to ride with King Arthur. But he had been joking, right? Of course, he had been. So why was there a portrait of the two of them doing just that?

It took Ike a moment to calm himself enough to think it through. Maybe the painting was recent? But why would Thaddeus commission someone to paint a portrait of him riding with King Arthur *now*? Didn't it make more sense that he and Arthur had posed for the painting all those years ago? Besides, the painting looked old. The paint itself was faded and the frame was cracked in two places.

Needing answers, Ike rushed down the circular stairway so quickly he almost fell. Then he hurried back through the banquet hall and all but barreled into the guard standing at the infirmary door.

"How is he?" Ike said. "Let me in."

He was surprised to hear such forceful words come out of his mouth. Then again, this was no time for being polite. And to Ike's surprise, his newly commanding tone worked. Perhaps the guard was already under orders to let Ike enter, but without a word, he stepped aside. Only then did Ike remember his manners.

"Thank you," he said.

Years of watching TV had set Ike up to find Thaddeus hooked up to machines with tubes going everywhere, surrounded by a team of doctors. Instead, the Order practiced a simpler kind of medicine. Thaddeus was alone, his stomach bandaged, lying peacefully in bed.

"Ah, so there you are," he said quietly.

It was still Thaddeus's voice—but a weaker version, as though a layer of richness had been washed out.

"Yes," Ike said. "It's me."

"Come in then. Have a seat."

Ike did as he was told, sitting on the side of the old man's bed.

"How are you?"

With great effort, Thaddeus raised an eyebrow and forced a half smile. "How am I? Surviving ... for now."

"You'll be fine," Ike said.

Thaddeus closed his eyes then opened them again, as if summoning the energy to continue.

"Maybe," he said.

Ike laughed. Was Thaddeus kidding?

"You fixed me up pretty quickly from the locust sting."

"True," Thaddeus managed. "But that was a locust. We have cures for that. And you're a boy. I'm an old man. Recovering from an arrow to my gut isn't quite as easy."

Ike was silent for a minute. He wanted to say something encouraging, but couldn't think of a single word. Besides, he couldn't wait any longer to ask.

"I'm sorry," he began, "but I was just in your room."

Ike expected the old man to be upset. But he was either too weak to be angry or didn't especially care.

"Oh, really?" he asked. "And tell me. What did you find there?"

"A portrait," Ike said. "Of you and King Arthur."

Thaddeus gently twirled his beard with his pinky. "So you saw the picture, did you?"

"Yes, I did." Ike began to pace, working himself up. "I also found a letter from my father who said he followed you to the Dark, Dank Woods seven years ago. He said he saw you raise a wand and call out something about Edward."

"My," Thaddeus said with a slight smile. "You've been busy, haven't you?"

Ike sat back on the old man's bed. "What's going on? Are you a wizard?"

Thaddeus smiled more broadly. "A wizard?"

"Are you?" Ike asked. "I have to know."

Thaddeus shuffled upward on his pillow. "Well, Ike. Since you *have* to know. You might say I'm *the* wizard."

"*The* wizard?"

"Yes, Ike. That's precisely what I said."

It hit Ike like a solid fist to the jaw. Momentarily stupefied, he sat back on the bed.

"*The* wizard?" he repeated. He looked the old man in the eye, not quite able to believe what he was about to say. "What are you saying? That you're ... *Merlin*?"

The man stared back, eyes twinkling. "I am."

"But how's that possible?" Ike gasped.

"By being blessed or cursed, depending upon your viewpoint, with a unique lifespan," the man said. "I guess you never studied your medieval myths in school. They would've told you Merlin lives for a very, very long time. And he lives backwards."

"Backwards?" Ike said.

"Yes," Thaddeus said. "If you think I look old now, you should've seen me back in King Arthur's time. I'm actually getting younger as the years go by."

Ike shook himself. Was Thaddeus insane? It was certainly possible. But then again, how else could Ike explain the strange series of events over the past day?

"If you're Merlin," Ike said, "tell me about Edward."

A cloud passed over Thaddeus's face. "Edward? Ah, yes."

"Who is he?"

Thaddeus sighed heavily. "I'm sorry to say that he was my son."

The surprises never stopped. It had never occurred to Ike that Thaddeus had a family.

"Your *son*?"

"Yes, and not a good boy, I'm afraid. You see, Ike. It was Edward who made the spell that conjured the locusts."

"What? But the credits on *The Fighting Dragons* say it was you."

"I'm well aware of what the credits say," Thaddeus said. "That's because I've been covering for my son's mistakes for over one thousand years. But it was Edward all along. He was a headstrong lad who wanted King Arthur to give him more power. But Edward wasn't a good magician. One day, after King Arthur wouldn't let him do a trick at a court dance, Edward threw a fit, a real corker, and cast the spell of the locusts. And then he couldn't figure out how to reverse it. And neither could I."

"So that's what you were doing in the Dark, Dank Woods?" Ike said. "Trying to figure out how to reverse the spell?"

Thaddeus sat up, not even leaning on the pillow. "Precisely," he said. "As I've been trying to do for the past fifteen centuries.

That's also what I was trying to do in my room the other night when my blasted cane exploded."

"But why were you using a cane?" Ike asked. "You have a wand, right?"

"*Had* a wand," Thaddeus said. "The cane is nothing but a largely ineffective back-up, I'm afraid. My real wand was stolen a month ago. By the wizard in the balloon, I think."

"Ah," Ike said. "So that's what you noticed right before the archer's final arrows?"

"Exactly," the old man said, lying back on his pillow. "It was decorated with fancy gems and trinkets but it was my wand all right. A Navy SEAL—Andre or one of the others—must've found a way to sell it to him."

Given the gravity of the conversation, Ike knew it was inappropriate. Still, he couldn't hold back a smile.

"What?" Thaddeus asked. "Is that funny?"

"No, no," Ike said. "It's the new wizard. You'll never believe it, but I think we figured it out."

Up went the eyebrows. "Ah, really?"

"Elmira did most of the figuring, actually, but yes."

"Well? Who is it?"

Ike took a deep breath. "Theodore Opal."

Thaddeus blinked. "Theodore Opal? The *businessman*?"

"Yes. He always wears loafers and we found custom-made loafer prints in the barn which matched the footprints my dad found in the Dark, Dank Woods. And the other day when the locust attacked me at school, Opal had your wand with him."

Thaddeus lay back on his pillow and looked to the ceiling.

"Amazing what you discover with the passage of time. Theodore Opal. So *he* was the mystery man seven years ago in the Dark, Dank Woods. Incredible."

"Maybe he was trying to steal your wand then?" Ike suggested.

"Maybe," Thaddeus said. "Or else looking for something he could find only there. The Dark, Dank Woods is a tangle of ancient plants and secrets. Even I don't know them all."

"Looking for something to get better control of the locusts, I'll bet," Ike said. "Elmira and I suspect he was the one who conjured them seven years ago." He smiled again. "And we sure don't think he wanted them to appear in Nevada."

"I'm sure he didn't," Thaddeus said. The old man laughed,

 but quickly grew serious. "But it's quite possible that my wand has given him more control over the spell this time. Perhaps that's why he's been able to make the locusts appear in New York."

"And your wand is probably also how he was able to get the Navy SEALS to conk out this evening before the attack," Ike said.

"Precisely," Thaddeus said. "He managed to make some sort of sleeping spell."

"But here's what I don't get," Ike said. "How does Opal know Edward's spell at all? Was it written down somewhere?"

Thaddeus shook his head. "Not that I know of."

"Then how did Opal find it?"

"That's a good question, Ike," Thaddeus said. "But I'm afraid I've run out of answers. Don't forget. Before the locusts came to Nevada, no one had used my son's spell for three hundred years. I have no idea how Theodore Opal discovered it."

Ike waited for Thaddeus to say something more. Instead, the old man rubbed his eyes.

"You need to rest," Ike said.

Thaddeus nodded. "I'm afraid I don't have the energy for much more of this. But if I might, there are a few more things to say before I sleep. The first is an apology."

"An apology?" Ike said. He was genuinely confused. "For what?"

"For not telling you who I really was earlier." The old man smiled, a bit sadly. "You see, I've run into problems through the years. When the truth comes out, people tend to think I'm batty. If I had told you I was Merlin the first time we met, you would've run like mad for home. You understand?"

Ike nodded. "Yeah, sure. Of course."

"I also know you'll want to tell the other children about me and that's fine," Thaddeus went on. "But let's not spread it any further, okay? You see, Ike, I'm not immortal, just extremely long-lived, growing younger as I age. An arrow can kill me."

Ike looked at the old man's wound. "But this one won't, you'll see."

Thaddeus patted his hand. "I've been lucky a few times in the past. Back in the tenth century, I survived an accident with a friend's sword. Hopefully, I'll be as fortunate now. But Ike, if I do survive this wound I'd like to live out my final days growing peacefully younger here in the Order. So please, do tell the other children to keep my secret quiet. Aside from Mr. and Mrs. Sussex, only two people in the entire United States know who I really am—the President and the Secretary of Defense."

Ike imagined what would happen if word spread that Merlin was living in Florida. Lowlife reporters would find their way past the Navy SEALS, clamoring for interviews, engineered to be as insulting as possible. The headlines would be absurd.

Arthur's Magic Man Alive

Abracadabra. It's Merlin

Swamp Man Sez He's Famous Wiz

"We won't tell a soul," Ike said. "And don't worry about this wound. You're going to be fine."

Thaddeus took Ike's hand. "I hope so. You know, son, your father would be proud of you."

Ike felt himself blushing.

"It's true. He used to talk about you a fair bit. And who can blame him? You're a good boy. But wait." Thaddeus chuckled softly. "I guess you're not a boy anymore, are you? You're a man now, Isaac Rupert Hollingsberry—a man who is up to any challenge. Your father and I will be watching over you, but the Order is in your hands. Your hands, indeed."

Thaddeus yawned, lay back on his pillow and allowed his eyes to close. When the old man started to lightly snore, Ike gave his hand a gentle squeeze and released it. Only then did he head out.

First things first, he had to report to the Sussexes then check on the dragons and the boat. As Thaddeus had said, the Order was in his hands. There was much to prepare.

Chapter Twenty-One

The other five children reacted to Thaddeus's news much as Ike had. Amazement turned to shock which gradually, when presented with the facts, turned to acceptance. It was a good thing, too—because with the locusts due in New York the next day, there wasn't time to spend ruminating over Thaddeus's improbable history as Merlin, the most famous wizard of all time.

Luckily, Kashvi's initial prediction about the state of the Purple Ship had been correct. A few minutes after midnight, she got the engine to run.

Even so, Ike still felt uneasy. Why had Opal traveled all the way to the Order only to botch the job? Wouldn't it have made more sense to do something to the dragons? Maybe. But then again, Ike had too much on his mind to fret about twists of good luck. Perhaps Opal had planned to  sneak in unnoticed during the banquet? Perhaps their counter-attack had disrupted his plans? Who knew?

Once the boat was repaired, Ike stopped at the barn to make sure the dragons were still all right, then found his way up the circular stairway to his room. Despite the high stakes of the coming day, he was so tired he fell right asleep—a good thing because the following morning began with the most unexpected conversation of his life.

At dawn, just as the first rays of the morning sun were inching under the curtains, there was a sharp rap on the door.

"Mr. Hollingsberry," a voice said urgently.

Half asleep, Ike hoped Thaddeus had called him.

"Mr. Hollingsberry. Are you there?"

Ike stretched and looked toward the door. Thaddeus never called him "Mr. Hollingsberry."

"Yes? I'm here."

"There's a phone call for you."

Ike finally recognized the voice. It was the headwaiter.

"Who is it?" Ike didn't know the Order even had a phone—maybe for emergencies. Then he had a thought. "My mother?"

Had someone thought to patch her through on the morning of the big battle?

"No. It's the President of the United States."

Ike sat up with a start.

"The *who?*"

"The President. With Thaddeus in the infirmary, she requested to speak to you. Shall I bring in the phone?"

Ike swallowed hard. Did he have a choice?

"Yeah … Sure."

The door swung open. The SEAL had traded in his waiter's uniform for fighting gear. In his right hand was a red cordless phone.

"You're not kidding me, are you?" Ike said. "This isn't another weird Order tradition?"

The SEAL shook his head. "No. It's her."

Ike nodded then glanced down at his clothes. Was it all right to speak to the President of the United States while wearing pajamas?

"She can't see me, can she?"

The SEAL covered the mouthpiece with his hand. "Don't worry," he said. "This isn't Skype. She can't see."

Ike was wide awake now—perhaps more wide awake then he had ever been in his life. More nervous, too. He took the phone.

"Uh, hello?"

"Yes, Ike?"

He recognized the voice instantly from years of speeches, press conferences, talk show appearances, and commercials. It was Francesca Mills, the Commander in Chief. For a moment, Ike felt almost too nervous to go on. But then he gathered himself. With Thaddeus in recovery—hopefully still alive—he was the head of the Order. He had to act it.

"Yes, this is he."

"You have a big day today, don't you?"

Her voice was warm but all business.

"Yes, Madam President," Ike said. His heart was pounding. "We do."

"Is everything ready? I hear you had an unexpected visitor last evening."

"We did," Ike said. "We think Theodore Opal is behind the locust attacks."

"Word got back to us about that late last night," the president said. "I have four government agencies looking for him now."

"Looking for him?" Ike said. "You don't know where he is?"

"He appears to be in hiding. But don't worry, we're looking hard. I hear Kashvi Changar has the Purple Ship running and the four fire-breathing dragons appear to be okay?"

"That's right," Ike replied.

"Good." The president paused, as if trying to figure out how to phrase what she wanted to say next. "I don't have to tell you how important this is."

"Yes, ma'am?"

"My advisors tell me that, according to the spell, our planes and guns won't do a thing against these locusts. We tried last time against the bugs your father fought."

"You did?" Ike asked. He knew the spell precluded the use of conventional weapons but he hadn't known the government had tried anyway.

"Oh, yes," the president said. "Our Air Force hit those locusts with missiles square on, but the bugs shook them all off and kept on coming. So even though you won't see us today, we'll be watching. We'll have your back."

"Thanks. That's good to hear."

"And Ike, I know about the prophecy, too. Much is at stake. Not only for America, but the world." To Ike's surprise, the president suddenly laughed. "That's an awful lot to put on the shoulders of an eleven-year-old boy and five other children, isn't it?"

"It is," Ike said. He almost wanted to laugh, too. What else was there to do? The whole thing was absurd.

The president's voice finally softened. "But you know what? I have a feeling you're going to do just fine."

"Thank you, ma'am."

"The whole thing is going to be entertaining, anyway. The ads for the *Return of the Royal Order* are running nonstop as we speak. Once you get to New York, we're going to film you like it's a reality show, happening in real time. Hopefully, people will buy it and when this is all over, no one will know the locusts were actually real. All they'll remember is great TV."

"I hope so," Ike said. Then he took a deep breath. Time to be positive. This was the Commander in Chief of the United States. "We're totally ready to go, ma'am. Don't worry. New York will be defended."

"That's what I like to hear, Ike," the president said. "One final thing. If you do run into Theodore Opal before we can grab him, do what you can to take him alive. We'd like to find out how he was able to conjure the locusts so we can make sure it never happens again."

"I understand," Ike said.

"Good. I'll be looking forward to watching you in action in just a few hours. Good luck."

"Thank you, ma'am."

She hung up. Ike dropped the phone then sat heavily on his bed. Heart thumping, he hadn't realized how nervous he had been.

"Did that really just happen?" he asked.

"It did." The SEAL grinned. "Game on, Mr. Hollingsberry."

"Yeah," Ike said. "Game on."

With the day of the battle upon them, Ike and his five Order mates changed into fresh tunics, new armor, and then ate a quick breakfast. While the others went to the barns to see to the dragons and the boat, Ike looked back in on Thaddeus, hoping the old man would be awake, maybe even coherent enough to dispense some final words of wisdom. Instead, Ike had to settle for the news that he was still alive. Laying on his bed, eyes closed, Thaddeus was breathing steadily, if with a loud rasp.

"He's going to be okay, isn't he?"

To Ike's dismay, the guard didn't answer right away. Instead, he dabbed Thaddeus's face with a damp towel.

225

"Let him rest," he said. "He has a better chance to heal. Besides, you have work to do, don't you?"

Ike nodded. As he had the night before, he squeezed the old man's hand. Then he hurried out of the room and took the main staircase to the entrance hall.

Before heading outside into the fray, Ike found himself stopping by the tapestries of the various members of the Orders of old. In the madness of the past couple of days, he hadn't had the chance to look at them closely. Brewster the Earl of Carrington, George Smith of Wellington, Joanne of South Bismarck and all the rest. Had they been nervous before their first battles? Had they been as scared as he was? What advice would they give him now? He knew he had to hurry—his troops were waiting—but Ike allowed himself to take his time, looking at each warrior one by one, studying each face, drawing whatever courage he could from their stern, brave poses. Finally, he turned from the last painting— a heroic image of one of his own descendants from the Second Order, Jackson Rupert Hollingsberry, sitting bravely atop a ferocious black and brown dragon.

"I can do this," Ike said to himself. Then a bit louder. "Yes. I can DO this."

Chapter Twenty-Two

The Royal Order had been transformed once again—that's what Ike saw the minute he stepped outside, squinting against the bright morning sun. A good fifty men and woman—all Navy SEALS, Ike figured—were bustling this way and that, turning the Order into something resembling a movie set. Cameras and lights hung from the side of the barns and castle. A man and a woman—Ike assumed they were the co-directors—were shouting directions, lining up cameras, and sending assistants running for whatever was needed. As for the dragons, they were already out, standing in a row outside barn one. To Ike's astonishment, each creature had a worker on a ladder who was combing out their manes. And nearby, Elmira, Alexandro, Lucinda, Kashvi, and Diego were seated in chairs, having makeup done and hair brushed.

And then things got even more surprising. The minute Ike crossed the bridge, an angular man in a sharply fitting suit was at his side, holding a microphone.

"Here he is, ladies and gentlemen. Isaac Rupert Hollingsberry."

The reporter all but shoved the microphone into Ike's face as a cameraman circled close. Clearly, they were filming some sort of live-promo to prime the audience for the main event.

"Tell the folks at home," the reporter continued. Ike assumed he was another Navy SEAL, pretending to be a TV host. "How does it feel to be the head warrior of the Tenth Royal Order of Fighting Dragons?"

"It feels good enough," Ike said. Then he quickly realized he had to do better. He was on TV, after all. "Actually, it feels great," he said, gathering his nerve. "We're ready to fight. In a couple of hours, these locusts are going to be history."

The reporter turned to the camera and all but screamed. "Did you hear that ladies and gentlemen? The locusts are going down. *Down.*"

The reporter swung back around and sidled even closer.

"Tell me, my boy. How's your dragon these days? That silver and gold flying machine?"

"Detroit? The best."

"Isn't Detroit the son of Dartmoor, the dragon your dad used to ride?"

"Yes, he is."

"It must feel wonderful to be following in your father's footsteps. Tell us about your Order mates. Are they up to a challenge this colossal?"

That one was easy.

"Absolutely." Ike said. "Alexandro flies Kansas City like a race car driver. And Lucinda has great aim with her sword."

"What about Elmira?" the reporter asked.

"Elmira?" Ike said. For the first time since the interview began, he smiled. "She's so smart she'll just talk the locusts' ears off."

The reporter guffawed and pivoted to the camera, like a mechanical toy on a taut spring. "You heard it here, ladies and gentlemen, straight from the next in line. Do they have what it takes to defeat the locust scourge? You're ding-dang tootin', they do. The locusts are going D—O—W—N—down. Don't believe me? Then see it for yourselves. Tune in later this morning for the premiere episode of *The Return of the Royal Order*. Until then, happy flying, everyone."

When the camera stopped, the reporter socked Ike playfully on the shoulder.

"That's exactly what we needed, Ike. Go get 'em."

With that, the reporter and the cameraman hurried off to find someone else to interview and Ike was left alone, breathless, and excited. This was happening in a bigger and more impressive way than he had even imagined. Yes, indeed, game on.

He took off at a sprint down the path to barn one.

"There you are," Sussex called. The Dragon Keeper was on his back, underneath Pittsburgh, holding what appeared to be a giant tweezer to the animal's foot. "Seeing to some last minute toe-nail clipping."

"Great," Ike said.

"Morning, Ike."

That was Mrs. Sussex. She was seeing after Kansas City's nails with a device that resembled a giant electric toothbrush.

"Hey there."

Then Ike felt someone grab his arm. Wheeling around, he found himself looking up at the woman he had seen giving orders.

"I'm Robin Underwood," she said. "Director of this little show. Mind if we get a little bit of make-up on that beautiful face of yours before you board the boat?"

Ike shrugged. "Sure."

Seconds later, he felt like one of the characters in *The Wizard of Oz*, newly arrived in Emerald City. After he had been guided to a lounge chair next to his fellow Order mates, a team of stylists descended en masse. One began combing his hair, while another shined and retied his boots and a third dabbed on rouge.

"This will help your face pop under the camera light," Robin Underwood said.

Ike's heart was racing, but more with excitement than fear. He had never cared much about celebrity. But now that he was undergoing star treatment himself? It actually felt pretty good.

The other kids were clearly enjoying it, as well.

"Ah, *si*," Alexandro called. "My grandmother will kiss the TV screen when she sees me. And that's not bad because the woman is one hundred and one years old."

"Whatever you do," Lucinda was saying, "don't mess with the hunting hat. This puppy is lined with octopus skin. That's what makes it sit perfectly on my head and keeps the sun out of my eyes and allows me to focus on what I've got to do. And today, that's to kill some locusts. Are we clear?"

To Ike's surprise, even Elmira seemed to have given in willingly to her team. Though initially skeptical, by the end of her makeover, she was unable to hold back a grin.

"Not bad," she said.

Ike hoped she saw what he did. With combed hair, a dab of Chapstick, and a smile, she was actually pretty.

Then there was Diego, who refused to allow his precious shaggy hair to be trimmed, combed, brushed or otherwise touched. His only concession to style was a new belt.

"It's hard to tend to dragons with underwear showing," he admitted.

Finally, there was Kashvi. Though a good six or seven stylists checked her hair, skin, and clothes, she was deemed to look so

231

naturally good she didn't require any makeup at all.

"All right then," Sussex said, emerging from Pittsburgh's underbelly. "Time to board the boat."

As Ike stood, he could see the cameras rolling. He had no idea what footage would be used or how the show would be constructed, but he knew everything he said from here on was for posterity. He was the commander. Time to embrace the role he was born to play.

"Are we ready troops?" he called in his most authoritative voice.

His friends responded in kind.

"*Si, si.*" Alexandro nodded. "*Pronto.*"

"Bloody well, yes," Lucinda exclaimed.

"Count me in," Diego said.

"Me, too," Kashvi said.

Finally, there was Elmira. With a look that could only be described as fierce, she glared defiantly at Ike.

"I've been ready since the day I was born."

"Okay, Royal Order of the Tenth," Ike cried. "Time to get the dragons onto the ship. Follow me."

Ike turned toward the boat and his five friends fell in line behind him. Meanwhile, Mr. and Mrs. Sussex and two other SEALS looped halters over Detroit, Kansas City, Seattle, and Pittsburgh's necks and led them behind. Ike had expected at least one or two of the dragons to resist climbing aboard the strange boat. But no. To Ike's surprise, each one marched right up the plank and onto the purple ship without a moment's hesitation. Maybe they had been born to play a role, too? Maybe they were as eager to prove themselves in battle as he was.

"There they go," the reporter gushed. "The beasts who will help our brave warriors save New York City from the locust scourge. Wait. Did I say, save New York? Correction. I meant to say, SAVE THE WORLD. Four dashing members of the Royal Order and their two Dragonflies."

All of a sudden, it was the kids' turn to board the boat. Ike went first. Of course, he hadn't done anything yet—he knew that—but moving up the plank onto the purple flying ship, he felt as though he was walking onto a stage to receive an award. Cameras were running. For all he knew, friends back in New York were already watching some sort of pre-show or commercial. His mother and sister, too.

Atop the ship, he turned and looked solemnly at the camera,  doing his best to convey a "take-no-prisoners" attitude. Then he stood aside as Alexandro, Lucinda, Diego, Kashvi, and finally Elmira came aboard. To Ike's surprise, she was lugging along the Order bylaws.

"What's that for?" Ike asked.

"This is the greatest dragon manual in history," Elmira said. "It might come in handy."

Ike nodded. "Good thinking. Put it in the pilot's cabin."

As Elmira scrambled off, there was another surprise. Sussex scrambled up the plank.

"Wait," Ike said. "You're coming, too?"

"If I may," the little man said. "You might need me for last minute dragon care."

Ike wondered if the Dragon Keeper was simply angling for another chance to fly. But who cared if he was? It would be helpful to have someone so knowledgeable along for the ride.

"Glad to have you aboard."

"Thank you, Sir Hollingsberry."

The little man scurried off to see to the dragons.

Just like that, it was time. Ike looked over his shoulder. Kashvi was already settling into the driver's seat in the small pilot's cabin. Diego took a seat beside her.

Ike turned back to the cameras. Instinctively, he knew what was expected of him now. A short speech. Thankfully, that fall, his English class had read Shakespeare's *Julius Caesar*. With no public speaking experience, why not steal from the best?

"Friends, New Yorkers, Citizens of the World," he shouted. "Lend me your ears."

Unfortunately, that was all he remembered. He would have to make up the rest as he went. As the reporter shoved his microphone under his chin, Ike summoned his nerve and went on.

"Today, I Isaac Rupert Hollingsberry, have the proud opportunity to lead a fine group of warriors into battle against a horrifying locust scourge—the same locusts that have plagued the Earth since the days of King Arthur. It is a difficult task. But rest assured, my team is up to the challenge. By the end of this day, not only will the bugs be wiped out of New York, but they will never threaten the good people of the world again."

Though trained military men and women, the Navy SEALS, clearly moved by Ike's inspiring words, applauded enthusiastically. Ike grinned, allowing himself a brief moment to suck in the adulation. But only a moment—there was work to do. Before the cheering died down, he yelled up to Kashvi in the pilot's cabin.

"Are we ready for takeoff?" he called.

"Ready, sir," Kashvi called back.

"Good. Start the engines."

Ike watched Kashvi flip a switch on the control panel. Then Diego proved his worth by pulling a lever. With a few more buttons pushed the boat started rumbling. Whatever Kashvi had done to fix the engine had worked. To Ike, it actually seemed to be humming more easily with fewer bumps and grinds.

The boat began to move across the field.

"And they're off, ladies and gentleman," the reporter cried. "Get ready for take-off."

But to get in the air, the boat had to pick up speed and in a short distance. Accordingly, Kashvi slammed the throttle all the way to the dashboard. As Ike and everyone else held on to whatever they could, the boat trembled and took off like a shot, barreling across the Order grass.

"Fun, eh?" Alexandro called.

"Yes," Ike said. "Fun."

Lucinda pounded on the ship's railing. "Go, go, go."

The boat trembled again and went even faster. With a scrunching creak, the two orange wings popped out of its sides. And then, so smoothly it was barely noticeable, the boat was in the air, gliding five, then ten feet over the Order.

"Yee-haw!" Diego called from the pilot's booth.

Ike saw the distant figure of the reporter talking like mad and the SEALS cheering. Then Kashvi pushed another lever all the way forward and the front of the boat angled sharply up. Just like that, they were over the swamp, with the sweep of the Everglades spreading out magnificently below them.

"It's beautiful, eh?" Alexandro cried.

It was hard to disagree. Like many other times in the past few days, Ike felt as though his life had turned into an insane dream. Three days ago he had been a student. Now he was riding a flying ship into battle.

"New York here we come," he cried.

"And after we take care of those locusts, I'll see if they've got any crocs in the Central Park Lake," Lucinda shouted. "I'll put the lot into half-nelsons."

"Yes. And while you do that, I'll wrestle a lion in the Bronx Zoo, eh?"

"Ah, dream on, mate."

Ike laughed. True, they were nowhere near New York yet, but what a great beginning. With such a magnificent take-off, what could stop them? Nothing.

Then he felt someone tap his shoulder.

"Ike."

He turned. It was Elmira.

"Amazing view, isn't it?" Ike exclaimed. "Can you believe it?"

Elmira glanced quickly over the side. Though the Florida landscape stretched out majestically below them, she looked no more excited than if she had caught a glimpse of a crosstown bus.

"You'd better come back to the pilot's booth. There's a computer screen on the dashboard that's showing some interesting developments."

"Developments?" Ike asked. "What developments?"

"We've got to get to New York in a hurry. The first locust just appeared over the Hudson River."

Chapter Twenty-Three

Ike scrambled up the narrow flight of stairs to the pilot's booth. It was a small room with two swivel chairs in front of a control panel of switches, buttons, and levers. On the back wall hung 8x10 glossies of the members of the Ninth Royal Order—Ike's Dad, Cassandra Carrington, Phillip O'Leary Smith, and Antonio Cortesi. The bylaws lay on a small table in the far corner.

"What's this?" Ike said, pushing through the door. "We have another locust? Already?"

"Sure do," Diego said.

"See for yourself," Kashvi said. "We're picking up national news through the computer."

She nodded toward a small monitor on the dashboard. Just as Elmira had said, there was another enormous bug, swooping over the river.

"According to reports, it showed up ten minutes ago," Elmira said.

Just then, Alexandro, Lucinda, and Sussex bustled up the stairs. Soon the entire crew was crammed into the small cabin.

"What's the bug doing?" Ike asked.

"For now, not much," Diego said. "Hanging out, it seems."

"Hanging out?" Alexandro said. "It looks to me like it's beginning to get some exercise, eh?"

It was true. Indeed, at that moment, the giant insect was angling over Riverside Park. Then as it curved back over the Pier to the river, the camera picked up a reporter, standing at the boat basin.

"Yes, sir, ladies and gentlemen," the lady said. "Never in the history of television have we seen such a beautifully made robotic bug."

The camera angle widened to reveal a second reporter, a short man with a pencil thin mustache.

"You've got to see this to believe it, friends. This is one real-looking fake insect."

"Those two reporters are with the government, right?" Ike asked.

"They have to be," Lucinda said.

"Yep," Elmira said. "Doing whatever they can to make everyone believe this is all part of a pre-planned TV show."

"Well, they need to work a little bit harder," Kashvi said.

"What do you mean?" Ike asked.

"The people on TV," Kashvi said. "They look terrified."

It was true. The camera angle had widened even more to reveal a crowd of New Yorkers, standing by the railing to the river, pointing at the giant bug. Though one or two were smiling, most were obviously shocked, alarmed and otherwise petrified. In a single sweep of the camera, Ike counted two babies crying, a toddler throwing a tantrum, four teenagers ducking behind a trash can, and a man in a three-piece suit taking a running leap into the river, probably figuring he'd be safer in the water. Then the locust swooped low, buzzing the heads of three joggers, who all hit the pavement. As the mighty bug rose back over the river, a policeman drew his pistol and fired. A direct hit. But the bug kept on flying as though it hadn't felt a thing.

"That thing is like Superman," a man in the park cried. "It can't be killed."

The crowd began to panic. Three more babies and two boys in baseball uniforms began to cry as assorted others, boys, girls and men and women of all ages, sprinted for Broadway.

"No, no, people." the first reporter cried, running into the crowd. "Don't you see? This is what makes this show so brilliant. The bug only *looks* real. It's all for the TV show. Before we know it, fake dragons will be arriving aboard the famous purple flying Viking ship. And those dragons will be led by none other than Isaac Rupert Hollingsberry."

To Ike's surprise, there he was suddenly on screen, footage filmed less than an hour earlier as he had walked out of the castle.

"Whoa," Diego said. "Looking good, dude."

"It's interesting," Elmira said. "While your actual looks are exactly the same, you seem stronger somehow, more fierce." She nodded to herself, as if making a mental note. "I should blog about it."

Though Ike didn't reply, he felt both embarrassed and pleased. He would never equal his father's natural stature, but in his short time at the Order he had taken on the swagger of a leader.

"That's right," the second reporter's voice said over Ike's picture. "This young man is a fine actor, following in his father's footsteps."

"It's an inspiring story," the first reporter said. "What a tribute to his fallen dad."

Suddenly, Ike's self-satisfied appraisal of his own appearance turned to a wistful sadness. Just like that, his father was on-screen in full fighting regalia. Ike didn't know if it would ever get easier to appreciate a picture of his father without regretting the time they had missed together—probably not, but thankfully, seconds later, the camera was back on the gargantuan bug.

"That's one monstrous insect, all right," the first reporter shouted.

The second reporter laughed. "It sure is. And look. There's locust number two."

Ike and crew pushed even closer to the TV.

"A second bug?" Elmira said. "Already?"

It was true. The on-screen camera shifted. A second bug, even larger than the first came into view, circling over the Hudson.

"It looks like Thaddeus's wand really has made Opal more powerful this time around," Ike said.

The other children and Sussex nodded gravely.

"It sure does," Kashvi said.

"That certainly is a large insect," the first reporter cried, while the camera remained focused on the new arrival. "I sure hope that purple boat gets here soon."

"Me, too," said the second reporter.

The camera cut back to the reporters, both doing their best to appear unconcerned.

"Stay tuned to see what happens," the first reporter said. "It's coming at you later this morning."

"Righto." reporter two said. "The world premiere of *The Return of the Royal Order.*"

The show went to a commercial, ironically for a new bug spray. For a full second that seemed more like a minute, the cabin was quiet. Slowly, Ike realized what was happening. Everyone was waiting for him to say what they should do next. They were waiting for him to lead. Even Alexandro and Lucinda.

"Kashvi," Ike began. "How fast can you get this boat moving?"

"We're close to maximum now," she replied.

"Take her all the way up then," Ike said.

He turned to Elmira. "Why do you think the first locusts aren't attacking anything yet?"

She seemed like the most likely person to know.

"I would guess Theodore Opal now has the capability to bring more than two bugs through the portal at a time."

"You think so?" Alexandro asked.

Elmira nodded. "He's probably waiting until a critical mass of bugs have gathered. He probably wants at least four or five before he makes his move."

It was frightening—Ike and his friends would have to fight more bugs at once than his father had.

"But wait a second," Ike said. "The president told me they were trying to bring Opal in."

"I'm sure they are," Lucinda said, "but that still doesn't tell us what the bugs will do. Even if the government has Opal, the insects might still be under his control."

"Right," Ike said. "Maybe he's programmed them to take over city hall?"

"Or Central Park," Kashvi said. "That's where Opal wants to build his hotel."

"Or maybe they'll attack different parts of the city at once, eh?" Alexandro said.

"It's hard to say," Sussex said.

"It is," Elmira agreed.

"But whatever he does, we'll be ready," Diego said.

Lucinda looked out the pilot window.

"New York City!" she shouted. "Help is on its way."

But first they had to get there. Out of nowhere, the boat bucked wildly and with such force, Alexandro smashed into Lucinda, who careened into Elmira who fell to the floor.

Holding desperately to a railing on the wall, Ike looked to Kashvi. "What was that?"

She nodded out the window. "The weather, that's what. Hold on, guys. We've hit a storm."

In a blink, the wind had turned fierce. The boat shook again. Then the sky opened up. Driving rain hit the windshield, coming in such powerful gusts it was hard to see.

"Can you get us out of this?" Ike shouted.

The boat was rocking back and forth as though on a violent and wavy sea.

"I can try." Kashvi called.

"Sussex and Diego!" Ike yelled. "Make sure the dragons are okay."

"Got it," Diego called.

As Sussex and Diego struggled out the door, Ike found his way to the copilot's chair while Lucinda, Alexandro, and Elmira, back to her feet, held on the best they could.

"Talk about a tropical storm," Elmira called.

"And a doozy," Lucinda said. "I can't see a blooming thing."

"What does the weather service say?" Ike called.

The boat lurched violently to the left.

"Can't say," Kashvi said. She was gripping the wheel with all her might. "The TV and electronics have gone out."

"So we're lost?" Alexandro cried.

"Not lost," Kashvi said. "Just out of communication for a bit. Everyone hold on. I'm going to take this puppy above the clouds."

Kashvi pulled back hard on the throttle. The engine screeched and whined—clearly pushed to its limit. But the boat began to climb.

"Yes," Lucinda cried. "It's working."

Or was it? Just as the ship's bow began to rise, the boat bucked twice and shook. Then the bow pointed down. Kashvi gripped the wheel with both hands.

"There's not enough power," she cried.

"Are we going down?" Elmira called.

Kashvi was too busy at the controls to answer. Or maybe she didn't want to verbalize what everyone knew. Without some sort of miracle intervention, they were in big trouble.

"Is there an emergency engine on this thing?" Alexandro called.

"I wish," Kashvi shouted. "I'm giving it all it's got."

Another gust of wind pushed the boat's bow down even farther. Again, Ike had to hold on to keep from falling over. The rain was driving so hard it was as though a row of fire hydrants had been opened on the windshield.

"This is not good, eh?" Alexandro shouted.

"So you've figured that out, have you?" Lucinda shouted back.

Then Ike got an idea. A wild, even desperate, idea, yes, but one still worth trying—especially when the alternative was crashing into the ocean.

"Alexandro. Lucinda." he snapped. "You're coming with me." Then he wheeled to Elmira. "You stay here and help Kashvi keep this thing in the air."

"Where you going?" Elmira yelled.

"To get us some extra power."

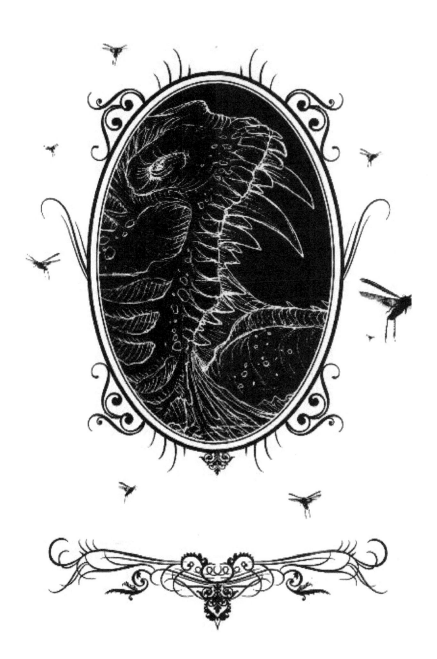

Chapter Twenty-Four

With Alexandro and Lucinda close behind, Ike lurched toward the exit and made his way down the narrow stairway. Seconds later, the three children were at the door to the deck. The rain outside was so loud, Ike had to shout to be heard.

"We're headed to the stalls."

"The stalls?" Lucinda said. "Why?"

"No time to explain," Ike called. "Follow me."

The wind blew so hard it took all of them to push open the door. When they stumbled outside, they were soaked in a matter of seconds.

"Hold on," Ike called.

"Don't have to tell me that twice, mate."

"Watch where you walk, eh?"

"I'm doing my best."

Ike, Alexandro and Lucinda found the railing just as the ship lurched wildly downward and to the right. Barely holding on, they waited a moment for Kashvi to steady the boat, then began to move as fast as they could toward the stalls. But halfway there, the ship lurched again, so violently Alexandro was thrown into the air. To

Ike's horror, his new friend was suddenly hanging over the side, holding on by a single hand.

"*Ay!*" he cried. "*Mamma.*"

"Hold on," Ike called.

"We've got you," Lucinda said.

"Hurry. I'm slipping."

Indeed, he was. With Alexandro's grip reduced to two fingers, Ike grabbed his right arm and held on for dear life. A moment later, Lucinda had his left hand. Then they pulled with all their might.

"He's too heavy," Lucinda called.

Ike felt his hands slipping. But then—a bit of luck. The boat lurched again, this time tilting back to the left.

"Pull now," Ike called.

Using the momentum from the boat, the children were able to hoist Alexandro up and over the railing. All three fell hard on the soaking wet deck, then slid ten feet on their stomachs, straight toward the stalls, before coming to a halt in a tangle. Miraculously, Lucinda's hat was still on her head.

"You okay?" Ike yelled.

"*Si,*" Alexandro called. "*Buona.*"

"Come on," Lucinda said. "We're almost there."

Rain hitting their faces, they crawled the final few feet to the stall door. Ike pushed it open with his shoulder and the three children rolled inside, soaked but safe—at least for the moment.

"What's going on?" Sussex said, closing the door behind them.

"We're getting bucked like crazy," Diego said.

"I know it," Ike said, finding his legs. "Can we fly these dragons through the rain?"

247

Sussex's eyes went wide. "What? Into the rain? Are you insane?"

Ike was all business. "There's rope on this boat, isn't there?"

"Sure," Diego said. "In the back of the stalls."

"Get it, okay?"

"But I still don't see what you're ..." Sussex began. Then he paused. His mouth twitched and he wagged his head. "Yes. Yes, it's brilliant."

"Let's see if it works first," Ike said. "Get the dragons out. And get me that rope."

"Already got it," Diego yelled.

He threw it to Ike, who caught it in his right hand.

"Good," Ike said. "Listen up. Here's what we're going to do."

It took Ike no more than half a minute to explain. Then the crew worked fast. As the ship bucked and lurched and pitched, ropes were cut and tied around the four dragons' middles. Then the beasts were led out of their stalls into the pouring rain, two to the right side of the boat and two to the left. Ike went first, tying Detroit's rope to the mast.

"Okay," he called. "Pass me the others."

Working as fast as he could in miserable, terrifying conditions, Ike tied off the ropes for the other three dragons, then hopped back onto the deck. No doubt about it, the boat was angling downward. How far they were from the ocean, Ike couldn't be sure, but he knew they didn't have much time.

"Can they take off in the rain?" he yelled to Sussex.

"These dragons can do most anything."

"Okay," Ike called. "Give the order then."

That's all Sussex needed to hear. Holding his hands to his mouth, he craned his neck and shouted up to Detroit, "Git in the air, you stinking creature. Fly, I tell you. *Fly.*"

Detroit glanced down, eyes wide, drenched, and confused. For a moment, Ike worried he was going to refuse. But as Sussex continued to yell, the dragon seemed to get an inkling of what was at stake. With two mighty waves of his wings, he took off into the driving rain, pulling the boat up sharply to the right.

"Get Kansas City up there," Ike called to the other side of the boat. "Hurry."

Lucinda let go of the dragon's rope.

"Yaaa!" she cried, slapping his butt. "In the air with you. In the air."

Taking Detroit's cue, Kansas City was ready. With one powerful stroke of his wings, he was off, pulling the boat back to an even position.

"Pittsburgh!" Ike screamed.

"You next," Sussex called up to the dragon. "Yaaa. In the sky."

Now the dragons were fully with the program. But with Pittsburgh in the air, teaming with Detroit, the boat once again tilted dangerously.

"Seattle," Ike called. "Get him up there."

"Yaaa!" Alexandro cried. "You fly, eh? Fly."

And so he did, heavily beating his wings against the driving rain. All four dragons were in the air. For a second, it felt as though the boat was suspended, motionless. Then slowly, but surely, it began to rise. Then the dragons picked up speed, gaining momentum, pulling the boat higher and higher.

"Yes," Diego called. "It's working."

"Fly, you creatures," Sussex called. "Fly."

In the pilot's cabin, Kashvi and Elmira pounded on the windshield and gave Ike a giant thumbs up. With the engine revved to high, the boat pushed upward through the driving rain until it broke through a cloud and emerged on the other side of the storm into a blue sky.

No more rain. No more wind. They were safe.

Soaked, but elated, Ike and friends cheered again and hugged.

"Done like a true Hollingsberry," Sussex said, kissing his cheek.

"You're a genius," Alexandro said.

"For once, Alexandro and I agree," Lucinda said. "You wrestled this ship like a wild gator."

Ike smiled. Coming from Lucinda, it was the ultimate compliment.

But the time for celebration was brief. Now that they were out of the storm, Ike heard a familiar *thunk-a-thunk*. It was another military helicopter. A soldier spoke through a microphone that blasted out of the helicopter loudly enough for all to hear.

"We thought we had lost you."

Sussex laughed. "Ike showed us how to use dragon power."

"Good," the soldier called back. "The President of the United States has asked you to mount your dragons. Time to get ready."

Ike blinked. "Get ready? Already? But I thought the locusts were going to attack New York?"

"The storm pushed you north fast. That's the city over there."

Ike wheeled around and gasped. There they were—the gleaming skyscrapers of downtown.

"Better hurry," the soldier called. "Our most recent count has it at twenty locusts. And it looks like they're about to make their move."

Chapter Twenty-Five

Alexandro gasped. "Did he say twenty? *Mamma.*"

"Yes," Ike said. "It looks like Opal was able to use Thaddeus's wand to bring more bugs out at once."

"That's a lot of bugs," Diego said.

"And there are only four of us who can fly," Elmira said.

"Which means we have to kill five each," Lucinda said. "Piece of cake."

Ike wasn't so sure. Then again, the dragon's firepower gave them a huge advantage, didn't it?

Things were moving quickly. Another helicopter joined the first. A new soldier called out through another microphone and speaker.

"We're here to escort you the rest of the way into the city. Are your fighters ready?"

Ike looked to Alexandro and Lucinda.

"You bet," Alexandro said.

"Bring 'em on," Lucinda exclaimed.

"You heard them," Ike yelled back to the helicopter pilot. Then he turned to his crew. "Okay, everybody. This is it. It's happening. Diego. Run to the pilot's cabin and get Elmira."

"Already done."

Ike blinked. Elmira stood before him.

"Kashvi's flying by herself," she said. Then to Ike's surprise, she saluted. "Permission to board Seattle."

Ike had never saluted in his life. Even so, he did it for the first time.

"Permission granted," he said.

"Permission to retrieve Pittsburgh," Lucinda cried.

Another salute.

"Granted," Ike said.

"Permission to retrieve Kansas City."

"Granted."

Ike wheeled around to Sussex and Diego.

"Now that we're out of the storm, the boat will fly on its own power. Get to the mast and release those ropes. We need our four main dragons back on board fast."

"Done, sir," Sussex cried.

The little man and Diego scurried to the mast and began pulling on the ropes that were attached to the dragons.

"Over here, Detroit," Ike said, waving his dragon back down to the boat.

"There you go, Pittsburgh," Lucinda cried.

"Kansas City," Alexandro said.

"It's you and me, Seattle," Elmira said.

Like thoroughbreds being led into the starting gate, the dragon's competitive juices were churning. Having caught the excitement, they were hyped up, ready for action. Landing on the right side of the ship, Detroit craned his neck and let loose a thunderous roar. A moment later, Kansas City was at his side, then Pittsburgh and Seattle were there, too, snorting and pawing the quickly drying deck.

"All right," Ike called. "Everybody on. Sussex. Ladders, please."

"Ladders?" Lucinda cried. "No time for that."

She scurried halfway up the mast. Then with a manic yell, she jumped straight onto Pittsburgh's back. As for Alexandro, he ran full out toward Kansas City's rear then kept right on running up his tail. Duly inspired, Elmira took a flying leap at Seattle's side and dug in her fingernails.

"Hey," she called. "A little help."

Ike stuck his shoulder under her knees and pushed her up and on. By that time, Sussex was back with the ladder. Though Ike would have loved his own creative way of getting on Detroit's back, the animal was simply too tall. With a quick climb up the ladder he was on.

The two helicopters were on either side of Ike and crew, each with a cameraman leaning out the side, shooting film for TV. Ike looked toward the city. There was downtown, the new Freedom Tower and, beyond that, the spire of the Empire State Building.

"Commander Hollingsberry," the first helicopter pilot said. "The locusts are still over the Hudson."

"Good!" Ike shouted. "Follow us over after take-off." He turned to Diego. "Sorry you can't fly, too. But you stay on the deck with Sussex. I imagine we'll need your help before this is over."

Diego nodded. "Hey."

Ike looked down from Detroit's back.

"What?"

Diego smiled.

"This is cool, right?"

Ike gave Diego a thumbs up, then called to the troops.

"Members of the Royal Tenth Order. Let's do this."

He gave Detroit a slight nudge. The mighty dragon spread his wings and rose into the air. Moments later, all four dragons were hovering in front of the boat. And then they were off. With the boat and two helicopters following close behind, the four warriors sped toward Manhattan. In what seemed like seconds, they were over the south side of the island. They then veered west to the Hudson River.

Looking down, Ike saw city streets, buildings, cars, buses, subway entrances, and cabs. And then there were crowds of people, many pointing at them. What could they be thinking? Did they really believe this was all part of a show? That the dragons and locusts were fake? Or were they terrified, wondering if the world was coming to an end? Ike couldn't know. But *he* knew the locusts were real. It was up to him and his friends to defend the city. Soaring over the west side highway, Ike thought of Thaddeus. He only hoped the old man would survive to see them defeat the locusts once and for all. And what had Thaddeus told him the night before? He and Ike's father would be watching over him, rooting him on.

The memory gave Ike a burst of confidence—and not a moment too soon. Looking up the Hudson, he saw it—a black blot in the sky.

The *locusts*.

Ike felt his heart begin to race. He leaned into Detroit's neck and kicked, urging him forward. Not that the dragon needed much encouragement. He was flying brilliantly, soaring through the sky. Better yet, despite saving the boat in the storm, he didn't seem tired. If anything, the dragon appeared to gain strength with each flap of his wings. The same was true of the others. In fact, the dragons were flying so fast it wasn't long before the dark blot had grown in size. Then slowly it began to dissolve ... and turn into an array of twenty, or maybe more, giant bugs.

And then Ike saw the locusts coming toward him—a mass of

antennae, wings, feet and giant eyes.

"This is it," he called to his friends.

He took out his sword and raised it over his head.

The first wave of locusts were one hundred feet away.

Then fifty feet.

Then twenty.

Ike reached to Detroit's neck. This was going to be easy. Yes, the bugs were huge. Yes, they all sported giant stingers like the one that had killed his dad and nearly killed him. But because they wore the special Order armor, it would be nearly impossible for the giant bugs to land shots precise enough kill. And before the locusts were close enough to try, the dragons would blast them out of the sky.

I've got this, Ike thought. *I've got this.*

He leaned forward, placed his hand on Detroit's neck, ready to give the signal to incinerate the first locust in a burst of flame.

Three more seconds ...

Two ...

One ...

Ready.

Blast that locust.

Ike pressed on Detroit's neck. As always, before sending forth a plume of fire, the dragon craned his neck. He opened his mouth as wide as it could go.

And then ...

Nothing.

No flame.

Ike touched Detroit's neck again, pressing harder.

Again, nothing.

Not a single spark.

Then the first locust was upon him. And to Ike's horror, there was a man on its back. And not just any man—the flash of red hair revealed him immediately as Theodore Opal himself. Worse, he wore a wizard's cape and carried the cane Ike recognized at Merlin's wand.

"Surprised to see me, Isaac Rupert Hollingsberry?"

The answer was yes. Hadn't the President of the United States said they were tracking him down? Had Opal used the wand to escape? Ike didn't know. But he did know when it was time to cut his losses and give the rest of his troops their chance at glory.

"Get the locusts," he called to the others. "But bring Opal in alive."

"Got it," Elmira called, swooping in from above.

Ike steered Detroit out of the way, hopeful his friends could do what he couldn't. Looking down, he saw Kansas City, Seattle, and Pittsburgh crane their necks and open their throats as wide as they could go …

"Fire!" Elmira cried.

But then …

Nothing.

"What?" Ike cried.

"It's a spell," Elmira cried.

"But Sussex tested the dragon's fire last night in the barn," Ike called back.

Elmira came up to Ike's side.

"Some spells take a while to take effect. I've blogged about it."

"Yes. Opal didn't come to the Order to ruin the boat."

That was Lucinda, flying up from the other side.

"*Si,*" Alexandro shouted. "He came to zap the dragons with the no-fire spell. Just like he did to Dartmoor and the others seven years ago."

Ike looked toward the locusts just as they broke into a perfect formation—twenty giant bugs … flying straight toward them.

Chapter Twenty-Six

F our children on four dragons—without a flicker of flame between them. Even so, there wasn't a single instant when Ike considered turning Detroit around and hightailing it back to the purple ship. He was beyond that now, a warrior, too focused on victory to consider retreat. Besides, wasn't this what he and his friends had come to New York to do? To engage the locusts in battle? Yes, Ike had counted on having the dragon's flame as a key weapon in his arsenal, but wasn't history full of instances when outgunned and outmanned armies had carried the day?

And so as the locusts thundered closer, Ike exchanged resolute nods with Alexandro, Lucinda, and Elmira, then faced forward and raised his sword high.

Then he gave the command.

"Charge!"

The four dragons craned their necks, flapped their wings as one and thundered into battle. Just like that, Ike and friends were in the middle of so many locusts, there was no time to think, only react. They stabbed, punched and kicked, occasionally landing a direct hit that would send the locust wailing into the Hudson—all of it captured on film by the two swooping military helicopters and their cameramen. But more often than not Ike and his compadres only succeeded in pushing a locust away for a few seconds before it was able to reconnoiter for another attack. As a result, Ike found himself fighting off the same locusts again and again, coming at him stingers blazing.

Thank goodness for the armor. Ike lost track of how many times he had been hit and how many times it had saved his life. Twice? Three times? Four?

Alexandro wasn't so lucky. While maneuvering Detroit away from an incoming antennae, Ike heard a cry behind him. Out of the corner of his eye, he saw Alexandro grab his upper arm. Ike knew from personal experience he needed immediate medical attention.

"Get back to the boat," Ike cried.

"No, no. I can fight."

"That's an order."

Ike turned to face another locust, just in time to land a direct punch to the mouth, followed by a sword swipe to his stomach. Another hit. Another bug careened to its death into the Hudson. But Ike knew that a single locust death—or even a bunch of them—didn't make up for how hopelessly they were outnumbered. Yes, they were fighting valiantly. But they would never gain a true upper hand without the dragon's flame. But if Elmira was right and the dragons had gone fireless due to magic, what could they do?

But then, Ike saw him—Theodore Opal, still seated atop the largest locust of all, clearly laying back, waiting for the main army of bugs to defeat Ike and his crew before turning his attention to taking over the city. In a single instant, Ike had his plan. Wasn't Opal the one who had put the spell on the dragons the night before? Wouldn't he know how to reverse it?

"Yaaa," Ike called.

He gave Detroit a hard kick. Though tiring rapidly, Detroit expended a last burst of energy.

"Help me get through to Opal," he called back to Elmira and Lucinda.

The girls didn't have to be told twice. They maneuvered Pittsburgh and Seattle to his either side, wildly swinging their swords, swiping at anything that might be a locust.

"Hey, slimy bugs," Lucinda called, as she flew Pittsburgh into the swarm. "I'm going to be wearing half of you guys by lunchtime."

Out of the corner of his eye, Ike noticed she was already using part of a wing as a cape.

Elmira was equally brave, swooping low to kick a locust in the foot, then coming back up to stab another in the top of the head.

"That's five down," she called, as the bug crashed to the river.

Lucinda caught another in the chest with her sword.

"No, make that six."

The girls laughed. But if twenty locusts had come through the portal and six were dead, that still left fourteen to go. And who knew how many more were going to come? Or when they would stop? No doubt about it he had to reverse the spell. Leaning close into Detroit's back Ike guided the dragon through the field of locusts, swerving, zigging and zagging.

"This way," Lucinda called.

Ike cut to his right, took a shot from the stinger to his armor, and kept on going.

"Over here," Elmira cried. "I've got you covered."

Ike swung back to the left, then ducked as a locust tried to swipe him off Detroit's back. But even though the dragon couldn't breathe fire, he could still use his jaws. With an epic lunge, Detroit caught a piece of the locust's side and tossed him into the sky.

And just like that, Ike saw daylight, enough of opening to get to Opal. But the man was no fool—and braver than Ike might have guessed. Though he had spent the better part of the battle laying back, he now rushed forward to meet him. And though Opal didn't have a sword, he did have the wand. Ike had no way of knowing whether he had learned how to wield other spells with it, but he couldn't worry about that now. All he could do was lie against Detroit's back, feel the wind on his face, and get ready. But to do what exactly? Even if he had a shot at it, he couldn't kill Opal. The President wanted him alive. More than that, a dead man wouldn't be able to tell him how to reverse the spell. And until the dragons got their fire back, the locusts could not be defeated.

Ike needed to take a risk. And he knew what that risk had to be.

"Get ready, boy," Ike called.

Then he pulled up sharply on the reins.

The dragon responded quickly, lurching up and over Opal. Before he could talk himself out of it, Ike jumped and landed— *boom*—right on the bug's back.

Opal looked over his shoulder, shocked.

"What?" he called.

Ike forced himself not to think about the fact that he was sitting atop a giant flying insect that had oozy, scaly skin. He had only one goal in mind—get to Opal. Shimmying forward, squeezing hard with his knees, Ike soon got close enough to lunge for his waist.

"How do I reverse the fire spell?" he called.

The locust swooped down sharply. Clearly, Opal didn't have full control of the giant bug.

"What?"

Ike needed to get the information and get off before they

crashed. He shouted it into the man's ear, "Reverse the fire spell. How do we do it?"

"And give your beasts the power to destroy us?" Opal said. "Not a chance."

The locust veered sharply up. Ike found himself gripping Opal's waist just to stay on. He was balanced just enough to hold his blade to Opal's throat.

"Tell me where you got the spell to take away their fire," Ike shouted. "*Now.*"

He pressed the blade closer to Opal's skin, drawing a thin line of blood.

"The woods," he said. "I got the spell from the woods."

The locust veered wildly to the left. Ike had to hold with all his might to stay on. Even so, he managed to keep the sword where it counted.

"What woods?" Ike asked.

"The Dark, Dank Woods. I used Firebane."

"Firebane?" Ike exclaimed.

It rang a bell. Hadn't Elmira seen that name in the bylaws under a section about plants?

"When did you get it?" Ike asked.

"Seven years ago."

"Was Thaddeus there, too?" Ike yelled.

"Yes. Yes. He was there, too."

Finally, Opal caught a break. Flying wildly, the locust lurched sharply to his left, knocking Ike off balance long enough for Opal to take advantage. Back went his elbow, catching Ike square in the gut. Caught off-guard, Ike slipped to his side, only to be met with a second blow, this one to the head, delivered with the handle of Thaddeus's wand. One moment Ike had a sword to Opal's throat, the next he was holding desperately onto the locust's wing.

"Nice knowing you," Opal said. "Sorry that you won't be

around to see my bugs take over the city. It's going to be epic. Fantastic. The best takeover of a city ever."

And then Ike was falling—just like his dad—hurtling through the air toward the Hudson River.

It was a short moment that seemed to last and last. Looking up, Ike saw Opal's locust fly out of view, as well as the helicopters that had been filming the battle, too far away to save him. To his side was Elmira and Lucinda and their dragons, both rushing to help, but also unable to get to him in time.

Was this how his father had felt?

Falling through the sky, knowing all was lost?

Was there another next in line? Or would the locusts really destroy the planet?

He would never know. Ike closed his eyes and waited for the end …

Until he felt something snatch him out of the sky, breaking his fall. When Ike opened his eyes, he was staring directly at Detroit. The mighty dragon had done what Dartmoor hadn't been able to do for his dad. He had swooped out of the sky and caught him in his teeth. With a quick flip of the dragon's head, Ike was on his back.

"Detroit!" Ike yelled, hugging his neck. "Thank you."

The dragon let loose a roar as Elmira and Lucinda dove close.

"Are you okay?" Elmira shouted.

"Fine."

"What now?" Lucinda asked.

"I learned something about the spell," Ike yelled back. "It's time to regroup."

Chapter Twenty-Seven

Moments later, the dragons were back on the Purple Flying Viking Ship. Sussex, Diego, and Kashvi, who kept the boat hovering on automatic pilot, were there to greet them.

"We have new information," Ike called, jumping from Detroit's back to the deck. "Dartmoor and my father's dragons lost their ability to breathe fire because Opal found a plant called Firebane. That's why he went to the Dark, Dank Woods seven years ago. That's why he broke into the Order last night—to put the same spell on our dragons."

"He must've also tried to wreck the boat, too," Kashvi said.

"Right," Ike replied. "Luckily, you were able to fix it."

"So what next?" Diego asked.

Ike turned to Elmira. "It's good you brought along the bylaws. Firebane was listed, remember? Maybe there's some info we can use."

"I'm on it."

As Elmira jumped from Seattle and hurried to the pilot's cabin, Ike turned to Sussex.

"How's Alexandro? Did he make it back?"

The little man nodded.

"A flesh wound," he said. "He'll be okay."

Alexandro appeared on deck with his upper arm taped. "Sussex got the locust poison out."

"Good," Ike said.

"Firebane, eh?" Sussex said.

"Yes," Ike replied. "We're going to need to find something to counteract it."

Elmira emerged from the pilot's cabin, cradling the hefty bylaws in her arms, open to the page in question.

"*Exotic Plants of the Middle Ages: Uses and Cures.*"

"Nice," Kashvi said.

"Let's hope there's a cure for Firebane," Ike said.

Elmira plopped the book on the deck by the other children.

"Okay, here we go." She kneeled and ran a finger down the page, reading as she went. "Wurstrot, Thruttlethrush, Beetle Root, Beetle Weed, Hemstickle, Poison Radish—okay, got it. Firebane. *A small four leafed fern of the Middle Ages generally found under larger plants in heavily wooded parts of England.*"

"Like the Dark, Dank Woods," Diego said.

"Exactly," Elmira said.

"Good start," Ike said. "What else?"

"Something weird," Elmira said. "*The edible leaves of Firebane have been known to taste of lemon peel and goose livers.*"

"Goose livers?" Ike exclaimed.

"I said it was weird," Elmira said.

"What do goose livers even taste like?" Lucinda asked.

"You don't want to know," Alexandro said. "My grandmother

used to cook with them sometimes and *Mamma. Disastro.*"

"Whatever," Elmira said. "Listen up. This next part is good. *Though Firebane's small leaves make it difficult to locate, it was known by the wizards of King Arthur's time for its magical properties as an anti-incendiary.*"

"Anti-incendiary?" Diego said. "What does that mean?"

"That it can put out fire," Lucinda said. "That's what."

"So Opal was telling the truth," Kashvi said. "He did use the Firebane."

"Cool," Ike said. "So all we need now is the cure."

"*Si,*" Alexandro said. "What's it say?"

Ike looked to Elmira expectantly. Unfortunately, instead of shouting out an antidote in her typical hard-charging style, she was scanning the page worriedly.

"What's going on?" Ike asked. "Is there a problem?"

Elmira shook her head. "This section says what Firebane does all right, but it doesn't say how to undo it."

"What?" Kashvi said. "But the section heading says uses and *cures.*"

"I know," Elmira said. "But all I'm seeing are the uses."

"You're sure?" Ike asked.

"I've already double-checked."

"Where does that leave us then?" Alexandro asked.

"I'll tell you where, mate," Lucinda said. "With four dragons who couldn't light a match between them."

"Not so fast," Diego said.

"What?" Lucinda asked. "Do you see something?"

"I think so. Look."

Indeed, while the others had been despairing, Diego had dropped to his knees next to Elmira. He pointed at a tiny smudge by the section title.

"It's an asterisk."

"An asterisk?" Elmira said, looking back to the top of the page. "Wait. Isn't that a speck of dirt?"

"That's what I thought at first," Diego said. "Look closer."

Clearly skeptical, Elmira granted him another peek. A quick moment later, she looked back up, face blank with disbelief.

"It is an asterisk. Which means that I was ... *incorrect*."

Ike exchanged a quick smile with Diego. In a week of surprises, here was another. Elmira Hand had admitted to being wrong.

"Relax," Diego said. "Like I said, I thought it was dirt, too."

"Everybody misses things," Kashvi said. "It's part of life."

Elmira nodded. Maybe a part of other people's lives—just generally not hers.

"Anyway, check it out," Diego went on. "The asterisk directs you to a series of footnotes." He flipped a few pages ahead. "See?"

Indeed, at the end of the section on *Exotic Plants* was a half a page of tiny, faded print.

"Yep, those are footnotes, all right," Sussex said, peering over Diego's shoulder. "Read it, my boy."

Diego brushed his hair behind his ears then concentrated hard on the small text.

"Now we're getting somewhere," he said, as everyone gathered close. "It says, *Footnotes Cures, Remedies, and Assorted Antidotes*." He moved his finger down the page, reading as he went. "And we've got Wurstrot, Thruttlethrush, Beetle Root, Beetle Weed, Hemstickle, Poison Radish ... and wait for it." He looked up, excited, almost as though he hadn't believed it would actually be there. "Firebane."

"Yes," Kashvi cried.

"What's it say?" Ike asked.

"Turn to Appendix 14A."

Ike couldn't believe it. There was still more to do?

"I've got this," Elmira said. Recovered from the debacle of the missed asterisk, she hip-butted Diego out of the way and began flipping through the pages. "We've got Dragon Lore, Dragon Wingspan, Dragon Dietary Restrictions. All right, here we go. The Appendixes. Appendix 12, Dragon Skin Color. Appendix 13, Dragon Mane Texture. Ah. Here we have it. Appendix 14A."

"Read it," Sussex said.

"Okay," Elmira said. "Give me some space."

Dutifully, the other children and Sussex took a step back. But instead of beginning to read, Elmira's eyes went wide. Then she wrinkled her brow and bit her lower lip. Ike was instantly concerned. Had Elmira missed something else?

"What's wrong now?" he asked.

"This is so weird."

"What?" Kashvi said. "Is there another asterisk masquerading as a speck of dirt?"

"No, not that."

"Then what's wrong?" Ike repeated.

Elmira looked up, utterly dumbstruck.

"I can't read it."

"You can't read it?" Ike asked.

"Why not?" Sussex asked.

"Because it's complete gibberish."

"What?" Alexandro said. "Gibberish?"

"Yes."

Everyone pushed to get the best angle on the passage, resulting in a wild tangle of arms and legs that didn't allow anyone to see anything. Finally, Ike pushed the book to one side. True to

Elmira's word, Appendix 14A was penned in a strange, incoherent prose. The letters were of the standard English alphabet, but there wasn't a single recognizable word.

"What is this?" Ike asked.

"Don't know," Elmira said.

"Maybe it's a secret language used by Merlin and King Arthur?" Kashvi suggested.

"Or maybe it was a broken medieval printer?" Lucinda said.

"*Si*," Alexandro said with a smile. "This is a long book. Maybe nobody proofread the whole thing?"

"Oh, they proofread it," Diego said. "You can count on that." He looked to Sussex. "Are you thinking what I'm thinking?"

Sussex nodded, eyes glinting with excitement.

"What's going on with you two?" Ike asked.

Diego smiled. "That this gibberish isn't as gibberishy as it looks."

"What does that mean?" Kashvi asked.

"It means listen up."

Diego hunched over the text and began to sound out the strange language. "*Ish ... Fantsicle ...* "

"What are you doing?" Kashvi asked.

"Reading it," Diego replied.

"But why?" Ike asked.

Diego kept on going.

"*Prime ... Du hal-i-stick.* "

"Oh, please," Elmira said. "That makes no sense."

"*Non capisco*," Alexandro agreed.

"What he said," Lucinda agreed. "*Non capisco*, mate."

"Maybe to you and me," Sussex said, excitedly. "But not to them."

"Who?" Kashvi asked.

Sussex pointed at the dragons.

"Them."

Ike gasped. It was true. All four dragons were looking expectantly at Diego, almost as though they had been summoned. To top it off, Detroit snorted loudly and stomped his front right foot.

Sussex slapped Diego's shoulder.

"We've finally discovered it, my boy."

"I think we have."

"Discovered what exactly?" Ike asked.

Diego pumped a fist. "*Dragonish.*"

"*Dragonish?*" Ike said.

"Yes and double yes," Sussex shouted. "It has to be."

Diego and Sussex executed an awkward chest bump that knocked the little man, laughing, to the deck.

"It was in the bylaws under my nose for years and I never even knew it."

"I know," Diego called. He helped Sussex back up, then tripped over his laces and fell down himself. "It's crazy."

But while they saw cause for celebration, the others remained dubious—no one more so than Elmira.

"Sorry to ruin your party," she said, "but there is no mention of such a thing in the historical records."

"Then you've been checking the wrong records, my friend," Sussex said, helping Diego back to his feet. "I've been saying it for years. Myth has it that the first Dragon Keepers could speak to the dragons in a language that has been lost."

"All right, then," Elmira said. "If it's *Dragonish*, tell me what it says."

"Yes," Ike said. "Translate it."

To Ike's surprise, Sussex shook his head, good naturedly. "Translate it? Oh, no. We couldn't possibly do that."

Ike blinked. That was news.

"You couldn't?"

"Why not?" Kashvi asked.

"It's too difficult for the likes of us," Sussex said.

Diego nodded. "We'll need Dr. Bernie J. Wong and maybe even a whole team of linguists and animal experts to figure it out completely."

"So what are you saying?" Ike said. He was becoming increasingly exasperated. "We need to contact Dr. Wong and a team of linguists and animal experts to reverse the Firebane?"

Diego laughed. "No, no. Relax. Just because we can't understand it yet doesn't mean we can't *speak* it."

Ike was as confused as he had been since he had gotten mixed up with the Royal Order. "What do you mean?"

"I mean I can sound out the words," Diego said. "As far as we know, this is a spell to reverse the Firebane as set down by the first Dragon Keepers—and my guess is that they cleverly wrote it in a language the dragons will understand. All we have to do is recite the whole thing to the dragons and the spell will be reversed."

"That's bonkers," Lucinda said. "Dragons can't understand humans."

"They just did," Diego said. "What about your aunt? Didn't she talk to animals?"

"Sure, but she got eaten by a snake."

"So I'll get eaten then," Diego said. He turned to Ike. "Hey, it's worth a try, isn't it?"

Ike nodded. What other choice did he have?

"Come on," he called. "Give Diego some room. Time to hear some more *Dragonish*."

Chapter Twenty-Eight

As Diego lugged the bylaws toward the dragons, the two helicopters hovered closer, still filming. Ike looked up and nodded to the pilots. Indeed, he had been so consumed with what to do about the Firebane that he had temporarily forgotten he was on a TV show being carried live across the country. Thankfully, it was proving easy to play his part. Reality had handed him a better storyline than any script.

"How long is this going to take?" Ike asked Diego.

"Not long. But I think we should do it one by one. I'll start with Detroit."

Statuesque as ever, Ike's dragon was already ready, clearly eager to get back in the sky for the next battle. Diego held the hair out of his eyes, hit his knees before the bylaws and squinted again at the small print.

"All right, then," Ike said to his friend. "Bring it."

But instead of immediately reciting what was there, Diego began to mutter quietly to himself.

"What are you doing?" Elmira asked.

"Practicing," Diego said, without looking up.

"Practicing?" Ike asked. "What's to practice?"

"There's a fine art to speaking correctly to an animal."

"Could you maybe practice a little bit faster?" Alexandro asked.

Diego ignored him, refusing to be rushed. Ike knew better than to push it further. After all, Diego was a boy who had once spent a full hour trying to get a particular sounding "coo" out of a pigeon. With nothing to do but wait, Ike looked over the edge of the boat toward the city and willed himself to be patient. But it was difficult. Who knew what Theodore Opal had done in the past few minutes to solidify his advantage? Who knew how many locusts were loose in the city? They had to get the dragons up and flying now.

Thankfully, Diego had a firmer grasp of the situation's urgency than Ike had given him credit for. Just as Ike was considering snatching the bylaws away to say the spell himself, he heard his friend's voice ring out.

"Ish fantsicle prime du hal-i-stick."

Ike wheeled around. Diego was standing, looking Detroit square in the eye.

"Nish fantsicle bime du hal-i-snick."

All was quiet save the quiet whirr of the purple boat's engine and the *thunk-a-thunk* of the hovering helicopters.

"You're done?" Ike asked, nervously. "That's all there is?"

Diego finally moved his eyes off Detroit and pointed down to the book.

"Wanna see for yourself?"

"No, I trust you," Ike said, hurrying over. "So Detroit has his fire back?"

Diego nodded. "Try him out."

By this point, the dragon knew what was at stake. Without being prompted, the great creature took a drink of water from a trough on the deck, then sat back on his haunches. Then he craned his neck.

Ike held his breath.

This had to work.

But like Diego, Detroit was not to be rushed. Standing as tall as he could on his back legs, he took a deep, slow breath through his nose. Then he spread his mighty wings. And finally … he blew.

And out came …

Not a single flicker of flame.

Not a single spark.

Only a gust of hot breath.

"Cancel the fire department, ladies and gentlemen," a reporter cried from the first helicopter. "That's one flame-challenged dragon."

"Diego," Ike said.

"Well, that's weird," his friend said.

"You think?" Lucinda said.

"Maybe he's too tired after all that flying?" Kashvi said.

"He shouldn't be that tired," Ike said.

He suddenly felt like a fool. Had he actually put his faith in his lovable but wacky friend, a boy who absurdly claimed he could speak to animals? And had it done it all on national TV? It was crazy. Theodore Opal was almost certainly taking over New York neighborhood by neighborhood by now. They needed dragons who could breathe fire—and they needed them fast.

"Oh, wait a second here."

It was Diego, on his hands and knees once again, his head buried in the book.

"What now?" Ike asked, impatiently.

"This print is so darned small," he said. "Turns out I read

the spell a little bit wrong. *Ish fantsicle gime du hal-a-stack*—that's how it should go." Diego looked up to Ike with a smile. "You heard how different that was, right?"

"Different?" Ike said. "Not really."

"Really? Because the *prime* became *gime* and the *hal-i-stick* became *hal-a-stack*."

"Okay," Ike said. "But will it work?"

"Ah, wait a second," Diego exclaimed, grinning wildly. "Hold on. This could be even better."

"What?" Ike asked.

"There's another asterisk."

"What? Another?"

"Yes. That leads to an even smaller footnote at the bottom of the page. Let's see … hmmm … *Misha ish grandula*."

"*Misha ish grandula*?" Elmira asked. "What does that do?"

"I'm not sure, to tell the truth. But it looks like it's part of the spell. Anyway, listen up."

With no further ado, Diego once again looked Detroit square in the eye and recited the entire incantation. *"Ish fantsicle gime du hal-a-stack. Nish fantsicle bime du hal-i-snick. Misha ish grandula."*

He turned to Ike. "There. Done. In the books."

"Great," Ike said. "Please tell me it worked."

This time, the dragon didn't require a warm-up. Detroit spread his wings, opened his mouth and let loose a thunderous blast of flame that shot so powerfully into the sky one of circling helicopters had to swoop out of the way.

"Oh, my gosh," Ike shouted. "It worked all right."

"That's the biggest fire shot I've ever seen," Sussex said.

Diego laughed. "I know. That last little phrase must've given it some extra pop."

"Sure did!" Sussex exclaimed. "Our dragons are back in business."

Diego slapped him five. "Thanks to *Dragonish,* baby."

"Good going, mate." Lucinda said.

"Yeah, Diego," Kashvi said. "I knew you had it in you."

"I didn't," Elmira said. "But the minute we destroy the locusts, this is going into *Elmira Speaks.*"

"I'll take it," Diego said with a smile, then turned to Ike. "You happy?"

Ike laughed. "Happy? If I've ever doubted you about anything I am officially sorry, buddy. Quick. Say whatever you said to Detroit to the rest of them. Let's move."

Chapter Twenty-Nine

W hile the others looked on, Diego moved down the line, reciting the complete incantation to the remaining three dragons. Once Kansas City, Pittsburgh, and Seattle had proved themselves cured with their own blasts of fire, Ike turned to his troops. There they were, Alexandro, Lucinda, and Elmira, standing in a line, ready to give their lives to defeat the locust scourge. Ike was proud to be their leader. They would follow him anywhere and he would do anything for them.

"Okay, members of the Tenth Royal Order," he shouted. "Mount up."

Lucinda went first, jumping onto Pittsburgh's back from the mast of the ship. Then Alexandro ran up Kansas City's tail while Elmira took a flying leap at Seattle's side, dug in her fingernails and scrambled up. Once again, Ike took the commander's prerogative and waited for Sussex to prop a ladder onto Detroit.

"Troops ready?" Ike called.

"Ready, mate," Lucinda called.

"*Pronto*," Alexandro said.

"Always and forever," Elmira answered.

Ike gave Kashvi and Sussex a thumbs up and waved to Diego. Then he looked back to his troops.

"Let's do this."

Ike, Elmira, Alexandro, and Lucinda nudged the reins and the four dragons lifted off, hovering for a second by the side of the purple boat while one of the helicopters flew to Ike's side.

"Reports say Opal has split up his troops," the pilot cried through the megaphone. "He's blocking off Manhattan in four different spots."

Ike nodded. Four locations. Four dragons. He would have preferred to have stayed together as one unit, but the enemy had dictated that he and his troops go it alone.

"All right," Ike called back. "Where are they?"

Back came the answer. "LaGuardia Airport. The Statue of Liberty. The George Washington Bridge. Opal himself is controlling the largest swarm over Central Park."

Ike nodded and made some quick assignments.

"All right then," he shouted to his troops. "You heard the man. We're going to split up. Lucinda, you get to LaGuardia Airport."

"I'm on it," the girl said. "I'll follow the landing planes."

"Good," Ike said. "Alexandro, you take The Statue of Liberty."

"*Excelente*. When some of my ancestors came to America one hundred years ago, Lady Liberty was the first thing they saw. She's an old *amico*."

"Elmira," Ike said. "Go to the George Washington Bridge."

"Got it." Elmira flashed a rare smile. "I've always wanted to see what it was like to be a Jersey girl."

Ike smiled back.

"What about you?" Alexandro asked.

"Me?" Ike said. "I have a date with Theodore Opal in Central Park. Now, is everyone ready?"

"Almost," Elmira said. "How will we all communicate?"

Ike's heart dropped. Despite all the TV cameras, helicopters, and modern technology surrounding them, the Royal Order had never prepared for the dragons to split up in battle. Communicate with his troops? He had no idea.

"You guys wouldn't happen to have cellphones in your tunics, would you?"

It wasn't a good time for a joke, but what else was there to say? Luckily, Ike got an assist from an unexpected source. Though the men of the military weren't able to fight the locusts directly, they had been busy seeing to tactical support. As the president said, they had their backs.

"Here," the helicopter pilot shouted down. "Try these."

A moment later, four headsets suspended by tiny parachutes come floating toward the children.

"Oh, my," Alexandro called. "*Bella.*"

It was a beautiful sight. Ike watched his drop toward him then plucked it out of the sky. The earpiece itself was no bigger than a shirt button and the speaker was the size of a small marble—more cutting edge technology courtesy of the United States Government.

"Place it on your earlobe," the pilot instructed everyone. "You'll hear each other just fine."

The four fighters did as they were told.

"Hey," Ike said. "Everyone there?"

"*Si.*"

"Righto."

"Loud and clear."

Ike shot the pilot a thumbs up then turned back to his troops to issue final commands.

"When you get to your battle stations, await my orders. Good?"

The three answered as one. "Good."

"And remember. If we can, we want Opal alive. Got it?"

"Got it."

"All right then, members of the Tenth Order. Let's move."

Freshly rested, the four dragons thundered so quickly through the sky the two helicopters had to go into overdrive to keep up. As the dragons sprinted uptown, the troops began to peel off. At lower Manhattan, Alexandro said, *Arrivederci*," and veered toward to the Statue of Liberty. Elmira turned west to get to The George Washington Bridge. Farther up Manhattan Island, Lucinda found a plane to follow to LaGuardia Airport.

With a wave goodbye and a quick, "Good luck." Ike hung a left toward Central Park. No doubt about it—Lucinda, Alexandro, and Elmira would have their hands full. But Ike knew he had the biggest job of them all—a showdown in Central Park with one of the most famous men in America.

Flying rapidly, Ike soared over Madison Square Garden then made his way over the bright neon signs of Times Square. Ironically, the next landmark was the gaudy Opal Grand, featuring a glittering sign that read, *Opal Industries: Redeveloping New York One Building at a Time.* Up ahead was Carnegie Hall. Then, two blocks from the park, Ike spotted a distant blot on the horizon.

There they were, his adversaries. An entire swarm of locusts, waiting to fight.

"Yaaa!" Ike cried.

Detroit zoomed over Sheep's Meadow, Wolman Rink, up to the edge of the zoo. A giant crowd, including a gaggle of reporters, had beaten Ike there, anticipating the showdown. Ike drew his sword and brought his dragon to a halt above the zoo's seal pond, fifty feet from the locusts. And what a swarm it was. There were a good thirty of them, one larger than the next.

"I'm here," Ike said into his earpiece. "Is everyone in position?"

"Yep. At the Bridge."

"*Si.* At the Statue."

"Just arrived at the airport."

"I've got around twenty-five locusts here at the zoo," Ike said. "What about you guys?"

"About the same here, I think," Lucinda replied. "Right by the main runway, just sitting there."

"I count twenty-five on the Jersey side of the Hudson," Elmira said. "They see me all right but they aren't coming close—at least not yet."

"Lady Liberty is covered with giant bugs," Alexandro reported. "But they're calm for now."

"Got it," Ike said. "Okay, then. Await my command."

In truth, Ike was slightly surprised. He had assumed the locusts would launch a full frontal attack the minute he and the others arrived. But apparently, another strategy was in play. So what were the insects waiting for? The exact right moment to make their move? More reinforcements? Ike hoped not. It felt strange to be cut off from his three friends. Perhaps that was Opal's plan? Separate the dragons. Divide and conquer. Then again, maybe Opal wasn't all that worried about Ike and his troops anymore. Maybe he had something else in mind.

Ike was about to find out. Just then, the locusts buzzed more loudly and flapped their wings. Then the swarm parted. Within seconds, the locusts had broken into two groups, revealing the largest bug of them all—Opal's. As before, the man himself was sitting on its back. But now he was attired in the full regalia of a wizard, complete with a flowing red cape, knee-high boots, and the traditional magicians' cap. Most importantly, he held Merlin's wand.

As Opal stared Ike down, the shouts from below came fast and furious.

"Wow. Opal is on the TV show, too?"

"Sure looks it. He's wearing a dress."

"No, it's a cape. The dude is dressed like a wizard."

"Wild. Celebrities will do anything for a little PR these days."

"Opal is here," Ike informed his friends through the headset. "Let's wait and see what happens."

"Are you sure?" Elmira said.

"We could still take out our bugs, eh?" Alexandro said.

"I know," Ike said. "But if Opal finds out you've attacked, he might do something crazy. We want him alive and we don't want anyone here to get hurt."

A few people on the ground began to inch nervously toward the zoo exits. However, the overwhelming majority of the crowd remained rooted in place, looking up, shouting, fascinated. That included a group of children, standing by the monkey cages. Out of the corner of his eye, Ike noticed two of them waving in his direction. With a closer look, Ike was so surprised he nearly fell into the seal pond. It was the Branford sixth grade class.

"Yo, Ike, we've been watching you on TV." It was Jimmy Barschdorff, a kid who sat in front of him in math. "Awesome dragon. Can I get a ride?"

Ike couldn't resist shouting back.

"Maybe later." He nodded to Opal, still eyeing him from atop his locust. "I've got to take care of some things first."

Then the rest of his class began to call out.

"Check it out. Hollingsberry is on a dragon."

"It's a fake dragon, dude. It's part of a TV show."

"So what? It's still pretty cool, right?"

Despite the severity of the circumstances, Ike had to smile. He was the first kid in the history of sixth grade who had upped his school cred by appearing on the back of what most people still assumed was a brilliant reconstruction of an actual mythological creature. Not bad. Still, not everyone was so impressed.

"Don't get so hot on yourself, Hollingsberry."

Ike recognized the voice immediately, Harrison Opal.

"Who cares if you're riding a fake dragon? My dad's on a fake locust, okay?"

"Yeah." It was Dirk Sher, sidekick number one. "And locusts are way cooler."

Sidekick number two agreed.

"Way, way cooler," Molly Willowinski shouted.

"I bet they paid my old man like ten million dollars to do a guest spot on this show," Harrison said. "Hey, isn't that right, Dad?"

With his son's question, Opal finally found the perfect moment to take control of the proceedings.

"Actually, Harrison," he bellowed. "I appeared for no fee."

Slowly, dramatically, Opal rose and stood directly on his

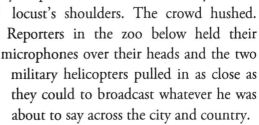

locust's shoulders. The crowd hushed. Reporters in the zoo below held their microphones over their heads and the two military helicopters pulled in as close as they could to broadcast whatever he was about to say across the city and country.

"Hear this, citizens of New York." Opal began. "You think this is a TV show, do you? Well, it's not. This dragon before me is completely real."

Ike blinked. What was Opal doing?

"Real?" a girl shouted from down below. She had climbed up

the edge of the monkey cage. "Are you serious?"

"Indeed, I am," Opal continued. He held Merlin's magic wand above his head. "This cane is actually a wand. And it gives me control of one hundred very real giant locusts that are guarding the airports and roadways into the city. And they are the biggest locusts in the history of the world. Fantastically huge. Which means one and only one thing. After years of kowtowing to the losers in the Mayor's Office and the City Council, I can do whatever I want. You see, as of this moment, *Opal controls everything.*"

Ike couldn't tell if the crowd was buying it.

"He's acting," Ike heard a man say, finally. "That's gotta be it."

Most of the crowd seemed to reach the same conclusion.

"Yep."

"Can he sing, too? He should be on Broadway."

"Give my dad an Emmy," Harrison called. "Best Actor Portraying Himself on a Giant Insect."

"You heard it here," Ike heard a reporter cry. "The Return of the Royal Order has a special guest star, real estate magnate Theodore Opal."

Out of the corner of his eye, Ike saw reporters roaming the crowd, grabbing interviews. Then he looked to Opal. The man was furious. Clearly, he had wanted this to be a moment that struck fear into the hearts of men. Instead, he was being portrayed as a charlatan willing to do anything for cheap publicity. In a matter of seconds, his face turned the color of his red hair.

"No, no, *no!*" he cried. "You don't understand. Quiet, I say. SHUT UP."

On cue, Opal's locust opened its mouth as wide as it could and emitted a sound that while not quite an actual roar, was frightening enough to shush the crowd.

"Perhaps I need to be clearer," Opal said. "My wand once belonged to Merlin. Yes, *that* Merlin. The one from the days of King Arthur. So let me repeat, this is *not* a TV show. As of this moment, Opal controls New York City."

"You heard it here, friends," a reporter cried immediately. "Theodore Opal claims to be a wizard."

"Not a chance," a teenaged boy called. "Building all those dumb hotels has turned him wacko."

"Not true!" Opal shrieked. He held the wand high. "Not only do I have Merlin's wand, which I have customized with some of New York's finest jewels, but chew on this—I am a direct descendant of his son, Edward."

Ike was so shocked he nearly fell off Detroit's back. So that's how Opal knew about the spell.

"Did you guys hear that?" Ike said into the headset. "Opal says he's related to Edward."

"My, gosh," Lucinda said. "It's in his bloody family."

"Now we know how he opened the portal," Elmira said.

Ike and his band realized Opal was almost certainly telling the truth, but with no knowledge of the history of the situation, most of the crowd thought he was kidding at best or crazy at worst.

"All right, then, Mr. Opal," a girl shouted up to him. She had shimmied halfway up a flagpole to be heard. "If you're so powerful, let's see it. Go ahead. Turn one of these seals into a frog. Better yet, turn that dragon into a rhino."

For a second, Ike was terrified. After all, who knew what Opal was capable of? And the girl had handed him the perfect set-up. All Opal had to do was to perform one small trick to strike fear into the heart of the city.

But instead of taking the cue, Opal hesitated. Ike allowed himself a small burst of hope. Could it be that Opal wasn't responding because he had no real idea how to wield the magic wand's mighty power? Yes, he had placed a spell on the dragons using the Firebane. But this was also the man who had first unleashed the locusts in Nevada and had needed seven more years to figure out how to get them to appear in New York.

The rest of the crowd joined the girl, baiting Opal, daring him to show what he could do.

"Yo. Turn that polar bear into a kitty cat."

"Then turn my tuna sandwich into a pizza."

"Make me taller, okay? Just two or three inches."

"Hey, I'd *love* bigger triceps."

"Forget the triceps," a lady shouted. "I want a bigger apartment."

As the individual shouts blended into a maddening cacophony, Opal was frozen.

"Yeah," Ike suddenly called out. "If you're so great, turn my dragon into a bowl of coffee chip ice cream."

"You want to see me use this wand, do you?" Opal sputtered. "Sorry, but that's not how this is going to work. The first proof of my power will come from my astonishing bugs. As I said, four groups of my mighty and magnificent locusts are stationed around the city."

"It's true," a reporter cried. "We have it on the satellite feed."

That's when Ike noticed a giant monitor, usually used to announce happenings around the zoo. The screen showed four separate images. Going clockwise from the left, Ike saw ...

Lucinda hovering on Pittsburgh above the runway at LaGuardia Airport ...

Alexandro and Kansas City facing off a horde of hovering bugs by Lady Liberty's head ...

Elmira and Seattle sitting patiently in the right lane of the Upper Level of the George Washington Bridge ...

The last frame showed Ike himself, sitting atop Detroit,

hovering over the zoo.

"I have you guys on screen now," Ike said into the headset.

"I hear you," Lucinda said.

"Still awaiting your order," Alexandro said.

"It looks like my bugs are waiting for Opal to give them some sort of a signal," Elmira said.

It was true. But what was the man waiting for? Was he scared and trying to avoid a fight? Or was he hoping to intimidate Ike and the Royal Order into surrendering with no bloodshed?

Or perhaps he was just wildly overconfident and wanted to milk the moment for everything it was worth.

"Look at that pitiful reptile, my friends," he cried, pointing to Detroit. "Sure, the beast can fly." Opal allowed his smirk to blossom into a triumphant smile. "But tell me, what sort of a loser of a dragon can't even breathe fire?"

Ike blinked. Had Opal really said what he thought he had? Had the city's most successful real estate developer in modern history been so busy planning his big entrance he hadn't seen what had happened on the flying boat? Apparently not.

Unfortunately, the press felt obliged to correct him.

"No, no," a reporter cried. "The dragons are fixed. They're flaming with the best of them."

"Yeah," a teenage boy shouted. "It was on television. Your locusts are gonna be toast—literally."

But the surprises continued. To Ike's amazement, Opal didn't believe them.

"If you saw it on TV, it was a special effect," he called. "I've done my research. Firebane is the best anti-flame plant in the world. There's no better plant. It's utterly fantastic. No cure for it."

Ike had to work hard to hold in a smile.

"Opal doesn't know the dragons are stoked and ready," he whispered to his friends.

"Nice," Elmira said. "Nothing like the element of surprise."

Oozing confidence, Opal faced down Ike. "Listen here, boy. I am more than willing to be reasonable. No one wants to see my locusts rip you into little bits. Surrender before anyone gets hurt."

"Surrender?" Ike said. "I don't think so."

Opal's eyes went wide. "I admire your courage, *Ikey*, but look at my bugs. They're fantastic. You're hopelessly outnumbered." Opal smiled more broadly. "But here's the good news," he called to the crowd. "When the dragons have been defeated and my locusts and I have demanded the mayor's resignation, I vow to rule this city with compassion and love. Yes, I might build some more buildings. Maybe a lot of them. After all, why does this city really need parks? There's plenty of grass in other parts of the state. Am I correct?"

"That's nuts," the boy on the flagpole called out.

"I like buildings," a man cried. "But don't we have enough already?"

"I told you he was crazy. That man is a menace."

Ike glanced down. The last comment came from the same courageous mom who had spoken her mind to Opal outside Branford a few days earlier. Then the shouts came fast and furious.

"I like grass."

"I like ballfields."

"I like parks."

"I like *cement*," Opal bellowed. "Miles and miles of fantastically hard cement." He turned savagely to Ike. "Don't you know when it's over? Are you sure you want to die on national television … just like your father?"

Ike willed himself to stay calm. He knew that Opal was trying to throw him off guard.

Detroit, however, was another story. Perhaps he sensed Opal had crossed a line. Or maybe he simply needed to clear his throat. But at that second, the mighty dragon exhaled angrily, letting loose a mighty burst of flame straight into the sky.

The crowd gasped.

"Did you see that?" a reporter called.

"Yes," a man called out. "It's like Old Faithful but with fire."

As for Opal, his eyes went wide. Even so, he gathered his wits enough to force a smile.

"No worries," he said. "We've still got more than twenty bugs for each dragon. We'll be fine, flame or no flame."

"I doubt it," Ike called. "These dragons have been re-tooled with fire that's stronger than ever."

"I still like our chances, boy. Your dragons are losers."

But Ike could see the chinks in Opal's confident façade. His lower lip was beginning to twitch. His trademark smirk was showing the first warning signs of collapsing into a worried frown.

Ike pressed his advantage. "I don't want to harm you and neither does the President of the United States. Surrender now and command the locusts back through the portal and no one gets hurt."

To mark his point, Ike gave Detroit a light pat on his neck. The dragon responded in kind, expertly aiming a torrid blast that singed the top of Opal's wizard hat.

"Hey, there kid," Opal cried. "Watch it."

Then Detroit fired again, this time singeing Opal's left ear.

"Surrender," Ike called.

"Not a chance," Opal called back.

He kicked his locust as hard as he could.

"Yaaa, boy. Yaaa."

To Ike's horror, Opal dive bombed straight for the crowd.

"Run for your lives," a woman shouted.

"Duck," a reporter called. "It's a lunatic billionaire gone mad on a bug."

It was true. Laughing, Opal careened wildly over the hordes, then turned straight toward Ike's class. Then quick as could be, he snatched up the first student he could get his hands on. Sidekick number two—Molly Willowinski.

Chapter Thirty

"What?" the girl cried. "*Help.*"

"Dad," Harrison called. "What're you doing?"

"Borrowing your friend for a moment." Opal kicked his locust again. "Yaaa."

Reporters jabbered like mad as the crowd pushed, shoved, pointed, and screamed. Soon Opal was back in front of his horde of locusts, holding Molly tightly around the waist.

"Okay, *Ikey*," he called. "Maybe your dragons are a bit more dangerous than I anticipated. But torch me now and you take the girl out, too. And just to be clear, if your other dragons torch my other bugs, I'll push Molly into the polar bear cage. It'll be fantastic. See how long she lasts."

"Don't!" Molly yelled. "They look really, *really* hungry."

"Hold fire," Ike whispered into his earpiece. Then to Opal. "You wouldn't."

"Try me."

"Dad." Ike could see Harrison waving frantically from below.

He had never seen him look so upset. "You aren't going to hurt her, are you?"

"Did you hear that?" a reporter yelled. "Opal's kid is pleading for his friend's life."

"Stand down, son," Opal called down. "I know what I'm doing."

"Dads don't drop their kids' friends into bear cages," Harrison replied. "It's totally uncool."

"It's up to Ike," Opal called to his son. "Tell him to withdraw and I'll let Molly go."

Harrison looked up to Ike. "Hey, buddy."

Ike couldn't resist.

"*Buddy*? You haven't said a single nice thing to me in six years."

"Okay, so we've been a little bit mean sometimes," Molly cried, struggling to get free. "I get it. But it's all been in fun, right?"

"Fun?" Ike replied. "Since when is being nasty fun?"

"Young Hollingsberry is having it out with a class bullies." a reporter shouted. "Is this just a brilliant script twist? Or is it real?"

"Who cares." cried another journalist. "This is great TV."

"Okay, I'm sorry," Molly yelled. "There, I said it. And I mean it."

"Me, too, pal," Harrison said. "I take back everything I've ever said to you—even the good things. Come on. My dad is nuts, everyone knows it. Molly can be a pain sometimes, but does she really deserve to be bear food?"

Ike felt everyone's eyes directly on him. Sure, there was a chance that if he didn't back down, Opal might release Molly anyway. But how could he be sure? Harrison was right. Theodore Opal had gone nuts. Who knew what he was capable of?

"Okay," Ike called to Opal. "What's the deal then? I order the dragons to stand down, and you let Molly go?"

"Precisely," Opal cried. "But before I free the girl, I'll need to see you and your friends get back on your silly Purple Ship and return to Florida. That will give me time to take over the city and set up proper defenses."

"You're hearing it live," a reporter cried. "Hollingsberry won't torch the girl."

"I always said Ike was a good kid," Harrison exclaimed to anyone near enough to hear.

"A reporter here says we're about to stand down," Elmira said through the earpiece. "Is that true?"

"I haven't agreed to anything yet," Ike whispered.

Indeed, while Ike refused to be directly responsible for the death of a classmate, he couldn't stand by and let a madman take over the city.

"You know what to do," he whispered to Detroit. "Go."

With an intuitive grasp of what was happening, the dragon brought forth another precision *whoosh* of flame, this one burning off the remainder of Opal's hat and trimming the top of his famous red hair.

The crowd was stunned by the speed and deadly accuracy of the strike.

"Talk about a fastball!" a boy cried. "Get that dragon on the Mets."

"You ruined a nine-hundred dollar haircut," Opal sputtered, his hair smoking.

"Come on, Detroit," Ike said. "One more."

The next blast licked the bottom of the Opal's feet.

"Those were two thousand dollar shoes."

The bug began to buck uncontrollably.

"Jump," Ike cried to Molly. "The seal pond."

The girl didn't need to be told twice. With Opal struggling to stay on the raging bug, Molly flipped over its giant head and did a belly flop into the water.

"What are you doing?" Opal shrieked to Ike, as the two largest SEALS pushed Molly onto dry ground. "We had a deal."

"No," Ike yelled back. "We *discussed* a deal. I never said yes. Will you surrender?"

For a moment, Ike thought that he had done it—manipulated Opal into giving up without a fight. But Theodore Opal had not built up a worldwide real estate conglomerate by backing down. As he regained control of his locust, Ike noticed he was smiling—and not the relieved smile of a man who knows he has given his best and was finally ready to quit—but the crazed, demented grin of a man who has crossed so many lines he had nothing else to lose.

"Surrender?" he chortled. "Twenty giant locusts against one puny dragon? Not a chance. All right, my glorious bugs. The time is now."

The locusts buzzed so loudly it was as though fifty lawnmowers had been revved up at once. In response, Detroit smacked his lips and spread his wings as wide as they could go.

"All right then," Ike shouted. "It's your choice." He spoke into the headset, "Ready troops? It's time. On my command."

"Careful, ladies and gentlemen." a reporter cried. "It's about to get awfully warm around here."

Terrified, the crowd hit the pavement.

"Charge!" Opal shrieked.

"Fire!" Ike called. *"Fire."*

With a single awe-inspiring *whoosh*, Detroit took out the first four locusts in one powerful blast, incinerating them in plumes of dark smoke.

"Oh, my goodness," a reporter yelled, shaking. "Talk about a bug spray."

No fool, Opal saw a head-on attack wouldn't work—not with a dragon packing such intense heat.

"Separate," he cried. "Come at him from different sides."

"Come on, boy," Ike urged Detroit. "Up we go."

Ike nudged the reins and the dragon quickly gained altitude. From a higher vantage point, Ike was able to watch the locusts take positions for a counter-attack. One group of bugs gathered over Fifth Avenue, while another flew to Sheep's Meadow. A third circled into position a few blocks uptown.

Ike smiled. Yes, he was outnumbered. But while Opal clearly hoped to undercut Detroit's fire-power by attacking from three different angles at once, Ike saw that if he acted quickly, he could pick them off more easily.

The bugs over Fifth Avenue were the closest. Ike raised his sword.

"Yaaa."

Seconds later, he and Detroit were swooping over the edge of the park into the city streets. The first giant bug flew to meet them, stinger ready.

"It's all you, boy," Ike said.

Whoosh.

Direct hit. Bug down.

Then another came from the left.

"Over there," Ike yelled, tugging on Detroit's reins.

Whoosh.

Another gone.

Two locusts attacked at once, one from either side. While Detroit roasted the first, Ike took care of the second, slicing it firmly in the chest. With a piercing shriek, the locust dropped like a boulder.

"Watch it," a policeman called. "Incoming microorganism."

300

A deliveryman pushed a lady with a stroller out of the way as the insect crashed to Fifth Avenue with a loud splat.

But Ike and Detroit were far from done. No sooner had the slain locust hit the ground than three more came in from behind.

"Up we go," Ike called.

Again, Detroit rocketed skyward. As Ike had hoped, the locusts raced after him, fifty feet ... one hundred feet ... two hundred feet into the air. Then Ike turned Detroit on a dime and reversed course, dive bombing straight at the insects.

"You got 'em!" Ike yelled.

Whoosh.

Three more bugs gone in a single blast.

"Yes!" Ike shouted.

The first battle was over. The Fifth Avenue bugs were down. But Ike knew there was no time to ease up, not with more bugs left to kill—and that didn't even include chasing down Opal.

"Yaaa," Ike cried. "To Sheep's Meadow."

Perhaps the bugs there had witnessed what had happened to their cohorts on Fifth Avenue. Because instead of picking Ike off one by one, they had joined forces. In fact, as Ike and Detroit approached, all ten were flying furiously toward them, stingers out.

Ike pulled sharply on the reins, bringing them to a sudden halt, hovering in mid-air.

"What's he doing?" a boy called up from below.

"I'll tell you what," a reporter cried, as the locusts thundered closer. "He's giving up."

Not a chance.

"Okay, Detroit," Ike commanded. "Give it everything you've got."

The dragon coiled in his back legs and spread his wings. He inhaled as deeply as he could. Then he waited ...

The locusts were fifty feet away ...

Forty.

Thirty.

"Those bugs are going to eat that dragon for breakfast," a reporter cried.

At twenty feet, Detroit exhaled, hard and fast, pushing out an astounding torrent of insect-shattering heat, a monumental blast that took out all ten locusts in a single shot.

As the pedestrians below cheered, the dragon let loose an exultant roar.

"Yes." Ike whooped. "Good boy. Now for the last group."

He had the locusts on the run now. Even so, Ike never would have expected what happened next. When the remaining bugs saw them coming, they flew for their lives.

Ike was stunned. Then again, what creature wouldn't be terrified in the face of a fire-breathing dragon? Still, Ike knew what he had to do. This was no time for sympathy.

"Pick them off," he cried to Detroit.

Though the locusts were fast, Detroit was faster.

Whoosh.

Detroit got one over the ballfields.

Whoosh.

Another flamed out and fell in the 72nd Street Lake.

Whoosh. Whoosh. Whoosh.

Three more down, two more to go.

Flying for their lives, the remaining two bugs rocketed back to the zoo. That's where Detroit finally caught them, incinerated over the monkey house.

"Good boy," Ike said. "Got 'em all."

Or had they?

"Look out behind you," a policeman called from down below. "Incoming bugs."

Ike gasped. With Detroit unable to turn quickly enough, it

was all on him. By the time he was able to spin around on the dragon's back, another locust was at him. Luckily, Ike had just enough time to raise his sword at the last second and catch it in the neck. But as the first bug dropped, a second was there, as well. Ike waved his sword again—but missed. Before he knew it, he was being lifted into the air, suspended in the locust's jaws.

"Nooooo," Ike cried.

Then he heard a voice.

"Hello, Mr. Hollingsberry."

Opal. Of course. The madman was still on the bug's back.

"Let me go," Ike called.

"Let you go?" Opal cried with a laugh. "I'd love to. Because as you know, I would *never* kill a child. But unfortunately for you, my locusts live by an entirely different set of morals."

Ike knew what that meant. In another second, he would be bug food. He had only one chance. Grabbing his sword with both hands, he lunged backwards, aiming the blade over his head. With his body faced the wrong way, Ike couldn't even see precisely what he was swinging at. But he certainly felt it—the dull *thwack* as the blade hit its mark, smack in the middle of the bug's forehead.

The giant insect shuddered. Then it dropped, carrying Ike and Opal along for the ride.

"Detroit," Ike yelled.

For the second time that day, Ike had the surprising but thrilling sensation of being plucked out of mid-air. Seconds later, he was back on Detroit's back.

"Good, boy," Ike called, shaking with relief. "Good boy."

Doing his best to catch his breath, Ike looked to the zoo. Some people were looking up, mouths wide, terrified, while others were flat on their stomachs with their hands over their heads. But most were cheering his victory.

"Oh, my Lord," Ike heard a reporter exclaim. "That was either the best extermination job in history or one of the greatest special effects I've ever seen."

But it was no special effect—that much was clear to everyone by now. In fact, news reports were already coming in that the same thing had happened at the Statue of Liberty, LaGuardia Airport, and the George Washington Bridge. With a succession of hot, thunderous dragon-blasts, coupled with the daring flying and swordplay of Elmira, Alexandro, and Lucinda, the city had been saved.

Or had it?

Circling down for a landing, Ike saw him. Theodore Opal had somehow managed to jump off of the slain bug onto the back of the last remaining locust. And he was flying like mad out of the park—still holding Merlin's wand. Who knew what Opal could do with it? After all, he had taught himself how to bring groups of locusts through the portal. Maybe he was on his way to conjure up even more? Perhaps an entire army …

He had to be stopped.

The work of the Tenth Order wasn't over—not yet.

"Yaaa, Detroit," Ike cried. "Yaaa."

Chapter Thirty-One

O pal retraced the route Ike had taken on his arrival, flying recklessly over Wolman Rink, Sheep's Meadow, then out of the park and over Carnegie Hall. For a second, Ike thought Opal might stop at his own hotel, but no, the locust swooped over *The Opal Grand* then continued downtown, swerving right, left, up and down, barely in control.

Where is he going?

Now that the main horde of bugs had been killed, the United States military decided it was safer to show its presence. As Ike chased Opal into Times Square, a fleet of planes from the Air Force appeared in formation high in the air, overseeing the end of the operation. Close behind were the two military helicopters who had been with them all along.

Even so, Ike knew it was on him to finish off Opal's locust. With the spell in place, the bugs could still only be killed by a member of the Royal Order. But at the same time, to take Opal alive, Ike couldn't blast the insect out of the sky. He had to be precise. Kill the bug, but spare the man.

"Come on, boy," Ike called to his dragon. "Faster."

Opal was out of Times Square, still zigging and zagging like a man possessed. Ike needed to get to him fast, before he had a chance to conjure reinforcements. But then Ike did see reinforcements—but not a new swarm of locusts. No, these reinforcements were for *him*. His own troops. And here they came...

Alexandro on Kansas City flying up from the Statue of Liberty.

Elmira on Seattle from the George Washington Bridge.

Seconds later, there was Lucinda rushing down on Pittsburgh from The LaGuardia Airport.

"Greetings, mate," she cried.

"Smoked those locusts good, eh?" Alexandro said.

"I think I got a couple thousand cockroaches, too," Elmira said. "The George Washington Bridge has never been so clean."

"Fantastic," Ike cried. "But we have one more fight."

"Opal?" Elmira called. "He shouldn't be a problem. Look."

In his manic escape, he had pushed his bug too hard. Though Opal was kicking and whipping the insect like mad, the locust was zigging with less zag and zagging with notably less zig.

"His poor locust can barely fly," Lucinda said. "The bloody insect is exhausted."

Quickly, Ike gave the orders.

"We'll cut him off. Alexandro, block him from the west. Elmira, take the east. Lucinda—you stay with me."

His troops answered in rapid succession.

"Got it."

"Down with it."

"Smash that bug."

"Okay then," Ike said. "Charge."

And they were off. A dragon to the east, a dragon to the west and two straight on. Glancing over his shoulder, Opal gave his locust another couple of frantic kicks. But with the dragons gaining and nowhere else to go, he guided the bug toward the only place he could land, the Empire State Building. At the top of the spire.

"We've got him now," Lucinda called.

It certainly looked good. But the battle wasn't over. To Ike's horror, the instant he set down on the spire, Opal stood on the back of his exhausted bug and held up the wand. Ike looked anxiously toward the Hudson River. More locusts? Another portal? He had to move and move now.

"Let's blast him out of the sky," Lucinda shouted.

"No," Ike said. "Kill the bug on my orders, but we want Opal alive. I've got this."

Sensing all that was at stake, Detroit barreled head on to the Empire State Building. With a glance below, Ike saw swarms of pedestrians, running to keep up with the action. And overhead, there was a giant blimp, obviously there to film the action. Totally unfazed by media attention by now, Ike tuned out the cameras and aimed straight for the top of the spire.

"Give it up, Opal," he shouted.

"Dream on, Hollingsberry," the man cried as Ike whizzed by. "I'm only beginning. Get ready for something fantastic."

Opal looked toward the Hudson, held the wand as high over his head as he could and began to chant. "*Ish Grunnish Fraught de ...*"

Another spell.

Not on Ike's watch.

He had jumped on Opal once, why not again? He jerked Detroit back around and flew directly over the spire, then vaulted off, arms wide, and tackled Opal off his locust. Together, Opal and Ike slipped. Down, down they fell until—*boom*. They smashed onto the observatory.

Ike hurt all over. But first things first. He looked up to his troops, circling near.

"Get the locust. Get him now."

All four dragons opened fire. In a dramatic *whoosh* of flame, the locust was gone, burnt to a crisp.

"You killed him," Opal cried, rising shakily to his feet. "He was my favorite."

"They were locusts you conjured up to destroy the Earth," Ike yelled, standing up as well. "Not pets."

"What of it?"

"What of it? I'm taking you to the president."

Ike didn't see it coming—Opal's fist connected hard with his gut.

Ooof.

Ike hit the deck once again. Laid out on his back, he saw Opal grab Merlin's wand and begin to climb back up the spire. Gasping for breath, Ike forced himself back to his feet. Opal looked down from above him and laughed.

"Better hurry, boy. More locusts are coming. Then more after that. You'll never stop me. Just like your father couldn't."

If Ike needed motivation, he had it. He had never been particularly good at climbing ropes, but with a surge of adrenaline, he pulled himself up, up, up the spire. But Opal was climbing quickly, too. Soon the man was standing at the exact spot where he had landed moments earlier, at the top. Again, he held the wand high. Again, he began the chant, "*Ish Grunnish Fraught de …*"

Ike reached up, desperately.

"Stop," he cried.

Opal greeted him with a hard thwack on the head.

"Merlin's wand makes a great weapon, don't you think? Those opals are sharper than they look, aren't they?"

Holding onto the spire by one hand, Ike drew on every inch of strength to hang on then slowly regain his balance.

309

"I should kill you," Ike cried. He pulled out his sword. "Just like you killed my dad."

Opal laughed. "Then why don't you, boy?"

"Because the government wants you alive. And because I'm not like you. I'm not a murderer."

"Impressive," Opal said. "But who says I killed your father anyway? In fact, *who says he's dead at all.*"

Ike was so shocked he nearly fell to the street below.

"What's that supposed to mean?" Ike shouted.

"That nobody killed your father, that's what."

"That's crazy."

"Not it isn't. Don't you get it? *He isn't dead.*"

"But he fell to his death. Killed by one of your locusts. I saw him fall straight toward Lake Mead."

"Yes," Opal said. "But did you see him land?"

The words caught in Ike's throat. He hadn't. "But no one could have survived."

Opal laughed again. "Guess again."

"But how?"

"Still want to kill me, boy?" Opal suddenly leaned down, grabbed the end of Ike's sword, and held it up to his own throat. "Go ahead. Stab me. Do it. But then you'll never find out what really happened to your poor daddy. Your choice. Come on. Make up your mind."

Ike shook. Of course, he wanted to know more about his father, especially if he were really alive.

"Get down," Ike called. "You're coming with me."

Opal shook his head. "No, I think not."

Once again, Opal proved he was better able to use the wand as a weapon than for magic. Whacking Ike's chest, Ike slipped ten feet down the spire.

"You can hit me all you want," Ike called. "You aren't getting away. Look around you. You're still cornered."

It was true. Opal was surrounded by the two helicopters, circling planes, and dragons. A team of Air Force paratroopers appeared at the door of a third helicopter, ready to jump onto the spire if necessary to bring him in.

"Not getting away?" Opal called. "Don't be too sure about that."

He waved the wand again. Though Ike couldn't hear what he said over the whirr of the planes and helicopters, he could sure see what happened next. Just like that, Opal was surrounded by a brilliant burst of fire. A plume of purple smoke engulfed him. And then, when the smoke cleared ... the spire was empty.

Ike blinked, utterly stunned. Was it possible? Had Opal learned one more trick? It seemed so. He had disappeared. Vanished in a puff of purple smoke.

And then, still hanging desperately on to the spire, Ike saw a piece of glittering wood spin toward him. Leaning, he managed to grab it before it went careening down to the street.

It was Merlin's magic wand.

Had whatever spell Opal used to escape thrown it free? Probably ... but more importantly, had Opal spoken the truth? Was his father still alive? Or had Opal been playing with his mind, trying to throw him off guard so he could escape? How could Ike be sure? Had his father's body ever been found? Ike realized he had never asked.

Then he got another surprise.

"Hey, Ike. You did it."

Ike did a double take.

His mother? Yes, it was. Further, she was leaning out of some sort of strange flying machine. Then Ike saw who was at the controls—Kashvi's father. Once he got over his shock, Ike smiled. Mr. Changar had finally gotten the two-man flying thingee to work.

"Mom," Ike called.

His mother was so happy to see him she dragged Ike off the spire and into the contraption, crying tears of joy and relief.

"The locusts are gone," she said. "Dead."

Ike nodded.

"That's great," he said. "But Mom. Listen. Theodore Opal just told me something. He says Dad is still alive."

His mother nearly fell out of the homemade helicopter.

"He did?"

"Yes. Do you believe him?"

His mother didn't answer immediately. Instead, she looked toward the spot where Opal had just stood, then finally turned back to her son. "I would love to believe it, Ike. But right now, I'm just so happy you're safe."

Ike smiled. The last few days had been so busy, his mother had barely crossed his mind. He was a different person than the boy who had left for the Royal Order three days earlier. More confident certainly, a commander now. And able to fly a dragon.

"Look," Ike said. "I got Opal's wand."

"I see that. He certainly decked it out with lots of jewelry."

Ike was about to tell her that it really belonged to Merlin. Then he remembered the promise he had made to Thaddeus. No, he would keep the old man's identity quiet—even from his family.

"I've had some pretty wild adventures." Ike turned to Mr. Changar. "Kashvi, too. She saved the day. She fixed the Purple Flying Boat."

"I'm not surprised," Kashvi's father said. He looked over his shoulder and grinned. "Though Diego's parents and I were pretty surprised to discover they weren't on a sleepover."

Ike smiled back. "I knew they should've come up with a better excuse."

Mr. Changar shrugged. "I'll talk to her about it, of course, but I guess it's hard to be angry with children who helped save the world. You're all heroes."

"Come on," Ike's mother called. "Let's get this hero down on the ground so he can meet his public."

Moments later, Mr. Changar had his two-man flying thingee down in the middle of Herald Square next to Lucinda, Alexandro, Elmira and the four dragons. Immediately, onlookers and reporters began to push close, shouting questions and asking for autographs. Then the police pushed a path in the crowd, making way for a tall man in a tan suit. Mayor Andretti himself.

"Good job, my boy," he said, pumping Ike's hand. "Excellent job. You saved the city."

Ike allowed himself a small smile. Against all odds he *had* done it—not only saved the city but perhaps even the world. Yes, there would always be a few holdouts who would continue to insist the dragons and locusts had been part of an exorbitantly expensive TV show, but after the dramatic showdown at the zoo, and the remarkable spectacle of the flaming deaths of one hundred giant locusts, most everyone believed everything was real. But to make matters clearer, as the mayor went down the line shaking the hands of the Order members, a city appointed vet rushed through the crowd and held a stethoscope up to the chests of all four dragons.

"They're real, all right," he announced, after he had examined each one. "Those are heartbeats I am hearing, not the gears of a machine."

The crowd cheered anew.

"You heard it here, ladies and gentleman," reporters cried.

"And you heard it straight. These beasts are real, genuine, fire-breathing dragons."

Then to add to the excitement, the Purple Ship suddenly appeared over Macy's. On Mayor Andretti's command, the police cleared a small runway and Kashvi brought the boat in for a smooth landing on 35th Street. Moments later, she ran down the ramp and hugged her dad, while Diego and Sussex followed close behind.

"Ladies and gentlemen," the mayor intoned into a microphone. "I give you the saviors of our city. The Royal Order of Fighting Dragons."

Though Ike never knew exactly where it came from, confetti began to drop out of the windows of Herald Square. As the crowd cheered, a brass band began to play "New York, New York." Soon reporters were interviewing each of the Order members.

As he did his best to describe what it had been like to find out he was "the next in line", Ike overheard snippets of his friends chatting up the press.

Alexandro—"Ah, *si*. My mamma and poppa in Roma will be proud of me. Am I on air now? Hello Grandma."

Diego—"I've always had this thing for talking to animals. I think it started at age two. My folks and I were on Columbus Avenue and there was this chatty pigeon …"

Kashvi—"I do like to fix things. The purple boat wasn't that bad. Actually, my history teacher's Volkswagen was harder."

Lucinda—"This belt? That's a snake, you fool. My necklace? That's a killer centipede. See this hat? That's octopus skin. No, don't touch it. What was that? Of course, I wrestled them myself."

Elmira—"The biggest thrill is how this is going to affect *Elmira Speaks*. Being part of the Royal Order is going to really juice my follower count."

Soon enough, Ike's mom took her place next to her son.

"Hey, Mrs. Hollingsberry. How does it feel to have a son who saved New York City?"

She wrapped an arm around Ike's shoulders. "I've always been proud of Ike." She paused. "And I know his father is proud, too."

Ike froze. His father *is* proud? Is that what his mother had said? Did her use of the present tense mean she believed what Opal had said? That his father was really alive?

"We can always hope," his mother whispered.

Yes, hope. Anything seemed possible now that the locusts had been defeated and Ike was holding Thaddeus's wand.

"Hey, Mr. Mayor," a reporter cried out. "What's going to happen to the dragons?"

It was a good question. Ike looked over his shoulder. They could go back to the Order in the Everglades—that was the obvious choice. But the mayor had another idea.

"You know what? There's plenty of space next to the zoo where Theodore Opal was pushing to build his hotel. I am going to suggest to the city council that we build stalls for our dragon guests so they can come and go as they please."

As the cheers grew, Ike felt something wet slap across his back. He turned to see what had happened.

Was it possible? Had Detroit licked him?

"Did you see that?" a reporter shouted. "The dragon likes the idea."

All four dragons craned their necks and roared, releasing whooshes of flame a good one hundred feet into the air.

The mayor winked at Ike. "Looks like we've got four new New Yorkers."

"Yeah," Ike said, laughing. "It looks like we do."

Chapter Thirty-Two

Later that day, in the Oval Office, Ike finally got word that Thaddeus had pulled through. The president herself told him.

"He's a tough old guy," she said. "But he's going to be fine. And he's going to stay right where he belongs. Running the Order."

The president also filled in some final facts about Theodore Opal. With Ike's information that Opal was a descendant of Merlin, Hugh Seymour Livingston, Professor of Ancient Studies at Oxford in England, had enough intelligence to connect the final dots to the mystery.

"Apparently, just as Thaddeus told you, his son Edward was an untalented wizard who got lucky with one spell," the president said. "Thaddeus spent years trying to reverse it, but couldn't. The best he could do was to help Arthur create the Royal Order to fight the locusts whenever they returned."

"So Thaddeus never knew Edward had a family then?" Ike said. "He never knew Edward had descendants who kept the spell alive?"

"Right," the president said. "Luckily, most of the families

from Edward's line turned out to be good people. But the ones who weren't, well, they used the spell to create chaos."

"Ten times throughout history," Elmira said.

"Right," the president said. "Ten times. But The Royal Order of Fighting Dragons was always there to stop them."

It all made sense. But one thing still bothered Ike. "Why didn't Opal attack New York sooner once he had stolen Thaddeus's wand?"

The president shrugged. "I imagine because it took him a couple of weeks to figure out how to use it. Remember, Theodore Opal is a businessman, not a wizard."

That night, Ike and his friends were treated to a banquet at the White House. Before dessert, they were each presented with the Congressional Medal of Valor for their bravery. Then the president gave a short speech.

"These dragons and these children have proved instrumental in our country's defense," she said. "And I'm told members of the Order can stay on active duty as long as their particular dragons are alive and well. So as the Commander in Chief I have a request—that these six brave children, led by Isaac Rupert Hollingsberry, remain on duty."

"Yes," Diego shouted. "The Tenth Order lives on."

The president grinned. "I assume that means that you all accept?"

Ike answered for them all. "Absolutely, Madam President. We would be honored."

The evening ended with the White House chef serving sundaes aboard Air Force One. Back in New York, Ike, Elmira, Kashvi, and Diego were taken by limo to their homes. As for Alexandro and Lucinda, they were greeted by their fathers, Antonio

Cortesi and Phillip O'Leary Smith, both flown to the United States by the government.

A day later, Ike boarded the Purple Flying Viking Ship and accompanied the four dragons back to Florida. It was there at the Order, now surrounded by a metal fence to keep out tourists, that Ike finally had a chance to return Thaddeus's wand—the decorative opals were removed instantly—and catch up. On his first evening back, he and the old man sat on two lawn chairs in front of the drawbridge and watched Mr. and Mrs. Sussex let the dragons out for the nightly feed, fire, and fly. And it wasn't four dragons, but eight. With the antidote for Firebane in hand, Dartmoor, Loch Lomond, Northumberland, and Snowdonia were shooting flame as well as ever.

After watching Detroit and Dartmoor race back and forth over the swamp, Ike got to the question that had been on his mind since his confrontation with Opal—his father's disappearance. Was he dead or not?

Thaddeus gave his beard a twirl with his pinky and thought it over. He had recovered nicely. But even though Ike knew that Thaddeus, or Merlin, was aging backwards, the wound seemed to have taken something out of him.

"That's interesting news, for sure," he said, finally. "And I know that you and your family would like to believe it, Ike. But don't forget, Opal is a pathological liar."

Ike sighed. He had known the prospect of seeing his father again was a longshot, but he still hadn't been able to hold his hopes in check.

"Yeah, you're right," Ike said.

"On the other hand ..." Thaddeus went on.

"Yeah?" Ike said, hopefully. "There's an 'other hand?'"

Thaddeus patted Ike's shoulder. "The truth is, my boy, Opal was right about one thing anyway. I'm sad to say it, but we never did find your father's body."

"That's what Mom said. So maybe?" Ike stopped himself for a moment. "Maybe he really is still …?"

"The way I see it is this, Ike. If your dad is out there, he'll find a way to get in touch—one of these days. He loved you all too much to stay away forever."

Ike nodded. He could live with that. What other choice did he have? They sat silently for a moment, watching the dragons shoot plumes of fire into the early evening sky.

"Anyway," Thaddeus said, "as long as I'm able to do it, I have an Order to run. And correct me if I'm wrong, but you have to finish up sixth grade."

It was true. School. It seemed so foreign after all he had been through. But it was what Ike's immediate future held—homework, tests, and gym. After another day at the Order, he said a sad goodbye to the dragons.

"Don't worry," Sussex said as Ike boarded the airboat that would take him to the plane that would fly him home. "You can visit anytime. And the dragons will be up in New York this summer. That's only two months."

Time passed quickly. While Ike and his friends finished up the school year at Branford, Alexandro and Lucinda returned to their homes in Italy and Australia. Then in late June, they traveled back to New York to help Ike, Diego, Kashvi, and Elmira greet the Purple Flying Viking ship in Times Square. When Mr. and Mrs. Sussex marched all eight dragons off the boat, the cheers were so loud the New York papers carried pictures of Mayor Andretti sneaking in a pair of earplugs.

That summer, more visitors than ever stopped by Central Park to see the Order's new summer home. Most days, Ike was on hand to share stories of his adventures. Elmira was there, too, of course, ready to expound on dragon lore while Kashvi kept herself busy doing repairs on the Purple Ship and Lucinda and Alexandro raced dragons over the park, arguing over who was faster and braver.

Then there was Diego. When a careful reading of the entire Order bylaws revealed other passages of so-called gibberish, he and Dr. Bernie J. Wong joined forces to attempt to decipher *Dragonish*.

As for Theodore Opal, there was still no word. Ironically, as the school year wound down, Ike found himself feeling sorry for his son, Harrison. Knowing firsthand how hard it had been to lose a father who was remembered fondly, he could only imagine how much it must hurt to lose a dad under such awful circumstances. Also, Ike had been struck with how hard Harrison had fought for Molly when his father threatened her life at the zoo. Maybe he wasn't a lost cause, after all.

On the last day of school, Ike spontaneously asked Harrison if he wanted to help that summer at the Order. To his surprise, Harrison said yes, even going so far as to pat Ike on the back and say, "Thanks, Hollingsberry."

Then it got even better. On the first day of summer vacation, Ike received a long text from Thaddeus himself.

> See if Opal's boy wants to spend time with me at the swamp. Don't forget, as we recently discovered, Theodore Opal was a descendant of my son Edward—which means Harrison and I are related. I'm his great-great-great, and then some, grandfather. Perhaps I can be a good influence. Ask him to bring along his two sidekicks, too.

So Harrison, Molly Willowinski, and Dirk Sher spent their summer in Florida under Thaddeus's tutelage. Thaddeus texted Ike in late July.

> Those kids are tough nuts to crack, but a daily diet of scrubbing old dragon saddles and polishing ancient armor is slowly straightening them out. Tonight, I might even teach them how to play Shufflericketts.

Ike smiled. One day he still wanted to learn, too.

Finally, always and forever, there was Cameron Rupert Hollingsberry. Ike thought about his father every single day. Would he ever reappear? Would Ike ever get to know him outside of a few memories, fan pages, and blogs? He would be overjoyed to see him again, but also in need of some serious answers. Mainly, where had he been? Of course, Ike knew obsessing about it wouldn't do any good. As Thaddeus had said, if his father was still alive, there had to be a good reason why he had been out of touch.

In the meantime, there was nothing to be done but to live his life and hope for the best. Luckily, as the new Head Warrior of the Royal Order, he had plenty to keep him busy. After all, if Theodore Opal returned with another deadly swarm of locusts, Ike had to have his team ready.

So if you are in New York City over the summer, drop by Central Park. Most mornings, you can catch Isaac Rupert Hollingsberry leading his troops in training flights around the city. Afterwards, Elmira might offer you a ride on her street sweeper. Lucinda might show you her latest snake-belt. Diego and Detroit might speak *Dragonish* while Kashvi fixes your car and Alexandro's grandmother makes you dinner.

But whether you are able to visit or not, know *The Royal Order of Fighting Dragons* will live on, ready to rise to any challenge and fight any foe. And whenever the Order is next called to duty, you can bet that TV cameras will be there to catch every exciting second.

Elmira Speaks and the rest of the blogosphere is already buzzing with anticipation.

Be sure to tune in.

Acknowledgments

Special thanks to Andrea, Cassie and John Elish for listening to me talk about the Royal Dragons incessantly and offering great suggestions. Many other people read drafts along the way. Special thanks to Jill Weiner, Pam Moses, Harry Elish, Matthew Gartner, and my most excellent and perceptive (not to mention persistent) agent, Matt Bialer. Also thanks to the team at Vesuvian: Liana Gardner, editor extraordinaire, and Italia Gandolfo for giving birth to the Royal Order in such fine style. Biggest thanks for all to John Canaday who made brilliant suggestions on the manuscript every step of the way. John: I couldn't have written this without you.

About the Author

Dan Elish is the author of nine novels, including *The School for the Insanely Gifted, BORN TOO SHORT: The Confessions of an Eighth-Grade Basket Case,* an International Reading Association Students' Choice Award Recipient (Simon & Schuster), the book for the Broadway musical *13,* slated to be a movie by CBS Films, and *The Worldwide Dessert* Contest, which was recently optioned for TV. In addition, Dan is a writer of TV shows like PBS's *Cyberchase.* Dan has received fellowships and scholarships to the Bread Loaf and Sewanee Writers' Conferences and is represented by Matt Bialer at Greenburger Associates. He lives in New York with his wife and children

www.TheRoyalOrderofFightingDragons.com
www.danelish.com